I0838715

HARRY WARREN

AT LAST

Stacia Raymond

Mentoris Project
745 South Sierra Madre Drive
San Marino, CA 91108

Copyright © 2022 Mentoris Project

Cover photo: courtesy of the Warren family

Cover design: Suzanne Turpin

More information at www.mentorisproject.org

ISBN: 978-1-947431-43-0

Library of Congress Control Number: 2022930052

All net proceeds from the sale of this book will be donated to the Mentoris Project whose mission is to support educational initiatives that foster an appreciation of history and culture to encourage and inspire young people to create a stronger future.

Publisher's Cataloging-In-Publication Data
(Prepared by The Donohue Group, Inc.)

Names: Raymond, Stacia, author.
Title: At last : a novel based on the life of Harry Warren / Stacia Raymond.
Description: San Marino, CA : The Mentoris Project, [2022]
Identifiers: ISBN 9781947431430 (paperback) | ISBN 9798201319915 (ePub)
Subjects: LCSH: Warren, Harry, 1893-1981--Fiction. | Composers--United States--History--20th century--Fiction. | Musicals--United States--History--20th century--Fiction. | LCGFT: Biographical fiction. | Historical fiction.
Classification: LCC PS3618.A987 A8 2022 (print) | LCC PS3618.A987 (ebook) | DDC 813/.6--dc23

The Mentoris Project is a series of novels and biographies about the lives of great men and women who have changed history through their contributions as scientists, inventors, explorers, thinkers, and creators. The Barbera Foundation sponsors this series in the hope that, like a mentor, each book will inspire the reader to discover how she or he can make a positive contribution to society.

Contents

Foreword

First and foremost, Mentor was a person. We tend to think of the word *mentor* as a noun (a mentor) or a verb (to mentor), but there is a very human dimension embedded in the term. Mentor appears in Homer's *Odyssey* as the old friend entrusted to care for Odysseus's household and his son Telemachus during the Trojan War. When years pass and Telemachus sets out to search for his missing father, the goddess Athena assumes the form of Mentor to accompany him. The human being welcomes a human form for counsel. From its very origins, becoming a mentor is a transcendent act; it carries with it something of the holy.

The Mentoris Project sets out on an Athena-like mission: We hope the books that form this series will be an inspiration to all those who are seekers, to those of the twenty-first century who are on their own odysseys, trying to find enduring principles that will guide them to a spiritual home. The stories that comprise the series are all deeply human. These books dramatize the lives of great men and women whose stories bridge the ancient and the modern, taking many forms, just as Athena did, but always holding up a light for those living today.

Whether in novel form or traditional biography, these books

plumb the individual characters of our heroes' journeys. The power of storytelling has always been to envelop the reader in a vivid and continuous dream, and to forge a link with the subject. Our goal is for that link to guide the reader home with a new inspiration.

What is a mentor? A guide, a moral compass, an inspiration. A friend who points you toward true north. We hope that the Mentoris Project will become that friend, and it will help us all transcend our daily lives with something that can only be called holy.

—Robert J. Barbera, Founder, The Mentoris Project
—Ken LaZebnik, Founding Editor, The Mentoris Project

Prologue

In October 2001 in New York City, a revival of the musical *42ⁿᵈ Street* swept Broadway. Perhaps the post–September 11 audience, a solid mix of visitors and New Yorkers, flocked to it with such enthusiasm because the show has that feeling of being a perennial—one of those classics that blooms again and again in regional productions, schools, and community theaters. In truth, this 2001 production was the first Broadway revival of *42ⁿᵈ Street*.

What most people didn't know then and continue to be largely unaware of today is that *42ⁿᵈ Street* was not originally conceived of as a stage musical. The first adaptation of the eponymous novel by Bradford Ropes was a Warner Brothers movie musical in 1933. And as any lover of musical theater knows, the key ingredient in the secret sauce of a hit musical is, of course, the music. In this case, it came from the imagination of Harry Warren, who provided the toe-tapping celebratory melodies that would become part of our American DNA—first in the form of a Depression-era movie, then in the Broadway revival for a grieving American people picking up the pieces after an unthinkable tragedy almost seventy years later. Though the 2001 audience members were more well-heeled than their Depression-era counterparts, it was with the same fearless defiance that they opted for celebration and not surrender.

As a uniquely American art form, the movie musical has a power like no other. If there is one person more responsible than anyone for defining this genre and taking credit for its success, it is arguably Harry Warren, the first major American songwriter to write primarily for film. Even the tremendous weight of a Hollywood flop was not enough to keep a Harry Warren hit from breaking out. According to the National Archives, no other songwriter—with the possible exception of Irving Berlin—has contributed so much "to the canon of American popular song in the twentieth century as Harry Warren." Though not much has been written about this true genius, what does exist all plays into the same trope: Why isn't Harry Warren better known? The real truth of the matter is that even in today's digital world, with so much information at our fingertips, the public is rarely aware of who writes songs because it is focused on the performers.

It could also be true that Harry was not all that concerned about fame, but was simply doing his best to survive and thrive in an industry of fame seekers—an environment that made him feel he was supposed to toot his own horn, even if he was never truly comfortable doing so. To compare him with Irving Berlin in terms of name recognition paints this picture; Berlin insisted on having his name splashed all over the movie posters of films he wrote for, while the humbler Harry would never have dreamed of making that demand. This could be key to understanding the legacy of Harry Warren—a desire for attention for his music more than for himself. In the end, was he rewarded for this humility? If you consider that he had more top-ten hits on *Your Hit Parade*— forty-five to Berlin's thirty-three—the answer is yes.

The inversion of *42nd Street* starting out onscreen before moving to the stage parallels Harry Warren's life and career in a sense, because while he may not have been as well-known as he would have liked in his day, his musical legacy is immeasurable. Had Harry been alive in 2001 to see the salutary effect his *42nd Street* score was having on the broken hearts in his hometown of New York City, it would surely have put a smile on the face of the man Bing Crosby once described as a "genial curmudgeon." Harry would have delighted in being rediscovered by a new generation. He lived just long enough to see his beloved *42nd Street,* which had launched his Hollywood career, make it to Broadway the first time—even if it was bittersweet, due to some negative circumstances surrounding the production.

As a place of made-up tales—both the kind told onscreen as well as rumors about people in the business—the heightened world of Hollywood is famous for apocryphal stories that can become transformed as gospel truths. There's one that's been going around about Harry Warren for a long time regarding what happened at the Eighth Academy Awards in 1936. Despite being repeated in print multiple times, the only documentary proof that exists supports the fact that the incident never happened. So, did Harry himself have a hand in repeating this tale as a way to keep his name on the lips of the industry he simultaneously loved and loathed? Was this musical genius employing subterfuge and outsmarting everyone on this score? Up until now, perhaps it has been a case of "when the legend becomes fact, print the legend."

Chapter One

TUTI

S now fell steadily, bringing a welcome blanket of quiet over the city. Brooklyn, yet an independent city from New York in the year 1893, was still recovering from a massive hurricane four months earlier. Known as the Midnight Storm, it struck in the dark, unleashing a level of destruction never seen in New York City—flooding lower Manhattan, snatching roofs off buildings, and snapping apart some of the largest trees in Central Park, which was not yet forty years old. For Rachel Guaragna, a pregnant mother of ten, it was beyond nerve-wracking. She, her husband, and their children had barricaded the windows of their Brooklyn brownstone with every mattress and pillow they could find, hoping to ride out the storm.

This fresh memory shadowed Rachel as she walked home from the neighborhood Italian market, where she'd gone to pick up provisions for the family Christmas Eve dinner. *Il Cenone*, as it was called in her native Calabria, consisted of thirteen dishes centered on seafood, as meat was not to be eaten the day before Christmas, according to Catholic tradition. Rachel's pushcart was filled with cherrystone clams for *spaghetti alle vongole*, salted cod with sweet red peppers, cheeses and olives, and a panettone with dried Calabrian figs and dark chocolate. Evidence of the Midnight Storm could still be seen everywhere, like in the giant hole in the side of a warehouse where a crane had swung through, taking a large corner of the building with it. Rachel remembered the day after the storm, when the family went out to check on friends and neighbors and survey the destruction. Downed trees blocked streets, and children in Prospect Park were distressed by the sight of hundreds of dead birds that had fallen out of their branches after drowning in their nests.

Things were much calmer now, with the city under the spell of Christmastime. It was December 24, and Rachel and her family were looking forward to midnight Mass at Our Lady of Loreto. She entered their townhouse at 2218 Fulton Street, rolled her cart of goods into the kitchen, and lit candles to place in the front windows. Then, in an instant, the calm was but another memory—she gasped loudly and clutched her belly. As she steadied herself with one hand on the counter, Antonio came in from his boot shop on the ground floor, rushing to his wife's side.

"Call the midwife," Rachel said in a quiet voice, slowly lowering herself onto a chair. "The baby is coming early."

Antonio grabbed a pillow and placed it behind her back as he called out to his eldest daughter. "Carolina, *viene in fretta!*" he pleaded for her to come quickly. Antonio's adrenaline coursed through him as though this was his first time witnessing his wife go into labor, even though he'd already experienced it ten times before.

Carolina came rushing down the stairs and sprang into action, putting her mother's feet up and setting water to boil on the stove to help cleanse her in preparation for the birth. Antonio ran out the front door to fetch the midwife, and Carolina leaned in close to her mother.

"Mama, we can get help for you if your pain is too great," she said. "I know what it says in the Bible about childbirth, but even Queen Victoria was chloroformed for the birth of Prince Leopold, her eighth child."

"I'm glad you will have that if you need it one day," Rachel said, in earnest.

"I don't want you to suffer, is all," Carolina told her.

"I don't think there's time—this baby seems in a hurry to get here."

When Antonio returned with the midwife, they moved Rachel into the bedroom, helping her change into clothing that could be easily removed after the birth.

"I am sorry to have to take you away from your family today," Rachel said.

The midwife smiled. "We will have plenty of time to celebrate Christmas as soon as this baby is born."

As Rachel suspected, she did not have to labor long before a baby boy arrived a few hours shy of Christmas. For Rachel, it brought forth a deep reflection on the experience of the Blessed Mother.

"As though birthing a child isn't difficult enough. Imagine not having anywhere to go and not understanding how you came to be with child in the first place," Rachel told the midwife.

"It is a great gift to have a child born on this day," the midwife said, swaddling the newborn.

Antonio entered the bedroom just as Rachel was saying, "He will be specially blessed and glorify God every day of his life."

"A priest?" he asked.

"I don't know. I just know he will have some kind of special talent. I would like to name him Salvatore Antonio if you don't object."

"*Va bene allora,*" he said, agreeing wholeheartedly.

Like Christmas itself, the baby was a gift that would keep on giving—long after his birth and well beyond his lifetime. They all wished one another a *buon Natale* as the older children took over making dinner.

The family embarked on their first outing with the baby a few weeks later. Rachel and Antonio pushed the carriage down the walkway as the younger children played along the riverfront, following Antonio Jr., the eldest. They ambled south beneath the Brooklyn Bridge to a bench beside the East River. As the wind gusted, little Salvatore began to cry. Rachel took him out of the carriage and buttoned him inside her warm wool coat.

"What's the trouble, *Tuti?*" she asked, cooing his nickname.

"Perhaps it is too cold for him today," Antonio said.

After some nuzzling, the baby's crying ceased, and Antonio

fixed his gaze on the bridge. "It is hard to believe the bridge was just finished ten years ago," he said. "It seems like something that has always been here."

"Yes, it does," Rachel agreed, marveling at the modern miracle of engineering. "It brings me joy to know an immigrant built it. It shows all we have to offer."

"Has something made you fearful?" Antonio asked.

"I worry at times about our children and what they could face because of their heritage."

Fear had become almost palpable amongst Italians after an incident in New Orleans in which a lynch mob, seeing no need for a trial, dragged three Italians accused of murder out of a jail and into the streets and killed them.

"Seeing the bridge always makes me feel a certain kind of pride for the immigrant," Rachel said. "Hopefully, it will serve as a bridge between cultures as well. Father Moretti mentioned the German bridge builders in a homily once when he was talking about fathers and sons.

"Roebling, the father, crushed his foot between a boat and a piling while he was taking some measurements. He got tetanus and died. His son, who was just thirty-two at the time, had to take over the project. Then *he* became very ill and needed his wife's help. Had it not been for her, the bridge would not have been finished. Father Moretti used her as a symbol of the Blessed Mother because she was able to communicate his message to see the completion of the miracle. Mrs. Roebling was well educated and knew advanced mathematics and physics."

"I see," Antonio said.

"And do you know what her maiden name was?" she asked. He shook his head. "Warren."

"Warren?" he repeated in his Italian accent.

"Does it not sound a little like the first part of our surname, *Guaran*-gna?"

Antonio paused as he realized what she was intimating. "Are you suggesting we change our name? The name I've had for fifty years? *Il nome della mia famiglia?*"

"Many Italian families have done this, Antonio."

"Several of our own children were born here, so they *are* American," he countered.

Their conversation went quiet for some time. They became more chilled by the minute as the wind picked up.

"Best we get Tuti home now," Rachel said.

As they strolled home, they quietly weighed the wisdom of anglicizing the family name. Contrary to popular belief, names were not frequently changed by Ellis Island officials, many of whom had been immigrants themselves and commonly spoke several languages. When passengers were listed on ship manifests in first or second class, they were usually not questioned at all; it was mostly the passengers who traveled in steerage who were screened and rejected for their lack of skills or for illness. Most often, people chose to change their own names when they arrived as a way of taking on a new identity.

"When I came through Ellis Island, my interpreter did not even suggest I change my name. In fact, he asked if I knew the

Guaragnas of Palermo." Antonio stated his final thought on the matter with his Italian pride ringing through loudly.

Antonio and Rachel knew they were amongst the first great wave of immigrants after the unification of Italy's north and south, along with fourteen million other Italians who left for America between 1876 and 1915, embarking on a risky journey aboard overcrowded and barely seaworthy ships. Antonio left his home of Cassano allo Ionio in the province Cosenza in Calabria in the Italian south on November 21, 1887, and sailed on the vessel *La France* from Naples to Buenos Aires. As a bootmaker, he'd been told there was a demand from the gauchos of Argentina for strong, fine riding boots, so essential to their work. As it turned out, Argentina was not much of an economic improvement over Italy, and neither Antonio nor Rachel cared much for living there. When they decided to try again in New York, Antonio thought it best for him to go ahead of the family and find a place for them to live and a shop for his work. This meant Rachel making the voyage alone with the seven children they had at the time. It was a journey she barely survived, enduring wretched conditions and emotional trials well beyond what most can imagine. She made it through the experience by dreaming about what their new life would be like. In the letter in which he sent for her, Antonio described the home he'd found for them that had a space for his shop on the ground floor. She read one line of his letter over and over: *"La Statua della Liberata ti aspetta per dare il benevenuto a te e ai bambini"*—the Statue of Liberty is waiting to welcome you and the children.

~

When the family attended church on Sundays, little Tuti always sat motionless during the music, his feet dangling off the edge of the pew. On some days, the family lost track of him as they enjoyed fellowship with their friends and neighbors after Mass. But they always knew where to find him: in the apse of the church, trying to get a closer look at the organ. One morning, the choir director and organist, a kind young woman named Miss Pauline Schneider, told Tuti, "Go ahead, pick a note to play." Antonio, Rachel, and Tuti's brothers and sisters looked on as he enjoyed a special moment with Miss Schneider. As he placed his finger on a key and pushed down, a note rang out of the organ pipe. At the same time, a ray of light beamed through the stained glass, splashing Tuti in a rainbow of color. From that moment, he came to regard music as a special kind of magic. He looked up at Miss Schneider as if to say, *Did I do that?*

When it was time for Tuti to start school, Antonio and Rachel were still struggling with whether to change the family name. Ultimately, they opted to become the Warrens. Around the same time, Tuti's brothers and sisters suggested he go by Harry to prevent him from taking some of the teasing they'd endured as Italians. Tuti didn't particularly care for the name and often wrote "Salvatore" before "Harry" on his schoolwork, as though he wasn't ready to let go of his Italian identity.

All in all, Tuti's protective brothers and sisters made life in their Brooklyn brownstone boisterous and fun. When they weren't out playing football in the street with a ball that was actually a block of wood tied up inside a newspaper, they were listening to music or reading books. Some of Harry's early favorite titles were *Young Wild West Junior* and *Freddy Fear Not*. These stories became the foundation for his lifelong love of reading. Business was steady for Antonio and their home was alive with music, despite not having a piano. They loved listening to Italian opera, and Giacomo Puccini became Tuti's favorite. Driven by a desire to play music too, he became enamored with his father's accordion, teaching himself to play. Given the instrument's formidable learning curve, Antonio was impressed by how quickly Tuti was figuring it out. Antonio held music in high regard, just as he did the customs of the Old World. He insisted the children tip their hats for the doctor as a show of respect for those with education and a profession.

Still known as Tuti at home, Harry declared his wish to become an altar boy as soon as he turned eight. Ever since his first experience with the church organ, he'd consistently been the first one out the door for church because he couldn't wait for the music. He'd wait out on the sidewalk for the rest of his family, tapping his foot impatiently while loudly humming some favorite new melody. He began asking his parents if he could stay after Mass to listen to the choir rehearsals. He'd sit in the pews with his eyes closed, listening intently to every note and nuance. He proved himself such a devotee, and Miss Schneider saw how much he longed to learn music. She was impressed by all the time he spent there, while other boys his age were running around outside and playing games in the street. She invited him to become the youngest member of the choir and began working with him one-on-one, teaching him chords and scales.

"Harry, it is as if you already *know* music," she told him one day.

He laughed. "Sometimes it feels like I do."

"Well, it would not surprise me, for it is a gift from God. You already speak English and Italian, and now he's given you a third language with which to communicate. It's the universal language of the world that anyone can understand. Make sure Father knows you are grateful, for it is not a gift he bestows on all of us. Just a special few."

Harry rushed home to share the news of being invited to join the choir.

"Miss Schneider is starting a children's choir?" Rachel asked.

"No, I'm going to be in the regular choir! She said I could because I learned all the parts—soprano, alto, tenor, and bass."

Rachel and Antonio listened with pride as Tuti shared all he'd been learning. It was Miss Schneider who introduced him to harmony, at which point an entire new world opened up for him. His first time performing with the choir was on his tenth birthday, Christmas Eve in 1903. After Mass, Rachel went to thank the choir director.

"Miss Schneider, I made you these *scalidde,* a Calabrian traditional Christmas sweet."

Miss Schneider looked down at the beautiful plate of fritters shaped like small ladders. "Thank you so much, Mrs. Guaragna," she said. "Excuse me—Mrs. *Warren.*"

"In Calabria, it is believed the ladder symbolizes the possibility of rising to heaven," Rachel said.

"How wonderful. I will enjoy them with that very intention," Miss Schneider said, smiling.

"Calabria does not have a proper landscape for dairy cattle, so many treats there are made without butter, milk, or cream. We did not have sugar there either. Everything is sweetened with honey or *mosto cotto,* a cooked-down grape," Rachel explained. "Thank you for taking such an interest in our Harry. He is learning a great deal from you and talks of nothing but music."

"Harry has a God-given gift, of that I am sure. It is my great pleasure to teach him what I know. Before long, he will be teaching me."

Miss Schneider was not wrong about how quickly Harry would progress. By the time he was a young teenager, he could sight-read music.

One day when the boys needed haircuts, Antonio marched them over to the neighborhood barber, Frank de Rosa. When they walked in, Harry noticed musical instruments in the barbershop's window.

"Say, what's all this?" young Harry asked the barber.

"I sell haircuts *and* musical instruments," Frank laughed. "Would you like to try one?"

As Harry's older brothers took turns in the barber chair, Harry carefully inspected each instrument before choosing one to try.

"That's a clarinet. It's in the woodwind family," Frank told him.

"I love the sound," Harry said. He played each note through the clarinet, then gently put it down before moving on to the harmonica. He blew into it, and just as Frank began telling him about the other set of notes produced by sucking air in, Harry had already figured that out.

Harry began making daily visits to the barbershop to try the different instruments. Frank picked up on Harry's great sense of rhythm, and soon enough, Harry gravitated to the drums, which he taught himself to play.

When he turned fourteen, someone asked him to play in a dance hall band in Canarsie, the roughest part of Brooklyn. He told his father what it was like leaving on the 1:00 a.m. train from the Canarsie station: "You just hear one long whistle and see the policemen lined up with their clubs out on the platform at the next stop." Despite the tense circumstances of the gig, he almost couldn't believe he was getting paid to play music, something he would have happily done for free.

In the summer, he got a job selling fruit at the Yiddish Liberty Theatre in Brownsville, Brooklyn. He'd walk up and down the aisles, selling apples and oranges to the frequently sobbing audience taking in the melodrama. Harry always got a big charge out of Hymie, a policeman who worked at the theater patrolling the aisles before a performance, knocking hats off heads with his cane.

Brownsville was a predominantly Jewish neighborhood also known as Little Jerusalem, and before Harry knew it, he was picking up Yiddish. He had an incredible mind for languages. Many of the Jewish families he met at the fruit stand assumed he was Jewish until he told them he was actually Italian Roman Catholic. Upon learning this, some hired him to work as a *Shabbat goy*, performing tasks on the Jewish Sabbath that they were not able to.

One day at the barbershop, Harry became intrigued by the flute. Of all of Frank's instruments he'd tried, the flute was the trickiest. It would take time to practice and develop the correct embouchure, the position of the mouth, to play it. One day while Frank was in the middle of a haircut, Frank heard Harry struggling with the instrument.

"I'll tell you what," Frank said. "Why don't you take the flute home, where you'll have more time to practice?"

"You'd let me do that?"

"I'll make you a deal. When you learn it, you can demonstrate it, along with all the other instruments you now know how to play, for customers interested in buying them."

"Thank you, Mr. De Rosa!" Harry cried. He ran all the way home with the flute case under his arm.

Harry picked up on the fact that Frank booked a lot of musical acts for parties, bar mitzvahs, and other events. Once Harry had learned nine different instruments, Frank invited him to rehearse with other musicians at night after the barbershop had closed.

"*Fa maggiore*," Frank would call out, followed by another chord, "*Sol minore*." With Harry's highly attuned ear, he learned to follow the chord changes quickly. They went through song after song this way, late into the night.

"No matter what I play, you can keep up. How are you learning it all so quickly?" Frank asked.

"I study Puccini," Harry said, as if it was the most obvious thing in the world.

"Puccini, ay? Well, you have set yourself quite a high standard! But until you get as good as Puccini, how would you like to play engagements and get paid for it?"

"You mean like Mousie does?" Harry asked. That was Harry's brother Charlie, who'd been performing in a trio called Dunn, Warren, and Mack—a song-and-dance act Harry's sister Carolina would sometimes perform in too, whenever she could get away without their father knowing.

"Yes, like Mousie. It wouldn't interfere with your school; it would just be on weekends and occasionally at night if it's not too late. You'll have to get your mother and father's permission, of course."

Harry asked his parents about it that night at the dinner table as a Verdi record played in the background.

"It's remarkable how far you've come with your music without any formal lessons, Tuti," his father said.

"So, it's okay with you if I play engagements with Mr. De Rosa?"

"*E un onore essere chiesto*," Antonio said. He believed it was an honor for Harry to be asked.

Harry's mood was buoyant until he looked over at Carolina.

She was several years older and would have given anything for her father's blessing of her performing aspirations.

Harry was well aware of their father's disapproval of this idea for his daughter—one night when she and Charlie were both gone, Antonio had asked Harry where they were. Harry knew he couldn't lie to his father.

"I think they are performing together, Papa."

Harry watched his father grow angrier once these suspicions had been confirmed.

"Where, Tuti? Where are they?" Antonio fumed.

"I just know it's somewhere here in Brooklyn, that's all."

Antonio went to the other children to pry more information out of them. They watched him grab his coat and put on his hat. "I'm going to get the deputy to get your sister," he said, "because I know she won't come with me."

"But she'll go with the deputy?" Annie the eldest sister wondered.

"If I tell him she's underage, he'll have no choice but to remove her."

Antonio Jr. spoke up. "Papa, she's not underage anymore."

"You see?" their father scoffed. "She's forcing me into a lie on top of it."

Harry feared for his sister—he could just imagine what it must have been like for her getting ripped off the stage in the middle of a show. When his father returned home with her, she was still in tears. When she climbed in Harry's bed to comfort him, he whispered, "I'm sorry, Carolina."

"It's not for you to worry about, Tuti."

He was relieved she was not upset with him. In fact, she adored him—and would soon become a mother figure to him when Rachel began to fall ill.

On Harry's fifteenth birthday, the family went to midnight Mass on Christmas Eve. It was the first time Miss Schneider invited a string section to accompany the choir. The sound took Harry's breath away and he took it as a sign to follow music as far as it would take him. It was the best birthday gift he could have ever imagined—a vision of his future. A few days later, he went to see his godfather, Pasquale Pucci. Pasquale played in the John Victor Brass Band, a group of about a dozen players that toured Massachusetts, Pennsylvania, and New York with the Keene & Shippey and Harry Lukens' carnivals.

"Mamma is sick," Harry told Pasquale. "I think it would be best for her to have one less child around."

"Well, we need a snare drummer, and you've gotten pretty good," Pasquale said. "It only pays $12 a week, which would probably mean skipping a meal here and there."

"I'll do it! Please take me with you this summer, Pasqua."

And just like that, Harry ran away with the circus.

They spent the season traveling up and down the Hudson, stopping at all the towns along the way. Harry soaked up all he could about the lives of the colorful people he worked alongside and learned the tricks of the trade, such as the stagehands' code for alerting the next crew about performers who didn't tip.

The crew would tie a shoelace to that person's trunk to alert the next crew about the bum. Of all the performers, the animals were Harry's favorite. He adored the zebra, was amused by the trained bear, and kept a safe distance from the chimpanzee. When summer ended, Harry found himself once again working at The Liberty Theatre, this time as a stagehand—a step up from selling fruit to the hysterical vaudeville audiences the previous summer.

The seed had been planted. Once Harry had gotten a taste of show business, his future became clearer to him with each passing day. He wasn't even thinking about music specifically; he just wanted to be in the business one way or another. He was also increasingly drawn to another aspect of Puccini's operas: the way music tells a story.

One evening on the road, Pasquale came to Harry with terrible news. "Dear boy, your Mamma . . ."

Harry sat straight up and put his flute down. "Is she okay, Pasquale?"

"No, son. I'm very sorry. She's with our heavenly Father now."

Harry was just fifteen. He immediately returned home, where his father told him her body had just given out. Her last words had been about how grateful she was that all her babies lived.

After his summer tour with the circus, Harry did not return to Commercial High School, which was a relief for him. He'd always been a bit tortured about how beautiful their orchestra was, and he could never join it because he didn't play a stringed instrument.

Harry's sisters would have to take care of him now—Antonio was already sixty-five years old. At Rachel's funeral Mass, Miss Schneider chose selections she knew Harry would love; he cried during "Ave Maria."

After the service, he went up to Miss Schneider with the $75 he'd saved up working for the circus. "I'd like to give you this for the music program," he said.

She looked at the money in his hands and smiled, gently closing his fists around it. "It's kind of you to offer," she said, "but I would rather you use it to get that piano you've been wanting." Young Harry stared back at her. "That way, you can practice anytime and learn all the Puccini you'd like. You'll make your mother in heaven proud."

Harry wiped away a tear and turned to exit the church, feeling every bit like the motherless child he now was.

Chapter Two

THE BIRTH OF AN ART FORM

Losing his mother seared a scar on Harry's fifteen-year-old soul like an open wound cauterized by his silent fury. Teenage Harry didn't have the words needed to express his grief, even if he had been encouraged to do so. Instead, he followed the lead of his brothers and sisters, who rarely spoke of their mother, especially in front of their father. The silence on the subject was deafening. Harry interpreted it to mean no one in the family was suffering as much as he was, which forced him to nurse his ache secretly. The worst part was accepting no one would ever see him the way his mother did, which made it feel like a part of him had disappeared right along with her. The only thing left to do was try to live up to the person she always dreamed he'd be: someone extraordinary, even though he couldn't exactly see his way to that. His mother had often been moved to tears by her pride in all he had accomplished without any formal training. This had always confounded young Harry, but now he was beginning to understand.

He held the pile of hard-earned money in his hands, all

his savings from his summer touring with the circus and more money than he'd ever had before. He felt a certain pride in having skipped meals to ensure he wouldn't go home empty-handed. Part of him felt a tug back to Our Lady of Loreto to try once again to get Miss Schneider to accept the donation. He also knew in his heart she wouldn't. He reached up to touch the medal of St. Anthony that he wore on a chain around his neck, lifted it to his lips, and said a silent prayer to the patron saint of lost things. Knowing he would never be able to get back the mother he lost, he wanted to do the next best thing and fulfill her wishes, which for him meant acquiring a piano and continuing to study music. If anything, Harry felt more like his mother had been *stolen* from him—in which case it would still be under the purview of St. Anthony, and Harry knew how much his mother believed in the power of intercessory prayer as a way of expediting a message to God.

Harry bounded down the steps and over to the barbershop to ask Frank where to get a piano. Frank was finishing up a haircut as Harry walked in.

"Harry, my boy!" he greeted him. "Do you know I sold three more clarinets last week, thanks to you? Some folks came back in after they heard you demonstrating it last month." Frank went on to offer a gig to Harry at an upcoming wedding, which excited Harry, before he remembered why he was there in the first place.

"I came to ask you where to buy a piano. I need the best used one money can buy—for $75, that is." Harry laughed, feeling a little embarrassed.

"Wissner & Sons on Flatbush Avenue and Chandler Piano Company are both great," Frank said. "You should be able to find something good from one of them."

Harry thought maybe he should bring his brother Charlie along, but Charlie was a busy vaudevillian who was always off doing some show or another. Aside from that, he wasn't home when Harry returned. Feeling a tremendous urgency, Harry didn't want to wait a minute longer. It was a short walk to Livingston Street, where he looked at dozens of pianos in a few different stores before finally coming across a sturdy black upright. It was in good condition with all eighty-eight keys in working order. A salesman spied Harry and swooped in.

"The price includes tuning upon delivery," the salesman said.

"Is that so?" Harry asked. He sat down and started to play through some Scott Joplin ragtime tunes, starting with "Maple Leaf Rag."

"Hey, you're pretty good," the salesman said, brightening.

Harry progressed into various other pieces. "I call this the Joplin leaf medley," Harry said with a chuckle. "'Rose Leaf Rag,' 'Fig Leaf Rag.'"

"Not bad, not bad! How 'bout I give you the professional's discount? Free delivery."

It almost seemed too easy. "Hey, you wouldn't try to sell me something that's been kicked around, now, would you?" Harry asked.

"We bought it from St. Anthony's Church, so I'd be surprised if it had been kicked around, although I've come across some pretty tough nuns in my day," he laughed. "It was one of their older practice pianos."

Harry's interest piqued. "Did you say St. Anthony's?"

"Over on Manhattan Avenue in Greenpoint? Big red and white one, you can't miss it."

"Yeah, I know it," Harry said, reaching up to touch his St. Anthony medal, feeling his prayer had been received. "You got yourself a deal."

At Our Lady of Loreto, the choir rehearsed Giuseppe Ottavio Pitoni's *Cantate Domino.* Harry's heart swelled at the power of the Baroque piece they had been working on for weeks. But he grew antsy when rehearsal ran past the hour. At five minutes after, he waved a hand to get Miss Schneider's attention.

"Miss Schneider, I'm very sorry, but I have to go. NOW! My piano is coming!"

She smiled and stifled a laugh. "Okay, Harry. Go!"

As he scurried out the door, behind him he heard her dismiss the choir for the day.

Running home to meet the delivery truck, he passed a movie house with a "Help Wanted" sign and froze with even more excitement. He couldn't see in through the papered-over windows, but at the bottom of the sign in smaller print it read: "No Irish Need Apply." He was relieved—sometimes this kind of sign said, "Protestants Only," which would have disqualified him. He checked his watch and knew there wasn't time now— he'd have to come back. He took off running once again and arrived on his street just as the truck pulled up. Antonio emerged from the boot shop, wiping his hands on his work apron. Harry reached his father out of breath, sweat dripping from his brow.

"It's my piano, Papa."

"*Va bene. Brillante.* I wish your Mamma were here to see it. And hear you play it."

It was the first time his father had invoked his mother's name since she'd passed away. It made Harry feel her presence, as though she were there above them in the swaying trees. He wasn't expecting to feel so much new purpose from a piano, but it was unmistakable.

As he watched the delivery men struggle to fit the piano through any of their doors or windows, his excitement faded. Harry was crestfallen, pacing along the sidewalk as he awaited the bad news: the piano would have to be taken back. Antonio patted him on the back and quietly returned to his shop. Harry ran all the way to the store to talk to the salesman, who promised to send a different one that would fit. When the replacement arrived a few days later, Harry didn't care for it. He was disappointed by all the scratches and sticking keys. The salesman convinced him these things could be fixed, so Harry made his peace with it, and before too long, he was playing it for hours on end, blissfully unaware of its imperfections.

Blinded by the elation over his newfound focus, Harry nearly forgot to go back to the movie house to see about the job opening. A few days later, he rushed back there first thing in the morning before coffee or breakfast. But the sign was no longer in the window. He tried the door, only to find it locked. The business wouldn't open for another couple hours. He shrugged and began walking away when he heard a voice call out: "Can I help you with something, young man?"

Harry turned to see a man with a large ring of keys just arriving to open the place.

"I, uh, came about the sign that was up a few days ago," Harry said.

"The little *ragazzo* I hired never showed up for his first day of work," he said as he fumbled with the keys. He found the one to open the front door and motioned for Harry to come inside. "And here I thought I was a pretty good judge of character," he chuckled as Harry followed him into the darkened lobby. "I'm the manager, Joe Melillo."

"I'm Harry. Warren." He could see the name didn't make any particular impression. "My given name was Salvatore," Harry continued.

"Ah," the man said.

"And my last name used to be Guaragna," Harry added. Harry stood quietly with his hands in his pockets, not sure how this was supposed to go.

Joe asked what work experience he had, and Harry told him about his time serving as an altar boy and touring as a drummer with the circus. Joe raised an eyebrow with interest. "What about school?" he asked.

"I'm learning much more on my own."

"Everyone who works here starts as a candy butcher," Joe said.

"Oh, I can do that," Harry said.

"That's exactly what the last guy said!"

There was a moment of silence where Harry realized he was supposed to fill the gap with a convincing word. "If you hire me, Mr. Melillo, you can be sure I'll show up for the job."

"Okay, Harry," Joe said after thinking for a moment. "I'll give you a try. If it works out, you could take over as bag boy when Tony leaves next month."

"You mean be in charge of rubbish?"

Joe laughed. "No, see—the bag boy stands under the projector to catch the film as it comes out." This sounded to Harry like something he could do. "Can you start tomorrow? Ten a.m.?"

"Yes! I'll be here. Thank you. *Grazie mille.*"

"*E tu parli italiano?*"

"*Si, si, si,*" Harry said, confirming three times, as Italians are wont to do, that he spoke Italian.

"Well, why didn't you say so?"

Harry smiled and shrugged.

Harry loved working at the movie house. He could watch as many films as he liked and get sick to his stomach on candy. The best part of the job was something he hadn't even thought of at first: listening to the piano players who provided accompaniment for the silent films. Harry watched in awe how they improvised along with the mood and scene changes. This pairing was the birth of a powerful and lasting bond between music and film, and it was one in which Harry would have an enormous part to play.

One day, Harry struck up a conversation with Johnny, the

piano player who worked the same shifts as he did. "Say, you play some really great stuff," Harry told him.

"Thanks, kid. You play too?"

"I sure do. Just got myself a piano after I saved up playing drums with the Keene & Shippey carnival last summer," Harry said. "So, what other kind of work do you do?"

"I'm a song plugger." When Johnny saw confusion on Harry's face, he explained, "See, we go around playing all the songs music publishers want to sell the sheet music for. Vaudeville houses, nickelodeons, cafes, just about anywhere we can chase an audience or a performer down. I'm bringing in a vocalist next week to do some illustrated song performances. You ever seen one of those?"

"I don't believe I have," Harry said.

"Before the first film and during the reel changes, we do a slideshow of about a dozen hand-painted slides that illustrate a song. Sometimes they have a magic lantern effect—it's where you see things dissolving within the frame to make them disappear and reappear."

Harry became utterly enchanted with these illustrated song performances. He'd lose himself in the story as the slides went by and a talented female vocalist sang. He'd heard a few different singers who'd come through, but his favorite was a young woman named Norma Talmadge. After one performance, he approached her to say how much he enjoyed her singing. She said a curt thank-you before returning to her conversation with Johnny. Harry busied himself with tasks that allowed him to stay close enough to listen to their conversation.

"Sure, I can accompany you at that audition. Just get me the sheet music a day or two beforehand," Johnny told Miss Talmadge.

"Oh, thank you, Johnny. I'd hate to have to rely on just any old pianist who happens to be at Vitagraph."

"Important audition?"

"Oh, yes. They've hired me for background parts before, but this would be a featured singing role."

"Well, I'm sure you'll knock it out of the park. Get me that sheet music. Soon as you can," he called after her as she turned to leave.

"Will do. Toodle-oo," she said with a wave on her way out the door.

Harry asked Johnny about this Vitagraph place as they closed that night. When Johnny explained that it was a motion picture company out in Flatbush, Harry's interest was piqued. He couldn't get the name out of his mind, thinking about what it must be like to actually *make* the movies he was growing to love so much.

The next day, Friday, was when Harry usually dropped by the Brooklyn library to listen to recordings of Puccini and Tchaikovsky. While he was there, he stumbled onto a local history book and brought it into the listening room with him. Flipping it open randomly, he found a section on the explorer Giovanni da Verrazzano, the first European to discover the peninsula that would come to be known as Coney Island. This was clear on the other side of Brooklyn, which was not nearly as far for Harry as it had been for Giovanni, but similarly, it would be the discovery of a whole new world. He decided to find out for himself what this Vitagraph Studio was all about. Seeing how *vita* meant "life" in Italian, that in and of itself was intriguing. He also felt it was time to start discovering his own world outside of his neighborhood.

When Harry saw Johnny next, he had lots more questions.

"Does Vitagraph make some of the movies we show here?" Harry wanted to know.

"Sure they do," Johnny said. "They started out doing news-reels, but now they're doing everything. It's an amazing place. I've never seen anything like it. Catch the Brighton line and go out there. Anyone can be hired as an extra for the day."

"You mean for extra work they don't have anyone else to do?" Harry wondered.

"Extras are people who appear in the background of scenes who don't have any speaking lines. Regular Janes and Joes, you know? You just have to get there at the crack of dawn to line up if you want to be considered. You don't have to be an actor, but it's not paid either."

"No pay?" Harry said. "Hm." The truth was, this mattered little, because Harry saw it as a way into the business he now desperately wanted to be in.

On a day off from work, Harry took the elevated BMT train out to East Fourteenth Street and Locust Avenue in Flatbush.

As the train pulled into the station, he spotted a towering red brick smokestack reaching into the clouds with "Vitagraph" painted vertically down one side. He hopped off the train and walked the remaining blocks with newfound purpose. The place was as much a marvel as Johnny described. Harry walked the property's perimeter, taking in all the fascinations: giant props being moved from place to place, actors running around in all manner of costume, and lots of people shouting excitedly with what seemed to Harry like the urgency of life and death. He loved everything about it.

There was good reason for the excitement. As a new art form, movies were quickly becoming the public's preferred form of entertainment, threatening to put vaudeville out business. Vitagraph couldn't crank them out fast enough for the insatiable appetite. Peering into one of the windows, Harry saw a warehouse filled with workers—all women, handling strips of film like seamstresses cutting and sewing fabric. A young man stepped up beside Harry to peer through the window and gape at the efficiency of it all.

"Isn't this place the most amazing sight you've ever seen?" he said. "The first modern motion picture company in the country, with all the departments right here in one place."

Sure enough, as Harry looked around, he saw other buildings marked Costume Shop, Set Design Shop, Production Office, and so on. Vitagraph's production and distribution model would become the blueprint for all the major studios that followed, right through to the end of the studio system in the 1950s.

"One of the guys who started this place used to be a newspaper man, a cartoonist, J. Stuart Blackton," the man said.

"You don't say," Harry replied.

"When he was sent to interview Thomas Edison about his new film projector, Edison talked him into getting one of his own and some films. A year later, Blackton got himself a partner and built this place to go into competition with him."

"That's some ambition," Harry said.

Suddenly, someone from inside the casting office stepped outside and started speaking to the other hopeful extras. As the crowd eagerly gathered around, Harry struggled to hear what the casting assistant was saying.

"Hey, c'mon!" the guy said. "It looks like we're being called in." Seeing Harry's confused face, he said, "They're calling for men between eighteen and twenty-five. That's you, ain't it?"

"Sure, sure!" Harry's head was swimming as he ran off with his new pal.

Harry didn't get cast that day, but he didn't give up. He rode the train out to Flatbush several times before he was picked as an extra. He was chosen for a war movie, which meant he had to be fitted for a military uniform. As he caught a glimpse of himself in this look, he scarcely recognized the foreboding image staring back at him. Because film lighting had not yet been invented, the length of each shooting day was determined by the amount of daylight. Harry learned this from one of the fellow extras on set who had worked on the four-reel adaptation of *Les Misérables*.

"And they did *The Life of Moses,* which was one of the first feature-length films. No one was sure if folks would sit for more than one reel of film until that one," the guy told him.

After the war film, Harry kept returning to Vitagraph and getting picked for more productions. He was thrilled to learn the studio was even doing opera stories. Eventually, it seemed the time had come to quit the movie house. Joe Melillo was sorry to see him go but wished him all the best.

Working on set one day, Harry stumbled across a group of three-part harmony singers midsong. Harry stopped to listen and applauded when they finished. "You ever think about expanding into a quartet?" he asked.

The tenor, a young man named George Cullen, said, "As a matter of fact, we've been looking for a fellow who can double as a tenor or baritone."

"I have the range," Harry assured him.

"I should mention it's for no pay . . ."

"How does anyone survive out here?" Harry asked with a laugh. Still, he wanted to try out.

George and the other two singers were impressed with Harry's musical abilities and offered him the job. They began performing at parties, on street corners, and on the Vitagraph lot, where they hoped someone would overhear and want to feature them.

"Where'd you learn to sing so well, Harry?" George asked.

"Our Lady of Loreto. How about you?"

"My brother taught me," George said. "But he joined the service, so I had to start my own group."

George quickly became a good friend to Harry. The others in the quartet worked odd jobs on the Vitagraph lot and helped get Harry on the payroll as a property man. He was a quick study and hard worker, learning the system for procuring all the props needed for each scene and making sure to have them ready at the right time. The job paid $30 a week. In between films, he would be laid off, but he kept getting hired back one project after another. Soon, he was a familiar face around the lot.

Harry quickly learned why it was called the "hurry up and wait" business: it took a tremendous amount of coordination to get everything set and everyone ready for each shot. During the wait time, Harry usually found his way to the piano—which he oversaw as the prop man—to tinker with and practice pieces he was learning. Before long, his playing caught the ear of one of Vitagraph's stars, Corinne Griffith. She approached Harry at the piano.

"I've been listening to you play," she said. "You have such a nice touch on the piano." Harry felt himself blush. "Would you consider playing mood music while I'm doing my scenes?"

"To help you get in the mood?" he asked. Ms. Griffiths giggled. "Of course, sure!" Harry said, trying to move past his embarrassment.

"I'd like you start as soon as possible." She turned to call to the director, who was also her husband, clear across the set. "Webster? Webster, please come here, dear, and meet—" She turned back to Harry.

"Harry," he said.

"Harry. Come meet Harry!"

Webster smiled and signaled he was coming over.

"Webster, dear, this is Harry. He's agreed to play my mood music."

When Webster made his way over, he stuck out his hand for a shake. "I agree, your playing is top rate. Where'd you learn?"

"I've been teaching myself," Harry said shyly. "I play nine other instruments too. I've been working on trumpet and trombone recently."

"And you taught yourself to play *all* of them?" Webster asked incredulously. "Are you some kind of genius or something?" He and Corrine started laughing as Harry politely smiled. Even when people teed Harry up to talk himself up, he resisted it. Harry knew Webster Campbell, with his leading man looks, had started out as an actor, as many of the Vitagraph directors had. It felt quite strange to suddenly be having such a long conversation with the two most important people at the studio.

Over time, Webster's admiration of Harry's talent deepened, and he hired him to work on many more of his films. He told other Vitagraph directors to hire Harry too, so he could stay busy and avoid dreaded downtime. After a few months, Webster and Corrine went to Harry after wrapping for the day. "You're very talented, Harry," Corrine said. "We think you should be doing more than the mood music, so we can arrange to have you paid more. How does that sound?"

"What else would you have me do?" Harry asked.

"I'd like you to be my assistant director," Webster said. "Corrine tells me how much you like reading the scripts, so you'd just need to time the scenes for me and break them down for production, which I can show you how to do."

"Yes! I'd love to!" Harry said.

"Great. We'll see to it that you're transferred out of Props right away, so you can start next week."

Harry could hardly contain his excitement. He knew being an assistant director would be a lot of responsibility. He would have to keep track of costume changes and which way actors exited offscreen for continuity—tasks that would later belong to the new position of a script supervisor. He'd need to procure the raw film stock, deliver the shot footage for processing, and create a report at the end of the day that detailed how many shots were done. During shooting, he'd put down marks for the actors, measuring nine feet away from the lens so they wouldn't get any closer to the camera and go out of focus. He'd carry the tripod around for the cameraman, who grinded the film by hand— not an easy job, because the film buckled once it got too cold outside. This made things difficult working with the camera, or the "lunch box," as it was nicknamed for its appearance.

During one of his first days shooting on location, Harry learned that part of the job of the assistant director was to pay off the cops when they'd come around, because there was no system for permits. Cash was the key to solving most of the problems they encountered. Soon, cops began seeing it as an easy payout and were sure to visit each film crew.

Harry discovered the first thing he didn't like about working for Vitagraph through this experience: dealing with what he called "the skinflint studio bosses." At the end of each day shooting on location, he'd have to report to them how much he had to pay the cops off. No matter the cost, it was always too much for them, and they'd harass Harry over it.

One day on set, Harry had to help the prop department by starting up a Ford that was going to be used in a scene. He broke his arm while cranking it. This didn't slow him down much—he insisted he keep working once he had the bone set.

During the cold months, one of his other assistant director friends, Phil Quinn, invited Harry to sleep on his couch in Flatbush so Harry wouldn't have to ride the train back and forth so much in the freezing cold. Harry loved this life. Waking up early, working late into the night, and not making much money. Somehow it seemed like his calling.

Corrine and Webster wanted to see Harry do well. They recommended him for gigs at Brooklyn movie houses, vaudeville venues, and open-air theaters. Harry's love of opera and his ability to transpose for piano was deepening his understanding of music theory. Playing at movie houses and improvising along with the film in real time would prove to be an important skill for him. He surprised himself at what a natural gift he had for this. The more he played along with films, the more he wanted to write his own original songs. One theater he frequently worked at on Manhattan's East Side paid him $12 a week in nickels and dimes. When Webster and Corrine asked him how it was working there, he said told them it was great, except for being lopsided on the way home on the trolley car with all those coins.

One night while Harry was on the train, he ran into Johnny from Joe's movie house. Harry thanked him for first telling him about Vitagraph. It had changed his life and put him on a whole new path.

"Hey, Harry," George called out to him on the Vitagraph lot one day. "You have any plans yet to see *The Fall of a Nation*?"

"Is that the one with an original score played by a full orchestra?" Harry asked.

"Yes! It's at the Liberty Theatre. You wanna go Saturday night?"

The two young musicians found it incredibly exciting to witness this first—an entire orchestra, not just a piano, playing a live soundtrack. Harry's brother Charlie had done vaudeville shows at the Liberty; Harry had worked there as a stagehand, and as part of the stage crew on first performance ever at Brooklyn's Palace Theatre. But the Liberty, like so many others as vaudeville was on its way out, was quickly becoming strictly a movie theater, even more so now with this exciting development of a live orchestra.

The Fall of a Nation did not disappoint. Harry and George knew it signaled something big for movies. It made Harry even more eager to go to work every day on film sets. His next job was as the assistant director for a 1917 film that would be shot entirely on location on Long Island. *For France*, directed by Wesley Ruggles, was a World War I film with lots of battle scenes. The entire cast and crew descended on the area for the duration of the shoot, comprising top talent across all departments at Vitagraph. Early in the filming, some townspeople got whipped into hysteria after someone thought the town was being invaded by German Uhlan cavalry men on horseback. The costumes and props people couldn't help but take pride in their work for being so authentic. As assistant director, it was Harry's job to try to talk the locals down.

"Ma'am, there's nothing to worry about. We're here from the Vitagraph Studio in Brooklyn making a movie. None of this is real."

Several people were still not convinced. Harry had to show them the camera equipment and introduce them to some of the actors to prove they were in no danger.

One of the Vitagraph directors Webster Campbell had recommended Harry to was an Australian named Paul Scardon. When Scardon hired Harry to be his AD, it was another learning experience, including an exchange Harry had with a fortune teller on set. She'd been taking people aside one by one, and Harry couldn't help but be curious about what she might say about his future. He ducked into her tent.

After inviting him to sit, she closed her eyes and took his hands in hers. "I see you are going to move out of New York one day," she said.

"Really? But I love New York."

"You will win several medals of some kind and be very successful."

"But not in New York?" he wanted to clarify.

"That is correct."

He never forgot her words—because they mostly came true.

Harry loved the ingenuity of the burgeoning art form, which was developing new techniques all the time. Vitagraph created a rotating stage that could face east in the morning or west in the afternoon. With the advent of carbon lights, the studio was then able to shoot indoors by lighting through a glass roof on the set, which Harry described as looking like a French attic. But then too much light would get in, so the crew had to paint it and put the carbon lights inside—this was the beginning of lighting sets. Vitagraph's foray into night shooting came after the invention of arc lights.

Harry worked on many night shoots in Westchester County, New York, with British director Wilfred North. He learned that much of the time it was song lyricists who wrote the silent film subtitles, such as "Go Away!" and "Don't Come Home!"

One of Harry's next gigs that year was as an assistant director on *Over the Top*, directed by Guy Empey. It was on location in Georgia and marked the first time Harry had ever heard a Southern accent. It was another war film shot by an American who'd made a mark fighting alongside the British Army. Shooting trench warfare made Harry feel like he was in the war himself.

In the summertime, Harry picked up extra work as a pianist in the Catskills, where he learned more Yiddish. He didn't mind if anyone thought he was Jewish, if it meant being asked back to work again.

In the winters, he looked forward to the Vitagraph Ball.

No matter how extravagant the food was at the ball, Harry always made George go with him to Feltman's beforehand for what Harry considered the best hot dog in the world. One year, George Cullen suggested they bring dates to this event, which the studio hosted at Stauch's Pavilion on Coney Island.

"A date? Who would I ask?" Harry asked.

"Anyone you fancy," George laughed. "Have you not noticed all the young ladies who come out to hear us sing?"

Their quartet had become the official quartet of Brooklyn Heights; every neighborhood had its own. And it was true—they'd begun drawing quite a crowd of young people who loved the free entertainment.

George had been talking a lot lately about a girl named Joan he was growing fond of. "I've started visiting her every Wednesday on 'beaus' night,' A'course, it's only visits at her house—she's not allowed out with me."

"I don't know if I'd trust you either," Harry joked.

George swatted him. "Say," he said, "you should come along one of these nights and meet her friend who lives in the apartment downstairs."

"Oh, yeah?" Harry asked.

"Seems like a real nice girl. I think her name is Josephine."

Chapter Three

As the door opened for George and Harry on beaus' night a couple weeks later, Joan ushered them inside and took their hats and coats. She was a lively host and quite lovely—Harry could see right away why George enjoyed spending time with her. She invited them into the parlor, where she had set out iced tea and cookies. As they exchanged pleasantries, Josephine Wensler appeared backlit and framed by a doorway, as if she were the subject of a painting. She commanded Harry's attention with her robin-red hair and aura of mystery. He gasped at the sight of her, then quickly scanned the others' faces, hoping no one had heard.

"Hello, George," Josephine said, approaching them. Then she turned to Harry and let him speak first. He introduced himself, shaking her gloved hand.

The four sat together in conversation before breaking off into couples, with music playing in the background. Harry's heart raced and he felt as though he could almost *see* the electricity charging the air.

"Have you lived in New York long?" Josephine asked him.

"All my life. Born right here in Brooklyn on Christmas Eve."

"I've spent my whole life in this neighborhood too," she said, smiling. "I wonder why I've never seen you before?"

"I don't know. But I know I would have remembered you . . ." Harry didn't realize how smitten he sounded until it was too late. He didn't have much experience courting young ladies, so instead of putting on airs, he spoke simply and from the heart. It was an attribute that would serve him well in his craft.

Harry and Josephine hit it off, and Wednesday beaus' night visits became a weekly event. They laughed a lot when they were together, and Josephine soon became enamored with Harry's singing and piano playing. She was most struck by how humble he was about his talent. If Harry had been shy at first, he grew more confident with each compliment from her. She loved when he played "Come Josephine in My Flying Machine" for her, a pretty little waltz with lighthearted lyrics:

Oh, say, let us fly, dear
Where, kid?
To the sky, dear
Oh, you flying machine!
Jump in, Miss Josephine
Ship a-hoy
Oh, joy! What a feeling
Where, boy?
In the ceiling
Ho, high hoopla

We fly to the sky so high
Come, Josephine, in my flying machine
Going up, she goes! Up she goes
Balance yourself like a bird on a beam
In the air she goes, there she goes!
Up, up, a little bit higher
Oh, my! The moon is on fire
Come, Josephine, in my flying machine
Going up, all on, goodbye

Josephine was falling for Harry. "I'd like to ask my parents if they'd allow you to visit in our home," she told him.

That sounded wonderful to Harry. Only later would he learn of Josephine's decision not to tell him about her father's low opinion of Italians before introducing them. She'd hoped Harry, regardless of his heritage, would be able to win over her father. The following Wednesday, when Harry and George arrived for their visit, Josephine led Harry downstairs to her family's basement house to meet her parents. Harry found Jo's father stern, while her mother was much softer, almost mystical. Harry was happy to see Josephine took more after her mother.

A few days later at Vitagraph, George ran over to Harry. He'd been tasked to deliver some unfortunate news. "Don't shoot the messenger," George prefaced. "I was asked to tell you not to call on Josephine again."

"What? I thought we really hit it off," Harry said, disappointed.

"Oh, Josephine thoroughly enjoyed your company. Her father, on the other hand . . ."

Before Harry could find his words, a large film set was wheeled right through the middle of their conversation.

"Look around, Harry. There are plenty of fish in the sea," George said, trying to cheer him up.

"Not like Josephine. Not with *hair* like Josephine's! She's more mermaid than fish," Harry said dreamily.

"Oh, you've got it bad," George teased.

They both laughed. Then the smile slid off Harry's face as reality sank in. Harry respected Mr. Wensler's wishes, but he couldn't help periodically asking George if Josephine had begun seeing any other company on beaus' night. George said he'd seen her at Joan's house from time to time, but never with a male visitor of her own.

A whole year passed. One day, as Harry boarded a Manhattan-bound elevated train, he saw *that hair* again. He made his way to the front of the train car. As he turned to look at the woman's face, she noticed him right away.

"Harry?" she said, surprised. She motioned for him to sit down. Harry felt butterflies swirl in his stomach, just like when he'd first met her. "How wonderful to see you again!"

"It must be fate," he laughed.

She stared at him for a moment, and he hoped he hadn't said the wrong thing.

"I'm sure you're right. *Quite* sure." The intensity she attached to this statement took Harry by surprise, but he was intrigued.

"Forgive me. Sometimes I get such strong signals about things. My mother says it's because I was born with a caul."

He wasn't sure what she was referring to, so he covered with humor—one of his favorite strategies. "Is that like a calling? Hopefully, not to be a nun," he joked.

She giggled before explaining. "A caul is a veil over a baby's face at birth. It's extremely rare. My mother says it's the mark of something very special."

"I would have to agree," Harry said.

"Moses was a caulbearer. Oh, and if you've read Dickens' *David Copperfield*?"

"I have," Harry said. Then, remembering: "That's right! He was upset when something he was born with was auctioned off."

"Yes! Do you like to read, Harry?"

"I sure do. It's my second favorite thing, next to music," he said cheerily, considering her obvious approval.

"A caul is said to be good luck," Josephine said. She told him about how, in ancient Rome, midwives would steal them to sell because it was believed they could cure disease. Cauls were prized by sailors, who believed they protected them from drowning. In medieval times, they were seen as a talisman against evil. "My mother believes caulbearers may even have supernatural abilities—that we can see beyond the veil," she said, then stopped, suddenly self-conscious. "I'm probably making it sound like witchcraft. Forgive me if I—"

"No, not at all," Harry assured her. He found this fascinating. "It's God-given, I'm sure."

Her body language softened, and she smiled. "It's good to know you don't scare easily."

He scoffed at the idea. "Oh, no. As the youngest of eleven, I'm a survivor," he laughed.

"You have *ten* brothers and sisters? Your mother is surely a strong woman."

"Yes, she was," Harry said, his demeanor changing before her eyes. "She passed away when I was fifteen."

"Oh, you poor dear," Josephine said, placing a gloved hand atop his.

Harry lifted his eyes to meet hers and something unmistakable passed between them.

When the train reached Josephine's stop, Harry asked if he could walk with her. Taking in the sights and sounds of the Gilded Age of Manhattan, surrounded by skyscrapers and streetcars, Harry felt his spirit soar as he strolled along with this enchanting young lady. He spotted an open park bench and asked if she'd like to sit.

"Sure," she said, "I have a few more minutes before I have to meet my friend."

Harry left her at the bench to investigate a nearby food cart and returned with a bag of peanuts and two seltzers. He looked up at the statue towering above them. "Well, what do you know? It's Verdi. This is Verdi Square," Harry said, looking around.

"You Italians are rather proud, aren't you?" she teased. "He must be your favorite composer."

"Oh, no. My favorite is Puccini, without question."

"That's it!" she exclaimed. "That's how you can win over my father! By playing arias. He loves opera!"

Harry and Josephine went back to sharing beaus' night with George and Joan at Joan's house. This gave Josephine time to let her father know she'd begun visiting with Harry again. She knew he would come around to liking Harry if he would just give him a chance.

"He is a wonderful musician, Father. He's been learning your favorite aria, 'Celeste Aida,'" Josephine told him. "Would it be all right if I invited him to play it for you?"

Mr. Wensler reluctantly agreed but couldn't help being impressed by Harry's talent. He reversed his position and allowed Josephine to see Harry, who worked hard to win her father over, learning as many arias as he could with ten-cent sheet music he'd buy from Woolworth's: Verdi, Monteverdi, and, of course, Puccini. Harry was touched that Josephine's father loved opera almost as much as he did, and that Mr. Wensler finally began easing his stance toward Harry. Even though he agreed to allow Harry to call on Josephine, he would stomp his boot promptly at 11:30 each time Harry visited, an inelegant cue for Harry to be on his way.

On April 2, 1917, Harry and Josephine were on their way to the movie house when they saw the headline of *The New York Times*:

PRESIDENT CALLS FOR WAR DECLARATION,

STRONGER NAVY, NEW ARMY OF 500,000 MEN,

FULL CO-OPERATION WITH GERMANY'S FOES

They knew what this would likely mean—it was only a matter of time before Harry would be drafted. Having already confessed their love for one another, this turn of events brought forth a certain urgency.

"Josephine, I would like very much for you to marry me," Harry told her after the movie let out.

She put her arms around him. "I would like that too," she said, sealing it with a kiss.

They married on December 18 that year in a small ceremony, their hearts full of promise for their future together.

Mr. Wensler passed away not long after Harry and Josephine married, so the newlyweds moved in with Josephine's mother, Julia, along with Josephine's sister Amelia and her husband, Ernie, who owned an appliance store. Mrs. Wensler was a self-described healer who would lay hands on neighborhood children to cure their sicknesses. She felt strongly that Josephine was derelict for not using her caulbearer gifts, but the truth was that Josephine didn't feel any instinct about how to go about it. Her focus was on becoming a highly skilled seamstress who enjoyed making clothes for her new husband.

Harry tried to get into the Navy to avoid joining the Army, but he was turned down several times for reasons he didn't understand. When Harry's draft paperwork arrived, it was for the Army, but he refused to give up on getting in the Navy. Somehow, in time, he convinced the Navy to allow him to join its ranks. He began his naval training in the fall of 1918 in Pelham Bay in the Bronx. He wanted to join the entertainment troupe there, but he couldn't get in because it was already bursting with Broadway talent. Instead, he was stationed at Montauk Point on Long Island and given a job as a photographer. With his knowledge of motion picture cameras, he figured it couldn't be too difficult, so he studied basic composition and other elements of what made for a strong image. He was mostly grateful he wouldn't be too far from home so he could visit his new bride often.

Being out in Montauk felt like the end of the world, despite being only a hundred miles from New York City. Given the remote feeling of the place, Harry naturally became the entertainer, as the only sailor who could play piano. Once his cohorts learned of his ability, they demanded he play for them nightly. He'd play the hits of the day, like Irving Berlin's "Oh! I Hate to Get Up in the Morning"— a favorite among the troops —Van and Schenck's "In the Land of Yamo Yamo," and "I Don't Know Where I'm Going but I'm on My Way." It was during this period that Harry felt compelled to write original songs.

One evening, a civilian visited the base. As a few officers showed her around, Harry was performing a song for his comrades. Everyone was always quick to notice the presence of a woman and Harry saw out of the corner of his eye that she'd stopped to listen. Afterward, the officers introduced her to Harry.

"You're quite a talent," she said. "I'd like your help putting together some musical acts for the servicemen."

"Sure," Harry said. "I worked at Vitagraph Studios for a few years, so I know all kinds of performers, whatever you might be looking for."

"Vitagraph?" she smiled. "Fabulous!"

All it took was one of the guys to overhear. "Hey! Harry here's been holding out on us!" an officer announced to the room. "We're stuck here, bored out of our skulls, when you could be getting us Vitagraph pictures to watch on the regular?"

"Now, who said anything about that?" Harry asked.

"You just did!"

The spirited discussion drew more sailors around. "Say, what's all the excitement about?" someone shouted.

"Harry here can get us Vitagraph films!" the officer said.

"No kidding! Well, whattya waiting for, Harry?"

Harry looked at his commanding officer, unsure how to respond. The officer smiled and snickered. "I guess that settles it, Harry," he said. "You can take leave tomorrow to go pick up some films for us."

Harry saluted the officer and the troops erupted in cheers.

And just like that, Harry became the hero of his desolate naval base. This arrangement worked out well for him because each time he went back to Vitagraph in Brooklyn, he could stop in on Josephine and his family before heading back to Montauk with the film reels. During one of these visits, Josephine had some news.

"We're going to have a baby," she whispered in his ear.

He lit up with joy. "Really?" They exchanged ecstatic smiles. "How are you feeling?"

"I feel great—so far!" she assured him.

He took her in a deep embrace and gently placed a hand to her belly.

The joyful news deepened when Harry found out he'd only

have to spend less than half a year in the service. The irony at the end of his time was that he owed the Navy money for the partial cost of his uniform. Josephine had to come up with thirty dollars to "bail him out," as she described it. With his service complete in January 1919, Harry returned to Vitagraph, but production had slowed down. He ran into George and one of his old assistant director buddies, Phil.

"What was the best thing about your time in the Navy?" Phil asked him over hot dogs.

"That I only had to spend a year in it!" Harry laughed. "You know, no complaints. I had plenty of time to start writing songs."

"Well, you ought to play them for my brother-in-law, Al Piantadosi," Phil said.

"That's your brother-in-law?" George asked. "The great ragtime pianist? Didn't he write that song, 'I Didn't Raise My Boy to Be a Soldier'? That's quite an offer, Harry."

Harry thought so too, so Phil agreed to set up a meeting between them. He told Harry and George about how Al had recently became involved in a new organization, ASCAP, that was supposed to help musicians get paid when their songs were played publicly.

"Oh, I've read about it." Harry said. "Irving Berlin and Victor Herbert founded it a few years ago."

"Al says it's going to make it so songwriters can actually make a living."

"Wouldn't that be something?" Harry exclaimed.

～

When Harry finally met Al Piantadosi, things didn't go as he'd hoped. Al said there wasn't much he could do to help him just then—perhaps because the best song Harry had to play for him was about a sailor, which was too like one of Al's own songs. But Al encouraged Harry to keep writing. They would cross paths again, but in the meantime, Harry needed work. Next, he went to see Guy Empey, a director he used to work for, to see if he knew of anything.

"You speak Italian, don't you?" Guy asked, remembering Harry's ear for languages. "Go down to the Travelers Insurance company. Tell 'em I sent you. They insure all the stevedores in New York Harbor, and they always need guys who speak another language to work as claims investigators."

Harry took Guy up on this offer and was soon hired. The celebrating didn't last long, though—his first day on the docks, he realized the Italians there were all Sicilian. He couldn't understand a word of their dialect! Harry hated having to go home and give the news to Josephine. He didn't know what he was going to do next, but he knew he'd better figure it out fast with a baby on the way.

On one of their last nights out before the baby arrived, they went to see the film *Mickey*, starring Mabel Normand. It marked a turning point in film history, one that would have great relevance to Harry's career path. With the song "Pretty Mickey," the film was the first to ever use a theme song. The concept caught on, and theme songs were seen as the best way to publicize a movie. "Pretty Mickey" quickly became the go-to tune for movie house pit pianists and orchestras everywhere.

"They're going to want a theme song for every film now, just wait," Harry said to Josephine.

"Then that means they'll need lots of songwriters to write them!" she said.

In 1919, Harry and Jo welcomed Harry Jr., though they called him Sonny. They would go out for walks on Sundays in Prospect Park and stop for an egg cream or a strawberry charlotte russe. When Harry's brother Charlie stopped by to see the baby, he told Harry he'd heard Healy's Saloon out in Sheepshead Bay was looking for a pianist. Harry jumped on it right away. It turned out to be an excellent fit for him—he was familiar with many kinds of songs, and Healy's regularly hosted a German night, Irish night, Italian night, and more.

One day after he'd been playing there for a while, a couple guys walked in during his set. When they approached him on a break, Harry guessed by their demeanor that this wasn't the first bar they'd visited that night.

"You can play just about anything!" one of them said.

"Where'd they find you?" the other wanted to know. Before Harry could answer, the guy said, "I'm Billy Joyce, and this here is Jack Egan."

"You two are musicians?"

"And song pluggers extraordinaire, Jack said."

"And a little *farshnashkied?*" Harry laughed, using his favorite Yiddish word for "drunk." "I just wrote another new tune of my own today. Would you like to hear it? It's called 'I Learned to Love You When I Learned My ABCs.'"

"Hey, that's a pretty good title," Billy said.

Harry launched into his song and Jack and Billy bopped their heads along to the beat. "You've gotta come in and play this for our boss on Monday," Billy said.

Harry was ecstatic. When Billy took out a cigarette, Harry thought fast, striking a match on the bottom of his shoe to provide his new friend with a light.

"Really? Where's that?" Harry asked.

"Stark and Cowan Music Publishers," Jack said.

Harry couldn't wait to tell Josephine. He arrived home late, but she was still up with the baby. He spilled out the whole story to her and she smiled back at him, rocking little Sonny.

"Here, let me take him," Harry said. "I want to see what he thinks of my song." He hummed his tune slowly as a lullaby to his contented son.

The next day, Harry played his song for Rubey Cowan, co-founder of Stark & Cowan. Rubey liked it and asked if he had more.

"About a dozen," Harry said, "and I'm writing more all the time."

Jack and Billy vouched for some of the other songs Harry had played for them.

"I could use you as a song plugger. It pays $20 a week," Rubey said.

"Thank you, Mr. Cowan! That's very kind of you—*very* kind!" Harry said. "My wife will insist on making you dinner." They all laughed. And just like that, Harry was in the music business.

Chapter Four

ALLEYMEN

Harry had every reason to be excited about this new opportunity. The 1920s were shaping up to be a very good decade for songwriters. With the first public entertainment broadcast on radio in 1920, daily broadcasts followed in 1921. Before long, Harry's brother-in-law, Ernie, would have a hard time keeping a new gadget called the transistor radio on the shelves of his appliance store. Still, he set one aside as a gift to Harry and Josephine, who couldn't afford to purchase their own.

But things were about to change for the Warrens. During the roaring twenties, there was plenty of money to be made—even in 1917, music publishers sold two billion copies of sheet music. With each fifty-cent copy, the publisher could make $500,000 from the sale of a million copies and hitting the $5 million mark was not unusual. Harry was dismayed when Woolworth's, one of the biggest sellers of sheet music, stopped carrying it shortly after he started with Stark & Cowan Music Publishing. But it would turn out to be a minor blip with little effect on the vitality of the industry and his own earning power.

The beating heart of the music business was Tin Pan Alley, a moniker that described the cacophony of songs, singers, and piano playing that drifted out of the music publishing offices on West Twenty-Eighth Street between Fifth and Sixth Avenues in Manhattan. In the warm months when all the windows were open, Harry described it to Josephine as sounding like "the Tower of Babel!" Tin Pan Alley later moved further uptown, but what would remain was the symbiotic relationship between the publishing houses and the theaters—performers were dependent on songs, while the publishers were dependent on the performers to make them hits. One of Harry's first songs to work on as a song plugger was "Blue and Broken-Hearted," which Bing Crosby would eventually have a big hit with. Harry enjoyed performing the song, but being such a sensitive soul, he struggled with the inevitable rejection that came with the territory. He was also working "They're Wearing 'Em Higher in Hawaii," and even though Harry felt ridiculous pronouncing "Hawaii" like "ha-why-ya," he had to act like it was the greatest song ever written. For every hit and beloved classic, Tin Pan Alley produced many more low-quality numbers designed to appeal to the masses.

Rubey Cowan quickly became a mentor to Harry. There could be a lot of turnover with song pluggers, but Rubey took the time to teach Harry the ropes and do all he could to ensure his success.

"What you wanna do is start with one of the early vaudeville shows," Rubey said, "then hit the second show at one of the Loew's houses. After that, get to the final show of the day at one of the Keith houses, and depending on your luck, maybe you go after the singing waiters in one of the cafés on your way home."

"Sounds exhausting," Harry replied quite honestly.

Rubey laughed. "Welcome to show business, kid!"

Harry was one to wear his heart on his sleeve. Rubey didn't want him to lose that quality because it would serve him well in the craft of songwriting.

"You have a lot of talent, Harry," Rubey said. "The only way to develop it is by putting in the time. When you're not out there pounding the pavement, you're in here writing."

To prove how much Rubey believed in Harry, he and his wife, Grace, named their baby boy Warren. Ironically, Warren Cowan would go on to be one of the most sought-after publicists in Hollywood, while Harry did his level best to avoid publicity throughout his career.

Harry felt an incredible sense of belonging in Tin Pan Alley. He loved soaking up the culture of songwriters, publishers, and singers—a colorful community of personalities and artists all pursuing the same dream. It reminded him of Vitagraph Studios. He liked the idea that while most other people were gathering to play cards and talk politics, songwriters were coming together to work on songs. The selling part of the job didn't get much easier for him, however, due to his lack of natural showmanship. He felt awkward approaching performers he could see were getting accosted by song pluggers left and right. Harry detested being lumped in with everyone else. He'd grown up in a family that believed he was special, and this was the last thing he felt when dealing with people who viewed him as a pest.

His shyness did little to get him over the job's hurdles, such as getting past backstage guards. On the days he couldn't get into the theater, he was reduced to waiting around in the alley for a performer to step out for a smoke break, or to following them to a bar after the show.

"I feel like a damn wet moccasin," he told Josephine after a particularly long day.

"You're an artist trapped in the job of a salesman," she said empathetically.

"We had to go see Belle Baker to plug a few songs today," he told her. "It's not quite as bad when you're invited into someone's home. At least you know they halfway want you there."

"Belle Baker is fabulous!" Josephine remembered seeing one of her vaudeville acts.

"Sure, sure. You know who's not so fabulous?" Harry retorted. "Her little Herbie, tearing around the place on his tricycle and smashing into my shins!" Josephine laughed at the image of this. "You should have heard her. I'm doing everything not to scream out in pain as she kept going on and on about him. 'Look at that little doll. Isn't he wonderful?'"

Josephine laughed even harder until Harry gave in and laughed along with her. Harry knew he had to pay his dues, but the hardest part was supporting his family on $20 a week. It required incredible sacrifice, like skipping lunch most days or settling for a glass of milk and some ginger snaps. On one particularly hungry morning, when didn't know how he would be able to go without lunch again, he caught a break. When Harry arrived at the office, Rubey jumped out of his chair.

"Harry, we need to get this orchestration over to Ross Gorman right away," he said, shoving some sheet music into Harry's hands. Gorman was a virtuoso clarinetist and arranger who played with the Paul Whiteman Orchestra.

Harry was relieved to be spared a morning of song plugging. He arrived at Gorman's apartment and summoned all his courage before knocking. But when the door opened, Harry found Ross to be a friendly fellow. Harry followed Ross inside and began looking around the place. It was a well- appointed apartment with lots of books and art. Harry wondered if he'd ever be able to afford anything remotely like it. He was gazing out the window at the bustling street below when he decided he had nothing to lose.

"Mr. Gorman, I hope this isn't inappropriate, but I have a melody I've been working on, and I was wondering if I could play it for you to see what you think?" Harry asked. Ross motioned for Harry to sit at the piano. "Really?"

"Sure, let's hear it," Ross said.

Harry sat down and began to play while Ross listened intently. "Keep going," Ross said as he walked into the other room. He returned with his horn and jumped right in, playing with Harry—the two of them speaking through their instruments. Harry loved where Ross was taking his musical ideas.

"Great changes, Harry," Ross said. "Really nice tune!"

"Thank you! You know," Harry said, "I'm always working on finding something that sounds a little different than what's out there."

"How would you like to hear the Paul Whiteman band

play this?" Ross asked. Harry was in shock, unable to formulate a response. "I could have an orchestration ready for next Wednesday night and you can come hear it at the Palais Royale."

"Wow, really? Thank you, Mr. Gorman," Harry said.

"Call me Ross!"

Harry was so excited, he almost left the apartment without the package.

"Harry, the orchestration!" Ross called after him, holding up the envelope.

Harry laughed and retrieved it from Ross. He didn't have the heart to tell Ross it would be impossible for him to get into the plush Palais Royale on his paltry salary. Even on the weeks when he was handed a check on Friday, Rubey usually asked him not to cash it until Tuesday.

When Harry returned to the Stark & Cowan office, he ran into Scottish lyricist Edgar Leslie. Edgar had written the lyrics for the Al Piantadosi song "I'm a Yiddish Cowboy." When Harry first realized this connection, he told Edgar about meeting Piantadosi just after he'd gotten out of the service. Now Harry couldn't wait to tell him about Ross Gorman's offer.

"Harry, that's wonderful," Edgar said. "We'll make a night of it at the Palais Royale!"

"I'm afraid you'll have to go and tell me about it later," Harry said sadly.

"Unacceptable! This is a big moment for you."

"My wife would agree, but I think she'd say keeping us all fed is even more important," Harry chuckled. "You know, I can barely afford lunch at the Automat."

"I've got the money for both of us. You can pay me back later. Or don't—just get it cleared with the wife," Edgar said. "Take the night off from eating beans, for crying out loud!"

That night, Harry went home to the one-room flat he, Josephine, and Sonny shared. It was a humble home, where they had a kitchen table, a bed, and some plates. Sure enough, it was beans for dinner again. He happily ate them up and told Josephine what had happened that day.

"I told you that was a good song!" she cheered. Harry usually played all his new songs for Josephine first. She hadn't heard anything she didn't like yet, though she would never admit to being biased.

"Edgar said he would cover me to get into the Palais Royale," Harry said. "I wish you could come with me."

"There will be other times. You have to go!" Josephine said. "I'm sure you'll find a way to repay Edgar for his kindness."

Once again, Josephine was correct. After Harry's song debuted at the Palais Royale, it was decided that Edgar and Ross Gorman would write lyrics for it, and the song became called "Rose of the Rio Grande." As Harry's first published song, it surpassed his wildest expectations when it went on to become a hit and one of Stark & Cowan's biggest sellers. Rubey cracked open the champagne and issued Harry a promissory note for future royalties.

Perhaps it was due to this first success that song plugging became a bit more palatable for Harry. Rubey reassigned Harry to cover Brooklyn, where he felt more upbeat and productive on his home turf, lightheartedly telling Josephine, "Even the animal acts need music to play them on- and offstage. Now, what kind of plugger would I be if don't make sure the poor beasts have the right tune?"

"Especially with all your experience from the circus," she said, laughing.

With his first published song under his belt, Harry was on a roll. Another fixture of Tin Pan Alley who took notice of Harry's talent was the controversial figure, Billy Rose. Many complained about Billy Rose being a "cut-in artist," someone who consistently took more credit than he deserved, like providing a title for a song and wanting 50 percent of the royalties. But it was a calculated trade-off for Harry, who recognized Billy had the skills he didn't for aggressively working all the angles. Billy was forever trying out different writers in different combinations and pushing people to come up with something better than their first try. He was a force of nature and Harry was happy to have him in his corner, especially when he began producing Broadway revues and needed songs.

Making a bit more money meant Harry had some free time to spend with his family. One night, Harry and Josephine went to see the movie *The Enchanted Cottage*, leaving Sonny with Jo's sister. The film told the story of a young man injured and disabled in the war who met a young woman with her own physical disability. When they looked at each other, they didn't see the other's handicaps. The film moved Harry to tears, which touched Josephine deeply. She'd been waiting for the right moment to tell him they were expecting their second child. Feeling doubly stirred by Josephine's news, a dreamlike melody came to Harry in a rush of inspiration. They raced home so he could play it. He called it "By the River Sainte Marie."

Later that year, in 1924, Josephine gave birth to a daughter, Joan. Little Sonny struggled with the pronunciation and called her Cookie instead. As Harry's family grew and well-established musicians began doing his songs, Harry gained confidence in his work. "Rose of the Rio Grande" was recorded by Vincent Lopez, followed by Duke Ellington, which brought it to yet another level of popularity. Harry's excitement for this was tempered by the development that the publisher, Edgar Leslie Music, Inc., had gone out of business. Harry was unable to find out who took over the copyright, and by the time the promissory note came due, he couldn't cash it because the bank had failed.

This was just the beginning of Harry's mystification at the business of songwriting. Paul Whiteman, whose orchestra put Harry's first song on the map, was also busy commissioning work from other top talent in New York. This was the year George Gershwin's "Rhapsody in Blue" premiered at Aeolian Hall. With elements of classical music and jazz, it was part of a concert Whiteman billed *An Experiment in Modern Music*. An excruciatingly long show, "Rhapsody in Blue" was one of the last of twenty-six pieces performed that night, at which point the exasperated audience shot straight up in their seats as soon as they heard Ross Gorman's opening clarinet glissando. Harry loved reading about—he knew the glissando had begun as an exaggerated joke when Ross first played it for Gershwin. George loved the sound so much, he made it a permanent part of the composition.

Staying on top of business matters was enormously frustrating for Harry, who felt powerless over the lack of transparency and inability to track his own figures. He had a sinking feeling he wasn't being paid his fair share in royalties. He would complain to Josephine that he didn't know what to do about it, and he implored her to keep the radio on all day to count how many times his songs were played. She had an idea of her own to invest in the stock market, which she turned out to have a talent for.

Josephine was doing her best as a young wife and mother, but her main source of irritation was Harry's sisters, who were always inviting themselves over to teach her to cook. "Tuti, how can a German woman know how to properly feed an Italian?" Carolina would ask in Italian, right in front of Josephine.

"The least you could do is speak English, so I don't have to translate all the gripes," Harry said.

"Mama would *want* us to teach her," Carolina replied in English. Harry's sisters could convince him of almost anything by bringing his mother into the conversation. There were some days when he would opt to dine alone in the city instead of rushing home to the potential in-fighting between all the women in his life.

In 1924, once Harry's songs became bigger sellers, the larger publishing firm Shapiro, Bernstein & Company offered him the position of staff composer. It was there he started working regularly with two of the best lyricists around, Mort Dixon and Bud Green. Harry's peers clearly recognized his musicality as far more sophisticated than the typical Tin Pan Alley songwriter. He was shocked when Isham Jones, the famous songwriter and bandleader from Chicago, told Harry about his "biggest booster in Chicago," the songwriter Gus Kahn. Harry was as much a fan of Gus, who'd written "It Had to Be You" with Isham the year before. Harry began taking the train to Chicago to write with Gus, which he considered a great privilege. When Harry wrote "Maybe You Will, Maybe You Won't" with Billy Rose and Mort Dixon, it became his tenth published work. It was 1925.

One night back in New York, Harry decided to grab dinner before catching the train home. He went to one of his favorite spots, the oyster bar in Grand Central Station. As he pulled out a stool at the counter, he struck up a conversation with a rotund man sitting next to him. They talked about food until they realized they were both in the music business.

When Harry told him his first name, the man's eyes widened. "Harry *Warren?*" he asked. "You've written some great songs, my friend. I'm Al Dubin."

They compared notes about people they knew in common, like Billy Rose. Harry was impressed with Al's vocabulary and intellect. As different as they were, they had the most important things in common: love of food, family, and music. Al was a larger-than-life character and Harry took to him right away. Just like the celestial mural high above them on Grand Central's ceiling, it seemed their meeting had been written in the stars.

Harry and Al began crossing paths more and stopping to chat when they'd run into each other at Lindy's, the popular eatery songwriters frequented. Billy Rose wanted Harry and Al to write together, and as per usual, he put himself right in the middle of them for "Too Many Kisses in the Summer (Bring Too Many Tears in the Fall)." The song never broke out, but it led to future collaboration. Harry partnered with Bud Green again and they landed an instant hit in 1925 with "I Love My Baby (My Baby Loves Me)," tapping into the zeitgeist of the roaring twenties. The song created exactly the kind of momentum Harry had been striving for since he started out as an alleyman, and it was an almost mystical feeling to be seen as a herald—crafting a song that resonated with so many people and came to define an age. Emerging jazz musicians helped put this song on the map because, just like "Rose of the Rio Grande," the form was tailor-made for improvisation. Harry followed it up with "In My Gondola" in 1926 and other songs for the more sophisticated Broadway revue shows. That year, he wrote more than a dozen songs.

With his increased earning power, Harry and Josephine were able to buy their first home in Long Island's Forest Hills neighborhood. Harry invited Al for dinner and Josephine made a pork roast, for which Al lavished her with praise. This endeared him to Jo from that first moment, considering the culinary battle she was engaged in with her sisters-in-law. Everyone loved getting compliments from Al, who had a unique ability of making them sound like poetry.

After dinner, the conversation topic turned to business. Harry felt his career was more secure than ever. And now that he was working for Witmark, Remick, and Harms, another publisher that dispatched him to demonstrate songs directly for theater producers and recording companies, Harry felt song plugging was becoming more respectable. No more wet moccasin in the alley.

"I hear the catalog of songs is pretty strong this summer," Al said.

"Yeah, there's some good stuff. I gotta say, though," Harry said, "this thing with the summer catalog and the winter catalog makes it seem a little like selling dresses."

Al laughed heartily. "And did you hear about Warner Brothers snatching up Vitagraph?" he asked. "I'm taking the *Chief* out to the coast for a few weeks to work on a project for one of the studios."

"How exciting," Josephine said. "I hear wonderful things about California, though I do love my home here." Josephine often had girlfriends over for lunch—other newlyweds with whom she commiserated about being left alone more than they liked. She had also hired a housekeeper and nanny from Louisiana named Lucille.

When Al departed for the night, he and Harry made plans to go see the new Warner Brothers film *Don Juan*, which had recorded music and sound effects. In October 1927, the following year, Warner Brothers famously took things another giant step forward when the studio released *The Jazz Singer*, starring Al Jolson, the first feature-length film with synchronized recorded music and dialogue sequences. Harry wasted no time going to see it. As the credits rolled, he turned to Josephine and asked, "You know what Jolson's real name is?"

"Is this the set up for a joke?" she wondered, but Harry was serious. "No, darling, I don't know Al Jolson's real name."

"It's Asa Yoelson." He paused. "It's makes you wonder, doesn't it? Should I have been Sal instead of Harry?"

"The name isn't what matters. You're going to do amazing things."

"And you know this because a fortune teller told me I would?"

"I don't need a fortune teller. I was born with a caul, remember?" she said, playfully tossing popcorn at him.

Although Josephine would always try to get Harry's mind off his doubts about his name, he would never be totally convinced the right name could make all the difference in someone's success. He was sure about one thing, though: with *The Jazz Singer* grossing over $3 million and breaking the box office record, theaters everywhere would be rushing to install sound systems. Harry Warner, one of the four founding Warner Brothers, purchased three music publishing firms—Witmark, Remick, and Harms among them for $10 million—and assembled them into the combined Music Publishers Holding Corporation. Harry had been with Witmark for a while at this point, which meant he had some new bosses across the country in Hollywood, where the movies were now talking—and one of them had the very similar-sounding, anagrammatic last name of Warner.

73

Chapter Five

DEPRESSION? WHAT DEPRESSION?

Throughout the boom of the 1920s, many Americans believed the stock market would continue rising forever, shortsighted as that turned out to be. From October 24, 1929, known as Black Thursday, to October 29, Black Tuesday, the market plummeted. The Great Depression followed, wreaking havoc all through the 1930s. Broadway braced for the worst, yet the glitz and glamour that splashed across silver screens never ceased in this era. If anything, film productions became even more lavish. Judging by cinema output alone, one would never have known the country was in the midst of the greatest economic cataclysm it had ever experienced. Harry and his fellow songwriters—"scribbler" was the term for a lyricist in those days, and songwriters were "cleffers"—began to notice that the public had no interest in dwelling on their own struggles. In music, onstage, and onscreen, audiences longed to escape reality. Watching money being thrown around onscreen—both literally and figuratively—was aspirational. One of Harry and Al's first hits would be "The Gold Diggers' Song (We're in the Money)," a catchy tune that lifted peoples' spirits without leaving any residue of resentment toward Hollywood or Wall Street. It made people believe they would rise from the ashes of the Great Depression.

In addition to the era's seismic shift from silent films to talkies, the timing for Harry's career couldn't have been better if it had been scripted. With the advent of sound, film studios needed a tremendous amount of music quickly. As a staff composer now with Remick Music Corporation when the company was snapped up by Warner Brothers, Harry's career course was determined. Producers had grown tired of bidding against each other for rights to popular songs, which achieved nothing more than a windfall profit for the publishers. They quickly came around to the wisdom of buying up publishing companies to make themselves the owners of the copyrights. Broadway and Tin Pan Alley writers began streaming into Hollywood like the ever-present sunrays of Southern California. In the midst of the Depression, their earning potential was great—a typical alleyman made $200 a week but could bring in five times that in Hollywood. By 1929, the studios had over three hundred songwriters on their payrolls. The Rodgers and Hart Broadway musical *Spring is Here,* which had been part of the Remick catalog, became one of the first projects Warner Bros. chose to adapt into a movie musical now that the studio owned the music. Harry was hired to work on the film, which meant traveling to Los Angeles for the first time. He had no idea what he would be doing there, because the show already contained Rodgers and Hart's stellar music.

Harry's lyricists for the project were Sam Lewis and Joe Young, with whom Harry had collaborated earlier that year on his first-ever song for a motion picture, "Mi Amado" for Paramount Pictures' *The Wolf Song*, starring Gary Cooper. That assignment, however, didn't involve riding a train clear across the country to a land that would feel very foreign to him, even many years after relocating there. With mixed emotions, Harry packed a bag and boarded the *Chief*, to ride the rails for four nights from New York to Los Angeles. He traveled with his two lyricists and Ruby Keeler, the Canadian-born actress, singer, dancer, and much-younger wife of Al Jolson. The four of them took their meals together in the dining car, where Harry enjoyed the camaraderie of his traveling companions but didn't hold back on his misgivings about the project.

"I can't say I totally understand it," he said with a laugh over dinner one night. "How can anyone hope to outdo a Rodgers and Hart score?"

"They're going to toss out most of those songs," Joe said.

"And replace them with our new songs," Sam added.

"There's always a strategy in Hollywood," Joe went on. "They're not as concerned about music as they are about hits. They'll keep the ones from the original and package them together with our new songs, which of course *must* be hits."

They all laughed. Harry was beginning to get the picture, but he remained skeptical. "Hmm" was all he managed to say.

Ruby saw Harry was about to learn a lot about Hollywood. She'd had her own experiences, plus the benefit of her famous husband's business dealings, to know the industry's modus operandi. "Harry, you have to remember, it's show business— with an emphasis on *business*," she said. She saw the waitress coming toward them with their drinks and marveled at her clean, crisp uniform. "Aren't these Harvey Girls just darling?"

"Harvey Girls?" Harry asked.

"They work for the Fred Harvey restaurants all along the train routes," Ruby explained. Harry could not have imagined that, years later, he would work on an MGM musical called *The Harvey Girls*, starring Judy Garland, about this very thing.

The *Chief* stopped several times in Colorado and again in Albuquerque, where they got off the train to take in some fresh air. As Harry walked alongside Ruby, they struck up a conversation about some of their mutual friends.

"Gus Kahn and I saw you in *Show Girl*. You were great. I love that Gershwin tune, 'Liza,'" Harry said. "Ira Gershwin and I have been doing some writing together of late. He's one hell of a lyricist."

"I just adore him. And George! My god, the talent between the two of them," Ruby gushed.

When they heard the train whistle blow, they boarded the *Chief* for the final leg of their journey.

Arriving in downtown Los Angeles at the Santa Fe station, Harry gazed out the window, unable to believe his eyes. The depot was nothing more than a little red shack. He turned to his companions. "Did we take a wrong turn somewhere?" he asked. They all laughed, but Harry was dead serious. "It looks like we're in a small town in South Dakota!"

Ruby stood as the train came to a final stop. "It's a far cry from New York, Harry. You're right about that," she said.

As they disembarked, Harry couldn't get over it. "This is the worst place I've ever seen in my life," he complained. "It's downright *corny!*" His companions were in stitches, but Harry wasn't kidding. With this first impression, his image of Hollywood was shattered.

A car met them and took them to the Roosevelt Hotel in Hollywood, where the studio was putting them up.

"Did you know the Roosevelt is where the first Academy Awards were held earlier this year?" Ruby asked, trying to get Harry's mind back on the more glamorous side of things.

Of the original songs from the Rodgers and Hart stage production, the studio decided to keep only two: "Yours Sincerely" and "With a Song in My Heart." Harry and his lyricists wrote six new songs for the movie adaptation, and three became hits: "Cryin' for the Carolines," "Have a Little Faith in Me," and "Absence Makes the Heart Grow Fonder (For Somebody Else)." After production wrapped on *Spring Is Here*, he couldn't book his return ticket on the *Chief* soon enough. Unable to find one redeeming quality of Los Angeles, he saw the place as the end of the earth, certainly not the future. The city had no decent restaurants or delis, and he missed the esprit de corps of working with New York's songwriting community.

The entire way home on the train, he stewed about his experience with studio executive Hal Wallis during the shoot. With his background at Vitagraph, Harry knew his way around sets and had a solid understanding of production. While shooting one of their new songs, the songwriting team watched the cast perform it. Everything was going well until Harry noticed some of the lyrics were being sung wrong.

"Do you hear that?" he asked Joe and Sam.

"I think they know. Or maybe they changed it," Sam said.

"*Changed* it? Without asking us?" Harry was appalled.

"They can do that out here, Harry. It's not like New York."

"You can say that again," Harry said. He went over to Wallis between takes to point this out.

"What's the difference?" Wallis said, turning to him with a look of disdain. "No one knows what the real lyric is."

"Aren't you the head of production?"

"What's your point, Warren?" Wallis asked, irritated.

"Don't you realize the *correct* lyric is going to be published on the sheet music?" Harry asked incredulously.

Wallis shrugged as he found someone across the set to yell at and walked away. Harry stood there, shaking his head in disbelief. "And these guys all think they're so smart!" he scoffed.

Sam and Joe laughed—but not too loudly.

"What a useless pants presser," Harry growled. Wallis was just getting started as a thorn in Harry's side. *Spring Is Here* turned out to be a box-office flop, giving Harry an unmistakable feeling of schadenfreude, but even that couldn't stop his songs in the film from becoming hits—a phenomenon that would become a hallmark of his career.

Back in New York, with this experience behind him, things had been totally redefined in Harry's mind. He was forced to come to grips with the fact that it was always going to be a battle of highbrow Broadway, which held creative people in high regard, versus lowbrow Hollywood, where expediency was key and it was open season on songwriters. Nevertheless, the suits at Warner Bros. refused to leave Harry alone, eager to cash in on their acquisition of the music publishing houses. No matter how determined Harry was to stay in New York forever and write strictly for Broadway, he'd gotten a taste of Hollywood's great financial rewards. He hoped there was a way to straddle these worlds without completely succumbing to the temptations of money.

Harry went into Manhattan to see Billy Rose, who was then working as the lyricist for composer Vincent Youmans's show *Great Day!* in July 1929 at the Cosmopolitan. While in the theater during rehearsal, Harry's ears perked up when the pianist started vamping at the end of one of the dance numbers.

"Who's that kid subbing for Fletcher?" Harry asked Billy. He was referring to Fletcher Henderson, the regular rehearsal pianist who would go on to be one of the most brilliant arrangers of the Big Band era.

"Couldn't tell ya," Billy said. "Want me to go introduce you?"

Harry sarcastically waved him off and went over to say hello to the accompanist. "Say, what's that pickup you've been playing?" he asked.

The young man stood and extended his hand. "Harry Warren?" he said, sounding somewhat starstruck.

"Never mind me. Tell me about your piece."

"Just vamping, really. Fending off the boredom with all

the stopping and starting as the dancers learn their steps. But even Youmans said there's probably a song in there somewhere," the kid said. "When I come across a new melody, it's like a tapeworm—it's hard to get rid of!"

"It's *very* good. Kind of wish I'd written it myself," Harry admitted with a chuckle. "Say, maybe you should get with a scribbler and work on it. I know just the guy to write it up."

"That would be swell, Mr. Warren. I'm Harold. Harold Arluck—or Arlen," he said. "I'm thinking about changing it to a combination of my father and mother's names—Arluck plus Orlin equals Arlen. What do you think?"

"I'm the wrong guy to ask about names," Harry said. "I'd most likely give you bad advice. All I know is that you need to get with my guy and write that song. I'll set it up."

Harry arranged for Harold to meet with him and songwriter Ted Koehler at the Remick office in midtown.

"Harry tells me you've got a pretty good song going," Ted said to Harold after Harry had introduced them. "Let's hear it."

Harry watched Ted's face light up with excitement as Harold played. Ted smiled and nodded to Harry in appreciation. Before long, Ted had the lyric:

> *Forget your troubles*
> *Go on, get happy*
> *You better chase all your cares away*
> *Shout hallelujah*
> *Come on, get happy*
> *Get ready for the judgment day*

The sun is shinin'
Come on, get happy
The lord is ready to take your hand
Shout hallelujah
Come on, get happy
We're going to the promised land

Harry felt a thrill he'd never experienced watching the partnership between these two begin to blossom. Ted was a kind and generous soul, a good fit for the young Arluck, who settled on changing his name to Arlen soon after. Once they performed "Get Happy" for Al Piantadosi, who had a publishing subsidiary under Remick, Harold was offered a staff composer job for $50 a week. Buddy Morris, who worked for Remick at the time and would become a lifelong friend of Harry's, was flabbergasted by the song, correctly predicting it would be an enormous hit. "Get Happy" was put in the Broadway show *Nine-Fifteen Revue* and won audiences over instantly. Remick rushed to print the sheet music, and soon bands all over were performing it. Everywhere Harry and Josephine went, they'd hear it and smile.

"If it weren't for you, that song never would have happened," she said.

"You really think that's true?"

"Of course. There's a mystery to how a creative thing comes to be. Who knows? Maybe those two would have met eventually and written another song. But not *that song*."

Arlen and Koehler went on to write plenty of other unforgettable songs, and it was their soulful signature sound that led to them writing for the Cotton Club in Harlem. "Stormy Weather," "Between the Devil and the Deep Blue Sea," and "I've Got the World on a String" made it clear they were at the top of their game.

Meanwhile, Billy Rose wasn't letting a little thing like the Depression slow down his ambitions. His 1930 production of *Sweet and Low*—a vehicle for his wife, Fanny Brice—was in need of songs and he wanted Harry to partner up with Ira Gershwin, who had some free time while his brother George was working on an instrumental piece. Harry loved writing with Ira, whom he considered one of his loveliest friends and who always made him laugh. This was Harry's first show, and their songs "Cheerful Little Earful" and "Would You Like to Take a Walk" were both successful.

While working at the piano one day, Harry and Ira were inspired by Harold Arlen's name change and began talking about songwriters who'd changed their names.

"What was Irving Berlin's name before?" Harry wondered.

"Same as mine—Israel. Izzy Baline."

"Really? And your last name was?"

"Gershowitz." Ira teased, "What about you, Harry Warren? Are you sure you're even Italian?"

"What? You think I should go back to Sal or Tuti?"

"Hmm, Tuti Guaragna . . ." Ira mused. "I don't think Americans would have any idea how to pronounce 'Guaragna.'"

Harry laughed. "You'd just have to tell 'em it rhymes with *lasagna.*"

~

A few weeks after the show premiered, accusations began flying from Irving Berlin that Harry and Ira had stolen the idea for "Cheerful Little Earful" from him.

"Poor Irving," Harry said.

"So rich and so paranoid!" Ira laughed.

Ira and Harry took this in stride. Everyone in the songwriting business had grown accustomed to Irving Berlin's rants and delusions about people stealing his songs. It was widely known he could not read or write music and was forced to hum his ideas to copyists, who would write out the music and orchestrate it.

"He's always giving me grief for hogging George," Ira said.

"Is that what he calls it? That guy's got some nerve."

"He just doesn't want to accept that it's not that George is too busy to work with him, he just doesn't care to!"

That night, Harry went back to the Gershwin penthouse, overlooking the Hudson River, for dinner and cards. Ira's wife, Lee, was always hosting New York's elite. When they retired to the piano to share their latest works in progress, George brought out some of his favorite cigars while Harry and Ira told him about the latest dustup with Irving.

"I assume this time it's just as baseless as all his other accusations?" George asked.

"He's Irving Berlin! He doesn't need proof to make accusations," Harry exclaimed.

Harry was as surprised as anyone when he was nominated to be the director of ASCAP in 1929, a post he held until 1933. Four times a year, twelve songwriters sequestered themselves in a room to set about the process of appraising themselves and their seven hundred members. Each member had to be placed in one of eight categories based on their length of time as a member, and their works' popularity, merit, and relative time performed in places licensed by the society. The meetings started in the morning and always lasted well past midnight. Meals were delivered into the smoky room where the songwriters argued over classification, never wanting to demote anyone. Should a writer who had been inactive for some time be pushed down in category? The organization operated more like a trust than one paying a straightforward percentage, like in the days before radio when songwriters were paid as individuals directly by their publisher. The highlight of Harry's ASCAP tenure was welcoming Harold Arlen into the organization when he became eligible in 1930. Harry had become an indispensable mentor and friend to Harold.

The following year, Harry had another song debut on Broadway in the show *Wonder Bar*, starring Al Jolson, who sang Harry's tune "Ma Mere." Jolson was a prickly character Harry preferred to keep a safe distance from.

Perhaps it was due to Harry's career momentum, but the time had finally come for his celestial ballad written seven years earlier, inspired by *The Enchanted Cottage*. One of Harry's close friends, Jack Bergman, plugged it aggressively to a publisher, who bought it out of respect for Bergman more than legitimate interest in the song. The publisher was sure glad he'd taken a chance on it when "By the River Sainte Marie," performed by Guy Lombardo, became an instant hit. It remained on top for many months.

Billy Rose was staying busy at this time too—in 1931, he began producing *Crazy Quilt,* a further reworking of *Sweet and Low,* for which Harry contributed four songs, one with lyrics by Ira. The breakout hit, however, was one he wrote with Mort Dixon: "I Found a Million Dollar Baby (In a Ten Cent Store)." This song was one case of Billy earning his credit. He came up with the tune a few years earlier and presented it to another songwriter who wasn't interested, so he reassigned it to Mort and Harry. It all paid off when Bing Crosby recorded it. The song captured the public's imagination once again in an almost magical way, distilling the strongest sentiments of the time into a jaunty tune guaranteed to put a smile on even the saddest of faces.

When two of Harry's lyricist partners, Joe Young and Mort, were hired for *The Laugh Parade*, the producers decided Harry was the best choice to write the music. The show became Harry's first complete Broadway score, from which a massive hit broke out that would stand the test of time: "You're My Everything."

Hollywood studios continued calling on Harry while he was busy in New York and in a position to turn them down. Still soured by his experience with *Spring Is Here*, Harry agreed to contribute one song to the film *The Crooner*, as long as he was able to do it from New York. Warner Brothers accepted his terms, and Harry and his friend and lyricist Irving Kahal wrote "Three's a Crowd."

At a gathering at the Gershwins' penthouse, surrounded by modern French paintings and champagne, Harry was excited to play the song for the group. All the songwriters loved it.

Then it was Harold Arlen's turn. He prefaced his new song with the story of how it had come together: "Ted was getting fed up with me because you know how I like to walk. The rhythm sets up something in me where I get ideas. I never feel like they're going to come if I'm just sitting around!" Harold said. "So I convinced him to go on a walkabout and it was freezing outside. He struggled to keep up with me, but I told him to pretend we were marching in a parade. He finally got into it, imitating drums and trombones. By the time we got to the Brill Building, the song was nearly finished."

Harold proceeded to perform "I Love a Parade" and everyone erupted with applause, knowing Harold had another hit on his hands.

By 1931, nearly the entire New York cadre of songwriters had been to Hollywood at least once for what they called the "second Gold Rush." Harry never kidded himself about getting respect for his work in the movie business. But with the Depression dragging on, he felt the pressure to make as much money as he could while his career was on an upswing. The next time he would be convinced to board the *Chief,* it was for a project of a much bigger scale, one Warner Bros. was willing to bet the farm on. Producer Darryl F. Zanuck had a strong feeling about a novel called *42nd Street* he'd acquired the rights to. He knew it could be made into a hit movie with the right team, so he called Buddy Morris and asked for the best melodist Remick had. Buddy didn't hesitate to recommend Harry, despite his friend's well-known disdain for Hollywood. "You'll thank me later," he joked to Harry.

The biggest hurdle for movie musicals at this point was the fact that audiences had been growing weary of their trite plots. Warner Bros. had made fifty musicals in 1929, twenty in 1931, and a dozen in 1932. For Harry, the appeal of *42nd Street* was that he'd be working with Al Dubin. Harry had always been convinced the two of them would eventually hit on some great songs, despite striking out with their early attempts. Under contract with Warner Bros. and absolutely enamored with the Southern California lifestyle, Al had already moved his family from New York to Los Angeles. While waiting for an assignment from the studio, he'd been translating lyrics from German films into English. He was fluent in German, a fact that impressed Harry, given that Al, originally from Switzerland, came to the United States at age two.

Back on the *Chief,* Harry arrived to work on *42nd Street* in the summer of 1932. He thought about his former traveling companion Ruby Keeler and how happy she must be after being cast in it, her first film role. When he stepped off the train, he choked on the dry heat. Days later, a severe sandstorm blocked out the sun and turned the insides of cars into sandboxes overnight. Harry told Josephine the rental cars were death traps. "Al told me not to bother with them," he said. "Apparently, you never know if you can trust the brakes or not."

With Harry and Al in place to do the music for *42nd Street*, Zanuck added the third member of this creative trio: former Broadway hoofer and outlandish choreographer Busby Berkeley. It was all part of the perfect plan and the beginning of an extraordinary partnership that would produce some of the decade's best songs and biggest hits. Harry got another taste of the ways of Hollywood when he and Al first realized a screenplay hadn't even been written yet—they would be writing songs based on the galleys of the book. The script would later be written around the songs.

Harry found it eerie to be on the Warner Bros. lot during the Depression, when there was nary a soul wandering around. It was a ghost town with the commissary closed. The only upside of this was Al introducing him to Musso & Frank's in Hollywood, where they went most days for lunch. Harry marveled at how much Al ate, typically ordering two of everything—including steaks.

"Al, slow down before you eat the whole restaurant," Harry kidded.

"All for a growing boy," Al said, patting his belly. "Say, I'm heading down to Tijuana this weekend. Wanna join me?"

"And go looking for trouble? No, I better leave that to you."

"I am rather good at that," Al chuckled.

"What did you go and get married for if you're still so restless?"

"Maybe just to irritate my Jewish mother by converting to Catholicism so I could marry a shiksa showgirl," Al laughed.

"I can't wait to meet your wife and find out how she over convinced a good Jewish boy to convert," Harry said with a smile.

"I didn't know you were Catholic, Harry. You speak more Yiddish than half the Jews I know."

Harry laughed. "Now that's a *shanda*."

Al laughed so hard over Harry's use of the Yiddish word for "shame" that he choked. "Take it easy, fella," Harry said, patting his partner's back as he signaled the waiter for more water. Al gulped it down and wiped his watering eyes.

"C'mon, Al," Harry said, "you know the only difference between the Jews and the Italians are the hats." With that, Al chuckled uncontrollably once again.

When they returned to the lot after lunch, they ran into the secretary of the great Leo Forbstein, the studio's brilliant orchestrator and conductor. She was "a good skate," as Harry would say, describing the people in the business who were unaffected by fame, money, or proximity to it.

"Hey, how's it going with that guy you've been seeing?" Al asked her.

She was from somewhere in the South, and Harry and Al loved listening to her accent and her turns of phrase. Shrugging, she drawled, "I guess he's getting to be a habit with me."

Harry and Al exchanged a tickled look, recognizing what a great expression it was.

"Go ahead. You can use it," she laughed.

Al fished his signature stubby pencil out of one of his pockets to write it down on a napkin from lunch. "You're Getting to Be a Habit with Me" became one of the many great songs in *42nd Street*.

Later in the summer, Harry brought Josephine out for a visit. Al, a sports enthusiast, offered to take Josephine to the 1932 Summer Olympics in Los Angeles. Harry, who was always complaining about the heat, said he had no interest in sitting under the sun all day.

"It's not like it's not hot in New York," Josephine reminded him.

"Different kind of hot," Harry said.

When Al and Jo returned from the games each night, they brought back lots of souvenirs Al insisted on buying. Jo gleefully told Harry one night, "He even invited me to the jai alai games and the races in Tijuana next time you go."

"You two are quite pally," Harry said.

Josephine smiled. "Why should the boys have all the fun?"

Harry's original plan was to do the one movie and go back to New York for good. His salary of $1,500 a week made that plan hard to justify—it was more than he could have made working in Broadway theater for an entire year. Before buying a home in Los Angeles, Harry stayed at the posh Beverly Wilshire Hotel, completed in 1928. His future Beverly Hills neighbor, actress Marlene Dietrich, was a frequent guest there. The Beverly Wilshire catered to the Hollywood set, offering groceries onsite and the ability to open an account with Martindale Bookstore, which delivered to the hotel. This was a big perk for Harry. His first order was for *The Brothers Karamazov* by Fyodor Dostoevsky and *The Story of San Michele* by Axel Munthe.

Despite frequent run-ins with Hal Wallis and studio head Jack Warner, working on *42nd Street* was a satisfying experience for Harry and Al, who quickly proved themselves to be a formidable team, turning out one great song after another. They were surprised to be asked to do a cameo in the film, essentially playing themselves as songwriters, even though Harry thought their wardrobe "made them look like gangsters." Their bit was to rush up onstage and accuse the producer character of ruining their song. This called for them to write a terrible song, stretching Harry's musical muscles. The song was "It Must Be June," and the producer was played by Warner Baxter, whose character makes a mess of it while the songwriters protest, causing him to throw it out.

"Cut!" director Lloyd Bacon called.

Al turned to Harry. "Geez, how can we ever keep all these names straight? Harry Warren, Harry Warner, Warner Baxter, Warren William?" he asked.

Harry laughed uncomfortably—Al didn't realize his name was a bit of a touchy subject. "There's even another Harry Warren who works here in the lighting department. Sometimes we get each other's paychecks," Harry said.

Al leaned in and whispered to Harry, "Someone just let it slip that Warner Baxter is only being paid $125 a week."

As angry as Harry was to learn the studio was so cheap as to pay a leading man so little, it made him realize that by comparison to his salary, the studio did value the songwriters—they just never wanted to admit it.

Harry and Al were in utter amazement every day on the set of *42nd Street* while working with Busby Berkeley, the choreographer affectionately known as "the madman." They'd known him from Broadway but were now in awe witnessing Buzz discover the perfect medium to match his outsized imagination—achieving through cinema what would never be possible on the theater stage. Buzz's creative process didn't care to waste time explaining to producers and studio executives, who demanded excellence but never wanted the truth about how much his ideas would cost. Harry and Al loathed sitting through production and budget meetings, which not only bored them silly but had no bearing on their work. What moved Harry like nothing had before was stopping in a scoring session and hearing one of his own compositions played by such a large, top-notch orchestra. Despite it being a short instrumental piece he'd written for the background of a scene, tears came to his eyes as he listened to it fully orchestrated and conducted by Leo Forbstein. Experiencing his own music on such a grand scale was life changing. It gave him a sense of what it must have felt like for his hero Puccini, and he felt as though he'd glimpsed the divine.

As much as Harry tried to adopt Al's love of California, he just couldn't bring himself around to it. He knew his heart would always be in New York, despite Al constantly trying to sell him on the "California Dream."

"You're Italian. You should love the Mediterranean climate!" Al said.

"I think all the oranges have gone to your head," Harry laughed.

"You're just like Helen. She misses the hustle and bustle of New York too."

Nevertheless, Harry couldn't help but love the burly Swiss man and his outlook. Over lunch at Musso & Frank's one day, Al turned philosophical.

"I get great comfort out of the fact that our work doesn't hurt anybody. No one ever buys a song to get even," Al said. "I just wish I could get that Peg Entwistle out of my mind. I seem to be obsessing over it."

"The actress who jumped from the Hollywoodland sign?" Harry asked. "Did you know her?"

"No. That's what's so strange. But do you know what she wrote in her note?"

"Al, it's macabre. You can't worry yourself over these things. It's tragic, I know—"

"'If I had done this a long time ago, it would have saved a lot of pain.'" Al paused. "Isn't that awful? I've been thinking a lot about my mother lately. Did I ever tell you she was the youngest of eleven children, just like you? But she wasn't nearly as nice as you, Harry. Not half as nice."

During these moments, Harry noticed Al's tendency toward melancholy. Al always had both their best interests at heart, but Harry couldn't help worrying about his partner's insatiable appetite for food, booze, cigars, gambling, and women. Harry figured one of these things or some combination of them would inevitably lead to Al's demise. He marveled at his partner's ability to lead a double life of family man and Casanova.

But most of the time, Al was in high spirits and fun to be around, like when he begged Harry to let him in on the secret of the artichoke. "I have no doubt they're delicious, but how the hell do you eat it?" he'd asked.

When they saw Jack Warner across the restaurant having lunch with playwright Eddie Chodorov, they passed by and heared Eddie speaking in all his college expressions. As they got back in their car, Harry said to Al, "Wasn't it Mark Twain who said, 'Don't use a five-dollar word when a fifty-cent word will do'?" Al laughed.

Driving back to the studio, they did their best to figure out why such things impressed the hell out of Jack Warner and the other executives.

"I think he kowtows to people with a college education because he doesn't have one. That's all," Al said.

"Not having one sure hasn't stopped him from looking down on other people," Harry observed.

"It's disgusting, isn't it? It brings me right back to my mother and father, who were always disappointed in me for not becoming a surgeon."

"I mean, sure, show respect. Like my father always told us, 'Tip your hat to the doctor,'" Harry said. "You tipped your hat. That came from the old country. And you kissed the midwife's hand to show respect for the woman who delivered you. But don't *grovel*, for chrissakes."

"You and I have probably read more books combined than all these Hollywood people put together," Al mused. The pair were alike in finding little use for formal education, opting instead to become autodidacts led by their own curiosity.

Production on *42nd Street* wrapped in the fall of 1932. Harry brought Josephine to Los Angeles for the premiere in March 1933 and rented a car and driver to escort them in the parade to Grauman's Chinese Theatre. Crowds were packed tightly on the sidewalks all around the theater, with police lined up to keep things under control. Harry felt overwhelmed by the searchlights.

When adoring fans peered into the line of cars to try to catch a glimpse of the stars, Harry heard one who looked in their car say, "Aw, that's nobody." He never forgot how this shocked and stung him. Little did that teenager know the person he'd accused of being nobody would go on to almost single-handedly revive the Hollywood movie musical. *42nd Street* would become the most successful of its time, paving the way for another twenty years of the form and saving Warner Brothers from bankruptcy. All four songs Harry and Al wrote for the film became hits: "42nd Street," "Shuffle Off to Buffalo," "Young and Healthy," and, of course, "You're Getting to Be a Habit with Me."

Once the film had become a runaway success, Harry received a surprise phone call. Josephine found him at the piano with Sonny, who was becoming increasingly interested in music. Harry was trying to help his son stretch his small hand into the shape of a new chord Sonny was learning. "It's Irving Berlin on the phone, dear," Josephine said.

"Uh-oh, what did I do now?" Harry quipped.

Josephine rolled her eyes and waved him toward the phone.

"Hello, Irving. How are you?" Harry paused to listen. "To congratulate me?"

This got Josephine's attention.

"Well, thank you. Yes, it's a fine picture. I'm glad I had the chance to work on it. I knew Dubin and I would eventually write something worthwhile together!" Harry laughed and waited for a response. "You're right, I think everyone thought the movie musical was dead."

Harry looked at Josephine and shrugged. After Irving talked for another moment, Harry said, "Yes, as a matter of fact, I'll be in New York next week. You can't find a decent pastrami out here to save your life."

They exchanged a few more words before Harry hung up.

"He wants me to go see the movie with him in New York," Harry explained.

"So he's seen it or he hasn't?" Josephine wondered.

"I don't know. I just know he's ready to end the dry spell he's been in for the last few years. But I don't know what that has to do with me."

Harry met Irving outside the Strand Theater, where *42nd Street* had premiered in New York a few weeks before. Irving held up two tickets he'd purchased for the late show, and they went inside.

"I've missed New York desperately," Harry told him.

"Understandably," Irving said. "But it seems there's too much opportunity in Los Angeles right now not to take advantage of it. Who knows how long this Depression will drag on? Consider yourself lucky."

"I certainly do," Harry said.

"Now that *42ⁿᵈ Street* is a major success, I suspect they're going to be making a lot more musicals. Have you seen how much money it's making?"

Harry laughed. "No, Irving. They don't send me the accounting sheets."

"Maybe you should ask to see them so you can strike a better deal for yourself next time," Irving said.

"I'll keep that in mind."

"If there's one person I'd like to meet out there, it's your producer, Darryl Zanuck."

"I can introduce you, if you like," Harry replied out of reflex, somewhat naively.

"If you can arrange it," Irving said.

As was Harry's way, he made good on his promise. Before long, Irving Berlin's dry spell did come to an end, as Harry knew it would. It mattered little in Hollywood who was really to blame for things like Berlin's 1931 score for *Reaching for the Moon* being scrapped after the movie was recut into a straight comedy without any musical numbers. In the years that followed, Harry could only marvel at how Irving was able to get top billing even over the stars of a film, with his name always in much bigger print than anything else on the movie poster. Harry found it unbecoming, which is why he would never feel like a Hollywood insider. It was not a town built on humility, but it was one very interested in everything humble Harry had to offer.

Chapter Six

RELUCTANT RELOCATION

Harry could never have imagined spending eight years at Warner Brothers, writing music for thirty-three films. At the rate of about four films per year, it was clear the studio didn't have many qualms about burning out its top talent. Harry was an admitted workaholic learning to navigate the pressure on both sides—from his bosses to constantly produce, and from his family, who complained about not seeing him enough. But the frenzied pace would not be as kind to his friend and partner Al Dubin.

At the beginning, the team was unstoppable. It was the two of them against the world, as far as the studio was concerned. They learned early on that the production chiefs, not normally endowed with creative talent of their own, showed little respect for those who did, often treating them with contempt. The bosses belittled the songwriters and took perverse pleasure in wielding power over them. Harry and Al, though, had the distinct advantage of being smarter than the studio brass realized. All those outsized egos wrought internal power struggles in the executive suites and gave the savvy songwriters something to work with. When they first started at Warner Bros., they would rush over to play their bosses a new batch of songs all at once. It didn't take long for them to notice this would cause at least one song to be rejected as a matter of course. Once they started doling out the songs one at a time—voila! Hardly any songs were rejected. Another tactic involved pitting one ego against another. If Jack Warner had any reservations about a song, they would go to Hal Wallis dejected, saying how much Warner disliked it. This would all but guarantee Wallis would love it, and vice versa. These ploys worked wonders for Harry and Al, and as painful as it was for them to expend so much energy on it, they managed to have a few good laughs along the way.

After *42nd Street,* Harry had rushed back to New York to the Remick office, hoping there would be enough work to keep him busy there. He didn't realize he was in a new reality now because Warner Brothers had gotten a taste of his phenomenal talent; it would take little time for the studio to come calling again. Once it became clear they had a hit on their hands with *42nd Street*, they knew how much they needed Harry and Al for their follow-up, *Gold Diggers of 1933.*

Josephine begrudgingly packed Harry a bag once again. "How long are we going to keep this up?" she asked.

"Do you really want to live in Los Angeles? It's a godforsaken town, Jo."

"I'll move to the North Pole if it means my children get to see their father once in a while."

Harry looked over at Cookie and Sonny playing happily.

"Have a safe trip, Mr. Warren," Lucille sang out in her New Orleans accent as she made lunch for the children.

"I'll be back before you know it," Harry said, kissing Josephine's forehead.

When Harry arrived in Los Angeles, he didn't like it one bit more than he remembered. In fact, he liked it even less. He knew *Gold Diggers of 1933* was going to be produced the same way *42nd Street* had been, with two separate units. The first part would be the non-musical scenes directed by Mervyn LeRoy from mid-February to mid-March, then from mid-March to mid-April Busby Berkeley would shoot the musical numbers. Harry kept this schedule in the forefront of his mind, resolved to focus on the work and dreaming about getting back to New York as quickly as possible. He didn't like that Josephine was unhappy with him for being away from home so much. "If I didn't have Lucille and Alice, I couldn't bear the loneliness!" she would say, referring to their devoted housekeeper who'd quickly become part of the family and her closest friend Alice—a former showgirl who would later marry their friend, songwriter Irving Kahal.

Al was lighting a cigar as Harry walked into their office on the Warner Bros. lot. The room had nothing more than a piano, a chair, and an overflowing ashtray. Harry couldn't help but cheer up at the sight of his jovial partner. They picked up right where they'd left off.

"We gotta write a real scorcher for that Ginger Rogers. That girl's gonna be a star, you mark my words," Al said.

"I wouldn't dare doubt one of your predictions," Harry laughed.

"Well, in that case, you'd better not come with me to the track!"

"Not to worry, I have my own patented system for handicapping the races," Harry said. "Now, let's get down to brass tacks. The first song I've been thinking about is the opening number. It's got to be the kind of tune that makes your shoulders bounce up and down, you know what I mean?" Harry flipped open his notes. "I have an idea for it." He started it on the piano and looked over at Al for his reaction.

"Ooh, I like that! Keep it going," Al said. Harry continued playing several more bars. "How about, 'We're in the money,'" Al sang atop Harry's melody, bouncing his shoulders up and down to show Harry it certainly *was* that kind of tune. Harry smiled, urging him to go on. "'We're in the money, I'll tell you honey . . .' No, no. 'We're in the money, we're in the money.'" Al paused. "Then when it goes to that other section, 'We've got a lot of what it takes to get along.'"

Busby Berkeley poked his head into their office. "Whattya you two got for me?" the madman asked.

"This is what we're working up for the opening number," Harry said, launching into the rest of the song they had worked out:

We're in the money, the sky is sunny
Old man depression, you are through, you done us wrong, oh
We never see a headline 'bout a breadline today

And when we see the landlord
we can look that guy right in the eye

Buzz erupted. "I *love* it. So, here's what I'm thinkin'. We open on Ginger. Screamer close-up, battin' those lashes. Singing us right into submission! Then I'll have several lines of girls *wearing coins.* What do you think?"

"I don't think I've ever seen a girl wearing a coin. Have you, Al?" Harry asked. Then to Buzz, he said, "He gets out a lot more than I do."

"More like girls *as* coins," Buzz explained.

"Oh, *now* I get it," Harry said dryly. He and Al exchanged a knowing look; the sarcasm had failed to penetrate the madman's excitement.

"And giant stacks of quarters. Or even better, silver dollars. Each one as big as a swimming pool, piled up all the way to the ceiling!"

"Sure, okay," Al said, going along with him, doing his best to imagine it.

"Each girl will have a paper coin fan on a stick and reveal her face one by one in a movement canon as they come toward camera," Buzz said. He jumped up. "Great work, guys!"

Leaning over Al's body, Buzz helped himself to a cigar from the box. "Don't mind if I do!" he said.

As Buzz exited, Harry turned to Al. "Sounds like the costume department's got their work cut out for them—if you'll pardon the pun."

Al chuckled. "You're a wit, Harry Warren."

There was nothing in the script to suggest anything about a shadow waltz, a visually dramatic concept that later came to Al. Buzz ran with it, happily taking all the credit for what became the artistic highlight of the film. This was how designing a production number with the madman typically worked: There would be a production meeting in which Buzz would dazzle the studio bosses with a lot of mumbo jumbo, despite not having any clue yet what he was going to do. Then he'd return to the set, where sixty-plus chorus girls were on the clock sitting around knitting, playing cards, and painting each other's nails, waiting on him. Only when Harry and Al delivered a song could Buzz start to work his magic.

It was during the making of this film that Harry first experienced Dubin's disappearing act. He knew his partner had been spending more time at his Hollywood bachelor apartment than at home with his wife and two daughters. Al's wife was a former singer and actress from New York and a strict Catholic who'd sought an annulment from her first husband on the grounds that they had not been married in the church. Al first met Helen after he saw her perform in New York; he'd sent a note backstage, telling her he would love for her to sing one of his songs. Harry knew of some theater folks in New York who'd tried to warn her about Al's reputation, so he figured she must have simply succumbed to his charming side. She had a five-year-old daughter whom Al adored and treated as his own from day one. Harry reasoned Helen must have found this to be irresistible, coupled with the fact that Al agreed to convert to Catholicism so they could marry in the church.

As Harry got to know Al more, he could see that when Al's demons got the best of him, he'd retreat to indulge his many vices. Harry glimpsed Al's inner torment from time to time and could see him doing his best to work out all the hardships he'd suffered—the death of his beloved aunt after she was accidentally poisoned while visiting Al's childhood home; the cold nature of his mother, who used to chain him to his crib while she attended college classes; and his grave disappointment in his father's adultery and death at age fifty-three.

Harry figured the less he knew about what went on during Al's lost hours, the better. He'd cover for him if one of the bosses came around, but the truth was, Al would always return with wonderful lyrics. Harry felt he had no choice but to accept his partner's process, dysfunctional as it was. When Al eventually found his way back to the studio from any number of his hideouts—be it Hollywood, Mexico, or Malibu—it was never empty-handed. In the case of "Shadow Waltz," he walked in serenading Harry with the dreamy, romantic words:

In the winter, let me bring the spring to you
Let me feel that I mean ev'rything to you
Love's old song will be new
in the shadows
when I come and sing to you

Instead of giving Al any grief about where he'd been, Harry

just turned toward the piano and a gorgeous waltz flowed through his fingertips. There was no question he and Al spoke the same musical language, complementing each other in the most profound way. "Shadow Waltz" is still considered one of the most beautiful American waltzes ever written. When they played it for Buzz, he was reminded of a vaudeville act he once saw with a woman dancing while playing the violin. With this as his inspiration, he multiplied the image by sixty dancers each with their own violin, arranged in a Busby Berkeley signature kaleidoscopic design.

"Wait, I've got it!" Buzz told Harry and Al as he helped himself to another one of their cigars. "Not only will each of them be waltzing with their own violin, but each violin will be outlined in white neon for sequences in the dark, where we'll see nothing but the dancing instruments!"

Beguiled by Buzz's ambitious idea, Harry and Al couldn't wait to see if he could pull it off. When the day arrived to shoot the number and the dancers were getting wired to their neon violins, some started complaining about getting shocked.

"Darling, a little *Buzz* isn't so bad, is it?" the madman joked with one of the dancers.

She swatted him on the arm. "Very funny, Berkley. Why don't you try getting wired up and see how much you like it?"

Berkley's unit had been shooting for only four days when the real shock arrived. It was March 10, 1933, and they'd been working since 6:00 a.m. The cast and crew were exhausted and preparing themselves to be there again until after midnight. Harry and Al sat on set watching the rehearsal, in awe of the choreography of sixty neon violins and the elegant, curved scaffolding that went thirty feet high. Just before 6:00 in the evening, while in the middle of a take, everything began to shake violently, knocking the power out and plunging the soundstage into total darkness—except for a few neon violins, which began short-circuiting.

"Al?" Harry whispered in the dark.

"I'm here."

Harry reached out to Al's shoulder to make sure. "What the hell was that?" he asked. His voice trembled with the power of an aftershock.

"An earthquake!" Al said.

The chorus girls screamed in their highest register. Buzz's voice cut through the darkness: "Someone open the stage door!"

As the crew rushed to slide the giant soundstage door open and allow the outside light to pour in, a collective gaze went up as if it too had been choreographed—chins tipped in unison to take in the dangling Busby Berkeley, who'd been knocked off the camera boom and was hanging by one arm. The entire crew gasped as one.

"Don't panic!" Buzz yelled, struggling to pull himself up. "Everyone on the scaffold, just sit right where you are, and someone will help you!"

Harry called Josephine that night to tell her what had happened. "So you think you're ready to move to Los Angeles *now*?" he asked, trying to lighten the mood.

"Well, you survived it, didn't you?"

"I nearly croaked from the shock."

Harry heard the radio on in the background on the other end of the line.

"The news is reporting that the quake struck Long Beach," Josephine said. "It registered at 6.4 on the Richter scale. I don't know what the hell that is, but isn't Long Beach an awfully long way from Warner Brothers?"

"6.4 must be pretty big, then," Harry said. "I just don't know about this place. Nothing about it is to be trusted."

This experience did nothing more to endear Harry to the idea of relocating to Southern California. As the shoot began winding down with just two production numbers left, Ginger Rogers went to Harry and Al's office to hear the song they'd written for her. When they performed "I've Got to Sing a Torch Song," she was moved to tears. She quickly turned to Al, sniffling, "Cigarette me, big boy."

Harry and Al were tickled to be asked to appear in a scene in which the producer character falls in love with the girl after hearing her do the song. He then declares the film's songwriter character a genius before adding, "Fire Warren and Dubin." Sadly, Ginger's performance was edited out of the final cut of the film.

The other number that was entirely Al's idea was "Remember My Forgotten Man." Harry and Al had many conversations about the heart-wrenching sight of military veterans on breadlines. Al found it shameful the way society watched them suffer, seeming to forget their sacrifices. In contrast to Harry's uneventful military experience, Al had served on the frontlines in France, where he was exposed to poison gas that left him with permanent lung damage and a yearly bout of pneumonia. Harry was aghast the first time he saw Al cough blood into a handkerchief while they were working at the piano.

"My god, Al! We should get you the doctor," Harry said, watching him fight off a coughing fit.

"Nah, just a little beet juice," Al said, downplaying it.

Al, feeling loyal to the troops, told Harry how music had the power to save lives on the battlefield. Harry thought Al was being a bit dramatic until he explained: "I'll never forget one night in France, when I was doing guard duty in Belleau Wood, immediately after the Battle of Château-Thierry. I heard footsteps in the dark. I thought I was a dead man, or that I might have to kill a man, until I heard him whistling 'Hinky Dinky.'"

Harry had to laugh a little. He knew the song. "The polite name for 'Mademoiselle from Armentières'?"

"Yup. That's how I knew he was one of ours—it was such a popular song with the Brits."

One thing was certain: their song "Remember My Forgotten Man," appropriately written in a minor key, packed a powerful punch of a social message—the soldier who fought for freedom no longer being free. The studio moved it to end the film for the greatest impact.

After *Gold Diggers of 1933,* Harry returned to New York once again, hoping to stay on Long Island for good. Al happened to be back there as well, and actor Eddie Cantor summoned the pair to meet him at his hotel to discuss a new movie idea.

Eddie was a warm and kind man, which wasn't true of many in the business. Harry and Al ended up writing four songs for Cantor's movie, *Roman Scandals,* on a loan-out deal, in which one studio loans someone they have under contract to another studio—Goldwyn, in this case. The breakout song from *Roman Scandals* was "Keep Young and Beautiful." Harry was happy to be joined on this project with Harold Arlen and Ted Koehler, who contributed the song "Kickin' the Gong Around."

Over dinner in Manhattan, Harry gave Al the news. "I think we're finally going to do it," he said. "I found a place to rent in Beverly Hills and I'm going to bring the family out."

"I thought I might never see the day," Al said, grinning from ear to ear.

"I had hoped I wouldn't," Harry joked. "Sonny's excited— he loves trains—and Cookie can't wait to see the beach. Our housekeeper, Lucille, agreed to come too."

"This calls for champagne!" Al said, signaling to a waiter.

"The place is less than a mile from yours. I'll have Josephine talk to Helen to find out about schools."

"She'll be happy to help with all that," Al said. "You know she'll be pushing the parochial school."

Just as Harry and his family settled into their new home on a quiet, palm tree–lined street, Al began to escape to New York more frequently, despite their new project being underway. Harry sensed the pace was beginning to take its toll on Al, who'd never let him down before. He wanted to believe Al never would, but Warner Bros. took a different view and tasked Arthur Schwartz, a friend of Al's who worked for the studio, to start rounding him up and bring him back to work whenever he drifted. One such event happened during *Footlight Parade*. The film was set to star James Cagney, whom Harry found a delight to work with. Cagney had lobbied for the part, eager to show off his vaudevillian talent for dance the first time in a film. When Art returned to the Warner Bros. lot, Harry saw him walking to his office.

"Art, did you find him?" Harry shouted.

"He slipped right through my fingers when we were almost home," Art explained. "I found him having dinner at Dinty Moore's, just like you said. I told him we had to go straight away to the station and get on the *Chief*. He didn't put up a fight—ordered a pastrami to go, and off we went. He said he didn't need to pack anything; he just got on the train with all the lead sheets you gave him crumpled up in one pocket and a bottle of Mount Vernon rye whiskey in the other. Then he worked almost the entire time on the train."

"Did you bring me back his lyrics?" Harry asked.

"No, I thought he would be giving them to you himself. But when we got to Albuquerque, he got off the train to buy some jewelry and blankets for Helen and the girls and—"

"He never got back on," Harry said, finishing what was becoming an all-too-predictable story.

Harry was unexpectedly distressed by the situation. It wasn't unlike the other times Al had vanished, but for some reason he now felt the ground shifting below him—not as violently as the earthquake still so vivid in his mind, but threatening major destruction all the same. Harry could hold his tongue no longer.

"I keep telling Wallis and Warner they need more songwriters to cover the workload, but all they care about is the damned bottom line. We're not machines! They're killing this man. I hope they know that. I'm just not sure they care."

"I'll talk to them," Art said sympathetically.

Finally, the studio seemed to get the message that their most valuable songwriting team was on the ropes. So, they hired Harry's friend Irving Kahal and lyricist Sammy Fain to contribute the gorgeous song "By a Waterfall" for *Footlight Parade*. Two weeks later, Al reappeared with all his lyrics finished, and they were good. Art went straight to Harry and Al's office when he spotted Al back on the lot.

"What happened, Al?" he asked. "When we got on the *Chief* in New York, you promised we would be on the coast by Saturday."

"Oh, Artie, you didn't say which Saturday!" Al said with a hearty laugh, eliciting an eyeroll from Harry.

Given Harry's sustained workload and time away from home, Josephine began insisting Sundays be devoted to family. Even Harry found himself submitting to some of the charms of the City of Angels, such as the Venice Beach canals, where they could go for gondola rides, just like in the real Venice. As they stepped out of the boat one Sunday, Sonny looked up at Harry.

"Daddy, you have a song about a gondola," he said.

"You're right, I do." Harry smiled.

"I think I'll be a songwriter when I grow up too."

Harry felt his heart get so full, he thought it might burst. The moment was priceless, and he would never forget it. For as much as he was wrapped up in work, Harry enjoyed these lazy Sundays and prided himself on being a family man. At the same time, he knew he couldn't afford to take his eye off the ball for a second. It was a balancing act he would struggle with throughout his career.

Chapter Seven

With *Footlight Parade* finished, Harry received quite an unexpected call from the studio. He couldn't wait to tell Josephine about it, especially because he'd started to notice her enjoying some of the perks of being a so-called Hollywood wife. He found her in the kitchen, making one of his favorite Calabrian dishes, and rushed to turn down the flame on the stove.

"Jo, you're going to burn the garlic!" Josephine shot him a look. Harry put his hands up in a "Don't shoot" gesture. "You're not going to believe the call I just got," he said, before she had a chance to retort.

"Try me."

"Remember the short film we saw in the theater a couple months ago, before the feature? The one on Walter Donaldson?"

"Sure," she said. "You know how I love that 'My Blue Heaven' and *all* those songs Walter's written with Gus Kahn—'Makin' Whoopee,' 'Yes, Sir, That's My Baby,' and—"

"Sounds like you're quite the fan," Harry said, cutting in on her litany. "Just so you know, Walter might be making a fortune, but he's blown it all on the wrong horse a few times now."

"Well, aren't you lucky to have a smart wife to manage all the finances for you?"

Harry smiled. "Anyhow," he said, "I came in here to tell you the studio wants to do a short film like that with *me*."

She cocked her head to one side and put her hands on her hips. "Harry Warren," she teased, shooting him a come-hither look, "I do believe you're a star!"

"What was the name of the one we saw?" he asked.

"Something like, *Walter Donaldson, Popular Composer*?"

"Yes, that's it! Well, Ray McCarey is set to direct this one they'll be calling *Harry Warren: America's Foremost Composer*. It's going to shoot in New York in November."

"Congratulations, sweetheart. Let's go out and celebrate. I'll ask Lucille to feed the children and put them to bed."

"What about the *penne calabrese*?" he asked.

"I'll make it another time when you're not standing over my shoulder like one of your sisters!"

Harry was having a hard time believing he'd been chosen as the subject of a short film, considering all the friction with Warner Brothers. He'd been so busy working, he hadn't stopped to acknowledge the simple fact that it was *his music* defining Warner Brothers and the best in Hollywood musicals in the 1930s. He'd revitalized what had been a dying genre. The studio had come up with a list of eleven songs for the short film to be arranged in a medley—a mix of Harry's Tin Pan Alley tunes and movie hits.

Because Warner Bros. had purchased Remick, the company now owned Harry's entire catalog, and it was determined to promote all of it—even his songs pre-dating his time at the studio.

The setting for *Harry Warren: America's Foremost Composer* was a chichi cocktail party with about a dozen guests dressed in tuxedos and evening gowns. It opened with a superlative from the bartender: "Say, folks, how 'bout a little toast to our pal Harry Warren, one of the finest songwriters that ever lived?"

One of the guests replied, "I think he should make a speech!"

Seated at a grand piano, Harry stood with a hand in the air and said, "Wait a minute, speechmaking isn't my racket at all!"

Harry kicked off his medley at the piano, singing "I Found a Million Dollar Baby (In a Ten Cent Store)" with two featured female singers—one was Marjorie Hines, the voice of Betty Boop. She sang "Have a Little Faith in Me" and planted a kiss on Harry's cheek to set up the next song, "Ooh, That Kiss," which lead into "Cheerful Little Earful," followed by "Would You Like to Take a Walk?", "Cryin' for the Carolines," and "You're My Everything." The well-known dance team Marguerite & LeRoy took center stage in top hats and canes to dance a number in the parlor before segueing into "Shadow Waltz." For the big finale, Harry played "42nd Street" for the party guests as it dissolved into footage from *42nd Street* and its rousing title track production number.

Harry Warren: America's Foremost Composer could have been a major turning point for Harry. With the full backing of the studio to position him as a huge star, he could have leveraged this moment in any number of ways. Not known for performing his own songs, he could have used the short as a platform to perform more to raise his public profile, in the vein of Cole Porter or George Gershwin. He could have asked for greater compensation or tried to negotiate a percentage of his own publishing royalties, given that his contract with Warner Bros. had been a standard work for hire. Of course, there would have been risks associated with attempting any of these things, and at this point, Harry was content to keep things as they were. There was also the issue of how much publicity he even *wanted*, given that he was a shy and private person.

While out at the movies one night, Harry and Josephine happened to see *Harry Warren: America's Foremost Composer* shown before the feature presentation. Josephine squeezed his hand in the darkened theater. But instead of soaking up the joy of the moment, Harry was hit with a jolt of reality that left him feeling depressed; suddenly realizing the short film's only purpose was to campaign for an Academy Award for *42nd Street*, he felt he'd let his ego run away with him. And because no category for music or song existed yet, none of it would directly benefit him—it was all for the studio's glory. He felt like a pawn for allowing himself to think this was somehow a tribute to his music. He kept these thoughts to himself, knowing Josephine would scold him for not feeling more grateful. But when it was announced that *42nd Street* was nominated for Best Production (the equivalent of Best Picture today), Harry felt privately vindicated. Josephine, on the other hand, was proud of him. She didn't need a caulbearer's wisdom to know Harry was one of the main reasons the film was a success. The morning it was announced, she sent Sonny and Cookie to wake Harry with his coffee and the newspaper.

"Your movie might be the best of the whole year," Cookie said.

"Is that right?" Harry asked.

Sonny nodded rapidly to confirm this and gave Harry a hug. Harry looked at Josephine and said, "Maybe I should go back to being an assistant director, since they give Academy Awards for that but not for music!"

She glared back at him, exasperated. Sometimes his grumpiness really wore on her.

By now, Harry was used to receiving the obligatory phone call from Irving Berlin congratulating him on every milestone, but Harry sensed the calls carried an undercurrent of competition. It was as though Berlin was keeping score in a game Harry never signed up to play. Harry knew the Irving Berlin publicity machine was always in overdrive, so it didn't surprise him to see Irving on the cover of *Time* a few months later. He spotted the magazine on a newsstand and expected the article to be somewhat cringeworthy, but he brought a copy home to Josephine anyway.

"There's a reason you don't see any music in this photo," he said.

"Because he can't read or write music, I know," she said.

"You shouldn't get to brag about your musical ignorance in *Time* magazine." Harry began reading portions of the article aloud: "'His subject was old songs and he was worried for fear it would sound conceited to say—'" Harry started laughing so hard that he couldn't speak for a minute. "How does he get away with being so disingenuous?"

"You really want to know?" Josephine asked.

"Probably not."

"He's got chutzpah coming out of his ears. He believes his own baloney, which in turn, makes it easier for others to believe."

Shortly after the *Time* cover, NBC aired a five-part special on Irving Berlin's work. It seemed he was having a moment. With this, Harry noticed an odd feeling of his own—the more he saw Berlin seek the spotlight, the more he wanted to retreat from it. As much as Irving irritated him, it taught him who he didn't want to be. Harry was by nature more of an iconoclast than someone who aspired to be an icon. On one hand, he found it unbecoming for anyone to sing their own praises; on the other hand, he felt slighted whenever he wasn't properly recognized. The only people who truly understood the complicated nature of this duality were Harry's songwriter friends. Strangely enough, Harold Arlen was also a good friend of Berlin's.

"Irving only likes you more because you're a member of the tribe," Harry joked. "With me, it always feels like he's employing *The Art of War*."

"Irving probably doesn't even realize you're *not* Jewish," Harold said. "I know he wouldn't be the first person to think that—you speak more Yiddish than I do! I feel bad for Irving sometimes."

"You feel bad for him when he's the *alter cocker* always accusing the rest of us of stealing songs from him?"

Harry loved to kvetch about this kind of thing for hours on end over lunch at the farmer's market on Fairfax, on the golf course, or at the pitch and putt. He cherished his time with Harold and Ted when they were in Los Angeles. Their days writing songs for the Cotton Club ended along with prohibition in 1933, and they'd been asked to come to Hollywood to write for the film *Let's Fall in Love* the same year Harold had written "It's Only a Paper Moon." At Harry's urging, Harold soon relocated to Los Angeles and joined all the other New York songwriters who'd gone to the golden land of sea and sparkling swimming pools to wait out the Depression by working for the studios.

Harold trusted Harry's good counsel when Harold was conflicted about a job offer from Ira and Yip Harburg to write a Broadway musical that didn't include Ted. Having first introduced the two, Harry convinced Harold it would not damage his relationship with Ted to take the job—in fact, he'd be crazy not to. Harold and Ted would go on to work together again.

Harold confided in Harry about everything, including his complicated romantic relationship with Anya Taranda, an American-born Russian model and one of the original Breck Shampoo girls. Once Harold and Anya moved to Los Angeles, it was clear she would never be happy left alone. She wasn't social, and the only other wives she felt comfortable with were Josephine and Buddy Morris's wife, Carolyn. Once the Gershwins traded their adjoining penthouses in Manhattan for adjacent houses on North Roxbury Drive in Beverly Hills, Ira's wife, Lee, began hosting everything from lunches, dinners, and happy hours to pool and tennis time for songwriters and their wives. Lee was known and feared as a strong personality. Despite her liberal views on just about everything, she wasn't shy about sharing her displeasure over Harold and Anya not being married.

Harry enjoyed time with friends, but the truth was that he was more comfortable at work than at any party. In another loan-out from Warner Bros., he and Al went to work for *42nd Street* producer Darryl Zanuck, who'd resigned as the studio's head of production to set up his own company based at Twentieth Century, a year before its merger with Fox. One of the first projects Zanuck produced there was *Moulin Rouge,* for which Harry and Al wrote three songs, including "Boulevard of Broken Dreams."

One of the many perks of working on the Twentieth Century lot was composer and musical director Alfred Newman's 5:00 cocktail hour. Harry and Al quickly became regulars. Like all the other music folks on the lot, they enjoyed working with Newman. Harry and Al also appreciated Zanuck as a producer; he never said he didn't like a song, just, "Save it for something else." This experience gave Harry a taste of how different things could be working elsewhere. He'd been so busy, he hadn't given much thought to life after Warner Brothers, which he now realized was something to look forward to.

After a few drinks at Newman's cocktail hour one day, Al pulled up a chair next to Harry and threw back a shot of whiskey. "Helen asked me for a formal separation," he said.

"I'm sorry, Al. Is it maybe for the best? It doesn't have to mean divorce. After all, you are Catholic now," he joked to cheer him up.

"I think it's safe to say I'm an abject failure as a Catholic," Al said, pouring himself another shot.

After the loan-out with Zanuck, it was back to Warner Brothers, where Harry and Al began writing for *Wonder Bar* and *Twenty-Million Sweethearts*. Their next big hit came out of the movie *Dames*. "I Only Have Eyes for You" would become one of the twenty-five most-performed songs of the twentieth century. In a scene in which the songwriter character tells financial backers that "pretty girls are what make the business go around," he greets several lovely ladies parading through the office, specifically referring to "Miss Warren" and "Miss Dubin." Josephine was tickled when she heard her name invoked in the movie, but it was too late for any charm offensive where Helen was concerned.

The following year, Harry and Al were ecstatic when the Academy Awards finally added music categories, Best Score and Best Song. Harry felt proud of Gus Kahn, one of his earliest supporters, who received a nomination in each category in 1935. Harry had always felt a special kinship with Gus, and he was happy to see Sonny becoming good friends with Gus's son Donald. Meanwhile, Cookie's best friend was songwriter Richard Whiting's daughter Margaret, whom everyone called Maggie. Every Saturday, the two girls were chauffeured to Grauman's Chinese Theatre to see a movie and go for ice cream sodas afterwards.

～

Warner Bros. was on a roll with the Gold Diggers franchise and greenlit *Gold Diggers of 1935,* giving Busby Berkeley a chance to direct the entire film, not only the production numbers. With Warren and Dubin set to write the songs, Harry gave a lead sheet to Al, who surprised no one with his now predictable and tragic routine of dropping out of sight. He'd been renting a beach house in Malibu, and because his studio driver, William Moore, and his wife, Nina, had been staying with him to run the household, Al couldn't see how this was considered disappearing.

One day, Al called Harry excitedly, asking him to drive out to hear the song he'd just finished. It was a sunny day on the coast, despite it being the one part of Los Angeles that was sometimes socked in with fog. When Harry arrived, Al opened the door and ushered him inside. Harry's eyes were drawn to the gleaming Pacific just beyond the back doors of the cottage.

"This one is just for you," Al said.

"Al, you shouldn't have," Harry said, a hint of facetiousness in his voice.

Al explained further: "I know how much you miss New York. This one is postmarked from Manhattan. From me to you, going right back to that fateful day at the Grand Central Oyster Bar."

This piece of music Harry had written was unusual in the sense that he'd composed it without any clear idea of how it would be used and without using any cues from the script. It was a blank slate in that sense, and Al took full advantage of that to paint his partner a masterpiece representing Harry's deep love and longing for New York.

Harry was moved. He took the song back to the studio to play it for Buzz and Jack Warner. When Harry finished, he was surprised that Buzz didn't immediately jump for it. Harry looked over at Jack, hoping for a better reaction.

"Go back to Al and have him write another lyric," Jack said.

Harry was furious. It took everything in him not to completely lose his cool. He remembered something Cookie would say that she'd learned from the nuns at school: "Even when you're mad, don't be bad!" Hearing his daughter's voice in his head might have saved him from getting fired. He took a deep breath.

"I'll write a new song, if you foolishly insist," he said, "but under no circumstances will I ever divorce these words from this music. *Never.*"

Harry stormed out and ran into Al Jolson on the way back to his office. Al saw Harry was burned up about something. "Harry, are you all right?" he asked

"You can't believe these *idiots*! I mean, what a goddamn pencil-pushing pants presser!" Harry said, red in the face. "I just played him the most beautiful—"

"Wait, who? Which one?" Jolson tried to clarify.

"Doesn't matter, they're all the same. They're dimwits who've never had an original idea in their lives. Al just finished a gorgeous tune, 'Lullaby of Broadway,' and Jack had the nerve to say, 'Tell him to write another lyric.' That's it—I'm done with this place!"

"I'd sure love to hear the tune, Harry," Jolson offered.

Harry stood there another few moments, steaming. When

he cooled down, he followed Al back to his office and performed the song.

"Well, hot damn!" Jolson cried. "If they don't want it, I'll take it for my movie. That one's a keeper, Harry."

Jolson went to Jack Warner and told him he would happily take the new Warren-Dubin song, which predictably caused Jack to backpedal on his position. "Lullaby of Broadway" remained in *Gold Diggers of 1935*, and Warner would be very happy for reversing his decision for it.

The first clue about what a big hit it would be came on April 20, 1935. Harry, Josephine, and the kids gathered around the radio for the premiere of *Your Hit Parade*, sponsored by Lucky Strike. They listened as the announcer's voice came over the radio:

"Your Hit Parade! We don't pick 'em, we just play 'em. From north, south, east, and west, we check the songs you dance to, the sales of the records you buy, and the sheet music you play."

The number-two song was "Lullaby of Broadway." When they heard it, Sonny and Cookie cheered and danced around the living room. A tear came to Harry's eye, and he forgot everything else for a moment, witnessing his children's unadulterated joy.

One day, while the song had been getting near-constant radio play, Harry joined Ira and Harold to play a round of golf with Manny Seff, the screenwriter of *Gold Diggers of 1935*. Manny shouted just as Harry was teeing off: "Harry! You've been nominated for an Academy Award!"

Harry froze mid-swing as Manny came running toward him, out of breath.

"I just saw Jerry Kern in the clubhouse, and he got nominated for his song 'Roberta.' And you and Al for 'Lullaby,' and Berlin for 'Cheek to Cheek.'"

"Well, whattya know," Harry said. "That oughta show those sons of bitches!"

"I guess Warner and Wallis are wiping egg off each other's faces right about now," Ira said.

This was a personal triumph for Harry. The vindication was all he really needed. Harry's friends patted him on the back in congratulations.

"Looks like drinks are on you, Harry!" Harold joked.

"All right, all right. Are we here to play a round or glad-hand all day? I'm sure Berlin's got it locked up anyhow," Harry said, always uncomfortable with too much attention.

"Hey, don't let Kern hear you say that. By the way, you *gotta* see his hat today," Manny said. Jerry Kern was known for his outlandish golf outfits and coordinating hats.

"I hope it's his lucky hat," Harry said under his breath.

"What was that, Harry? Does that mean maybe you wouldn't mind an Academy Award after all?" Ira teased, always entertained by Harry's pawkiness.

Harry suddenly howled with laughter as Manny's ball hit a drainpipe and an owl flew out. "Hey, you got a birdie!" Harry joked. Everyone broke up laughing.

"I think I'll take this hole as a birdie, if you don't mind," Manny said. "Small consolation prize for not getting an Academy Award."

"It's only a nomination," Harry said.

"Oh, it's a win," Manny said.

"Don't jinx it!" Harold cried. Harold had a mystical approach to his songwriting process, fearing each great song he wrote could be his last. Harry was always tickled to learn of his songwriter friends' superstitions.

"Jerry finally stopped naming his shows with titles that began with an S, and look! He gets a nomination," Harry said. "*Sally, Sunny, Stepping Stones, Show Boat, Sweet Adeline . . .*"

Ira nodded, well aware of this. "Well, I'll be damned!" Harold said, feeling enlightened.

Harry wondered if Al had heard the news of their nomination, wherever he was.

When Harry finally did hear from his elusive partner, it was a phone call in the middle of the night. "Al, *where* the hell are you?" Harry asked groggily.

"Funny you should ask. I just finished the lyric to that gorgeous tune of yours, 'Where Am I?'"

"Great. And now I'd like to know, where are you?"

"Juárez, I think."

"Juár-ez the hell is that?"

"You know Juárez, Harry. Mexico. At the local cathouse. Now, listen!" Al began singing: "'Where am I? Am I in heaven, or am I really with you? Who are you? Are you an angel or just a dream that's too good to be true?'"

"That's beautiful, Al, truly," Harry said. "Now, can you get back here? We've got Forbstein's birthday on the stage day after tomorrow."

"Okay, Harry. I'll be there. And by the way?"

"Yes?"

"I just finished two quail and they were delicious."

Harry made a strange face at the phone and hung up.

Al made it back in time for Leo Forbstein's party. It was the only studio-sponsored event all year they actually enjoyed, when Warner Brothers's orchestra saluted its beloved music department head with parody songs and revelry.

As the holidays approached, it was a festive time. The *Los Angeles Times* reported that Harry, Josephine, Gus Kahn, and his wife attended a birthday party at the Trocadero for Johnny Mercer, thrown by Johnny's wife, Ginger. In a separate but related item, the paper printed: "Mr. and Mrs. Harry Warren left Friday for a pre-holiday jaunt to New York but plan to be back in time for Christmas." Harry cringed every time he saw something like this in print.

Then, on March 5, 1936, the big day arrived: the Eighth Academy Awards. The Biltmore Bowl, a ballroom in the exquisite hotel of the same name in downtown Los Angeles, held the ceremony. Frank Capra hosted, fresh off his win of Outstanding Production (Best Picture) the year before for directing *It Happened One Night*; he was now president of the Academy of Motion Picture Arts and Sciences. This was the first year people began referring to the golden statuettes as Oscars. Like so many other details surrounding this night, there is no one widely accepted account of how the awards got this nickname. One thing for certain, though, is that the ceremony back then was an "intimate affair"—Harry's own words for the evening, which consisted of a formal dinner and seating arrangements that grouped people from the same studio and film together. It was the first year for the category Best Dance Direction, and Busby Berkeley was nominated for *Gold Diggers of 1935*, along with Harry and Al. A black-tie affair, Harry donned a sharp tuxedo and Josephine stunned in a couture gown designed for her by Bess Schank in Beverly Hills. A top-notch seamstress herself, Jo had sought out the very best for the occasion.

After getting settled at their table, Harry excused himself to the men's room. When he returned, Buzz looked at him and noticed him fidgeting and patting his forehead with a hanky. leaned in to ask, "Is everything all right, Harry?"

Harry was surprised anyone noticed a change in his demeanor. "Yes, I'm fine. Never mind," he said.

Harry was a sensitive soul, and there's no telling what could have transpired on his trip to the men's room. Yet there is simply no evidence to support the notion of Harry getting turned away at the door or being mistaken for a gatecrasher, an oft-repeated tale. What seems more plausible is Harry's discomfort with being nominated the same year as Irving Berlin. Knowing how much more media savvy Irving was, Harry was likely anxious about being upstaged by Berlin *even if* he and Al were declared the winners.

When it was finally time for Frank Capra to announce the Best Song category, Harry and Al instinctively sat up a little taller in their banquet chairs.

"And the Oscar goes to . . . Harry Warren and Al Dubin for 'Lullaby of Broadway'!"

Jo looked over at Harry and beamed. She'd always seen the depth of his talent and she had never been prouder of him than in this moment. Everyone at the table raised a glass to the song-writing heroes. As he and Al stood to go receive their award, Harry felt Berlin's gaze on him, causing an impish grin to spread across Harry's face. Being honored in this way was something Harry never could have dreamed of growing up in Brooklyn, playing ball in the streets with a block of wood. He had the distinct feeling his life was about to change. He just wasn't sure how.

When they returned to work on Monday, Harry and Al felt absolutely no difference in the way they were treated by the studio now that they were Academy Award winners. It was almost as though the bosses went out of their way to ignore it. The movie *In Caliente* had been assigned to another song-writing team at the studio, right up to the moment that Buzz insisted on getting at least one song from Warren and Dubin to inspire him to create something extravagant. They were up to their ears with other work but delivered the song "Muchacha." Due to either Al's wanderings or someone's miscommunication about the schedule, Harry got a call from the studio early one morning, informing him that Buzz was blaming him for holding up production. Most everyone at Warner Bros. knew Harry's routine was to work late into the night and sleep until noon, so he was irritated at being called in under such duress. He dressed as fast as he could and rushed to the studio, where he found the set in total chaos.

Stuntmen were riding horses on top of treadmills. The poor creatures were utterly panicked by the contraption, urinating all over themselves and anyone else who happened to be standing too close. Jack Warner and the entire cast and crew were sitting around, waiting for Harry. Still irked to be taking all the heat for this, he grumbled all the way to the piano, where he sat down and leaned over to his musical secretary. "I'm about to completely improvise something," he said, "so I need you to remember what I play."

That Harry proceeded to ad-lib, no one could have guessed— they loved it all the same. It was these moments that made Harry appreciate the experience he got from working as an accompanist for silent films. He'd come a long way from the Vitagraph Studio in Brooklyn, yet those times suddenly felt very familiar as he watched horses bolt all over the back lot and people dive into bushes to avoid getting trampled.

It seemed to Harry that things were getting crazier at the studio all the time, or maybe it was just that signs of strain were beginning to show in him too. He had begun experiencing abdominal pain and had promised Josephine he would go to a doctor. He disliked doctors almost as much as he dreaded being summoned to Jack Warner's office. Those were the meetings that almost always began with, "You know we consider you part of the family here." When Al resurfaced shortly after the fiasco, the duo was called in for one such meeting with an extremely animated Jack.

"Ah, there they are, the golden boys!" Jack said. "I wanted to tell you personally that we just struck a very important deal with William Randolph Hearst."

"I thought he had a company set up over at MGM?" Harry asked.

"Yes, Cosmopolitan Pictures. He'll be moving the whole operation here, starting with Miss Davies's bungalow."

"What does this have to do with us?" Al asked.

"The deal is for four films starring Marion Davies, *featuring* music by Warren and Dubin!"

On the way home that night, Harry got stuck behind a huge traffic jam. "Oh, for crying out loud," he mumbled. Frustrated with not being able to move an inch, he pulled his car to the side of the road and got out to light a cigar. Leaning against the hood, his gaze went up to the long row of palm trees he usually didn't take the time to admire. He had to admit, some aspects of California were beginning to grow on him. Bringing his eyeline back to street level, he saw the source of the holdup: a giant structure making its way down Sunset Boulevard—Marion Davies's bungalow. As the massive thing lumbered down the road, Harry thought about how strange this all was—and even stranger, his own life was connected to it. He realized that when he got right down to it, he was partly to blame for the traffic jam that was causing him so much irritation. William Randolph Hearst and Davies were moving to Warner Brothers specifically for the Warren-Dubin team. It suddenly occurred to him that maybe he should ask for a raise.

When he went back to work after the weekend, he discovered the bungalow had been placed right next to the music department. This turned out to be convenient for working over long lunches. What wasn't so convenient was the tremendous amount of security around Miss Davies, which made it difficult for Harry and Al to get onstage. They were consistently turned away and would have to return to their office and wait for the phone call from the director: "Where the hell are you two? Get down here now!" Then they'd go back to the stage and try to explain things to the guards, but the same thing would happen all over again.

"You'd think she was damned royalty," Harry said.

"Well, her sugar daddy might be richer than royalty," Al said, shrugging.

"Jeez, is money all that makes the world go 'round?" Harry asked, sounding defeated.

"*And* music. Don't forget music. They couldn't do this without us," Al said, having one of his more clear-minded moments.

Keeping this fact in the front of their minds did little to alleviate the stress of the new Marion Davies era at Warner Bros., when they were often forced to play songs over the phone for Mr. Hearst. As kind and generous as Marion was with the cast and crew, Harry found her entourage tedious. She had her own organist, fiddler, and accordionist to play a march every time she walked onstage. It was all too much after a while.

When Harry finally went to the doctor, he was diagnosed with an ulcer, for which he was advised to work less and relax more. Josephine thought it might be helpful to join the Sun & Sand Club in Santa Monica, where they could put their feet in the ocean and enjoy cocktails and a nice meal. The kids could run around with their friends and talk about why they weren't members of the neighboring Jonathan Club, which had a reputation for racist and anti-Semitic policies.

Even with the new focus on carving out time for recuperation, Harry continued getting worked up over his mistreatment by the studio. One day while Harry dropped off Richard Whiting at home after golf, Richard's daughter Maggie ran up to the car.

"Uncle Harry, is it true you're replacing Harold Arlen on *Gold Diggers of 1937*?"

Harry looked at Richard. "She's reading the trades now?" he asked incredulously. "How old are you, Maggie?"

"I'm ten. Same as Cookie, Uncle Harry," she answered, exasperated. "Are you or are you not replacing him?"

Harry sighed, "Yes, it's true. Now, don't you have homework to do? What do you think your father and I are paying all this money to the private school for?"

"Even the nuns agree *The Hollywood Reporter* and *Daily Variety* are above my grade's reading level." She and Cookie attended Marymount, a convent school that required the girls to wear hats, gloves, and long stockings.

"Touché," Harry said, smiling as she ran back to the house. He turned to Richard. "Buzz complained he couldn't get anything going with Harold and Yip's score. Al and I are furious they would put us in such an awkward situation. All I can do is try to convince Harold we had nothing to do with the decision and tell him how much we resent it."

Harry and Al begrudgingly began working on the movie, quickly coming up with "Plenty of Money and You." When Hal Wallis came into their office to hear it, he sat down and flipped open the newspaper.

Harry said, "Are you going to read or listen to the song?"

Wallis ignored him. Harry and Al exchanged a curious glance and began playing anyway, but Wallis immediately got up to leave. "It's lousy," he said. "Write another song."

"No," Harry said. He finally called his bluff.

"It stinks. Write another song," Wallis snapped.

"*You* stink. Get another songwriter."

Once again, Harry and Al had to go back to the old playbook and exploit the ongoing feud between Wallis and Jack Warner to ensure their song made it into the movie. Harry was getting tired of this.

Somehow, Harry prevailed in getting Warner Bros. to hire Richard Whiting and lyricist Johnny Mercer for the film *Hollywood Hotel*, despite still being angry about how the studio had treated Harold Arlen and Yip Harburg. Harry knew Richard and Johnny had knocked it out of the park when they wrote "Hooray for Hollywood" for the film, and he was incensed when Wallis called him to his office to listen to all their songs submitted for the film.

"It's your job as producer to decide which songs stay or go. Don't try to shirk that off on a hired hand like me," Harry scolded. "If you don't want a hit as big as 'On the Good Ship Lollipop,' that's your problem." Harry was trying to stick up for Richard while simultaneously making Wallis feel like the fool he was.

Many Warner Brothers producers were former bookkeepers, like Sam Bischoff, who had a rabid gambling habit. Whenever Harry and Al reported to Bischoff's office to show him a song, they had to wait for him to call his bookie to see how his horses did. He bet on races all over the country, so it could take hours to play him just three songs. Gambling on the lot had become so pervasive that Warner Bros. had started tapping the phones— all except for Harry and Al's. When the gambling junkies got wind of this, they began barging into their office to place their bets. This caught up with the studio heads, and their phone was removed too. This may have been the last straw for Harry, who started leaving work in the middle of the day. When one of the bosses ran into him on such an escape and asked where he was going, Harry said, "To Hollywood. To call my wife. Get the phone back in my office." He huffed. "This place is turning into a damn daycare center. I've just about had it with all the *mishegaas* around here!"

That same year, the film *San Quentin* starred Ann Sheridan, who had recently signed a contract with the studio. Wallis came to Harry and Al and said, "We've got this girl and I want you to write a hit for her."

Harry laughed hysterically. Even he thought he was

beginning to sound a bit mad. "That's pretty good, ordering up a hit," Harry joked. "Say, is this *film* going to be a hit?"

Just when he thought working at Warner Brothers couldn't get any worse, a massive rainstorm washed out the Cahuenga Pass. Everyone was forced to stay on the lot overnight, and the property department issued blankets like it was wartime.

"Now I really feel like an inmate," Harry told Al as they waited out the storm.

"More like a prisoner of war. In a battle we're no longer winning," Al said, his voice melancholy. "I've been taking pills to get through the day and other pills to sleep. Now I have to go in for some surgery."

Harry feared for Al. He'd never seen him quite this down before. "Surgery?" he asked.

"A fistula in my stomach." When Al saw the confusion on Harry's face, he said, "I try not to ask too many questions. I just know I need the operation if I want to live."

Al went ahead with the surgery. While he recovered in the hospital, he was prescribed morphine for his pain. He quickly realized that with morphine there's no such thing as pain. He made fast friends with the drug, as well as with the nurse tending to him—once she intimated that she could arrange to keep his prescription bottle filled long after he'd left the hospital.

Al had only recently learned to drive and adding drug use to this mix was all the more dangerous. During one of his first attempts, he made it only a couple blocks before having to ask his daughter to drive the car home for him. The next time, he drove to Jerome Kern's one night, but he asked Harry to drive him back in his own car. As Harry started the engine, Al opened the glovebox in search of a handkerchief—that's when Harry noticed a gun. He knew Al hadn't been the same since the surgery. "What are you doing with a gun in there?" Harry asked.

"Better to feel safe, don't you think?"

"You don't feel safe without a gun? Since when?"

As Harry turned onto Al's street, Al abruptly grabbed the wheel. Harry struggled to right the car to narrowly avoid a row of parked cars.

"What the hell are you trying to do? Kill us both?"

"There was something in the road!" Al yelled. "Didn't you see it?"

"No, Al. I didn't see it because there was nothing in the road." Harry looked at Al feeling incredibly saddened. "What did you think you saw?"

Al stared straight ahead. "I don't know," he said, shaking his head. "I don't know."

The man Harry knew and respected was gone. It was time Harry came to terms with it. Despite Al having recently written what Harry considered one of their most beautiful songs—"September in the Rain," for 1937's *Stars Over Broadway*—he knew Al had done it in a heavily drug-induced state.

Some part of Harry thought perhaps it was best for the team to go out on this high note. He knew he needed to consider working with other lyricists. The first person who came to mind was Johnny Mercer, with whom Harry had worked before. Their first collaboration had been "I'm an Old Cowhand," for which Harry turned down co-writing credit, thinking it wasn't much of a song. But when it ended up in the Bing Crosby movie *Rhythm on the Range* and became a hit, Harry realized he'd miscalculated. He reminded himself not to make that mistake again.

The saddest part of this time was that it should have been one of celebration for he and Al, having just completed their hundredth song for Warner Brothers, "Ring Around a Romance," for *The Singing Marine*. Harry knew he'd be bringing about the end of the partnership by calling on Mercer to help him finish "Night Over Shanghai" for this movie. The song still needed some tweaking and Al was nowhere to be found.

When Al did resurface, he agreed to check into the Mayo Clinic. But as Harry predicted, Al was upset over Mercer being brought in. "It's like that old song of yours and Irving Kahal's, 'Three's a Crowd,'" Al told Harry.

This broke Harry's heart. They'd always been a team of two, and Al didn't want things any other way. They were forced to work as a trio for several films before Al demanded to be let out of his contract. He left Hollywood for good and never worked on another film. Harry didn't want his treasured partnership with Al to end on such a sad note, but he saw no other way.

Chapter Eight

BROKEN RHYTHMS

Bringing a new lyricist into the mix was not at all what would break Harry's rhythm. Quite the contrary, working with Johnny Mercer brought a welcome new tempo for Harry's creative output, something he gleefully noticed from the outset of their new partnership, even as Al Dubin overlapped with Mercer on their next few films for Warner Brothers.

Al resented having to work alongside another lyricist and Harry knew full well it signaled the end of the Warren-Dubin era. Still, he appreciated that Mercer was having a positive effect on him. No longer having to worry about sending out a search party for lyrics was a weight off Harry's mind. Now, if Al could not deliver, Mercer could pick up the slack, even if he was already working on another tune of Harry's. Johnny was a massive talent, and at eighteen years Al's junior, it seemed he had a hundred times the energy.

Harry hadn't realized it until he paused to look back at the last few years, but he now saw how he'd been entrenched in survival mode, pushing past signs that his own health was in dire need of attention. Johnny had a lightness of being that allowed Harry to let out a sigh after holding his breath for years. Harry called him "cloudboy," as Johnny sat for long stretches of time, contemplating just the right combination of words to create his extraordinary poetry. Harry found Johnny's deep Southern roots to be a refreshing new take on the work.

Harry appreciated being able to reclaim a small amount of personal time, allowing him to get back to the large stack of mystery novels by his bedside—on the top of the pile was *The Maltese Falcon* by Dashiell Hammett and *Murder on the Orient Express* by Agatha Christie. It was Harry's habit to order more books from Martindale's Bookstore than he had time to read, hoping he'd get to them eventually. In years to come, he would have to build more shelves to accommodate his ever-growing collection. He also now had more opportunity to enjoy time with his adoring circle of friends. He knew Josephine was happier when he tried to be social and strike a better balance between work and leisure, especially because Harold Arlen was quickly becoming a cautionary tale in this regard. Leaving Anya alone too frequently was causing major problems. When Anya was happy, she was *very* happy, but that seemed to be only when she was with Harold. Not nearly as busy as Harry, Harold began finding other reasons to be away from home to escape Anya's darker moods. Josephine loved Harold and Anya, but she feared for the couple's future together; Harold running away wasn't the answer. Some would accuse Josephine of being a handwringer, but oftentimes her predictions were spot on—whether it had to do with her being able to "see past the veil" or was simply common sense.

The swimming pool at the "Gershwin Plantation," as Harold called it, was one of Harry's preferred places to see friends—a relaxed, casual atmosphere with lots of people coming and going. Ira often filmed home movies of these halcyon days. Once, when Harold's parents were visiting, they decided they liked Harry the best of all of Harold's friends because Harry happily conversed with them in Yiddish. This compound was a sacred space where mutual respect and admiration was always front and center. The Hollywood songwriting cabal preferred to mingle amongst themselves, looking upon the larger industry of which they were a part as a viper's nest they did well to stay away from. Many of them believed whatever culture existed in Los Angeles was of their making, to a large degree. They often joked about it, trying to imagine what Hollywood would be like without their contributions.

"Silent!" Ira exclaimed, to great laughter.

"Insufferable," Harold added.

"Who would they have to kick around if it weren't for us songwriters?" Harry said, eliciting more laughter, marked by nods of acknowledgment. There wasn't one in the bunch who was immune from the indignities of working for the studios, though Harry felt it most intensely and never let anybody forget it.

A certain anticipation had been building in the Gershwin inner circle since early 1937, when George was asked to perform his *Piano Concerto in F* with the Los Angeles Philharmonic.

While wading into the pool on an unseasonably hot winter day, Ira shouted over to Josephine, who was sunning herself on a chaise lounge while throwing the ball for Ira's inexhaustible dog, Tony: "Jo, you think we'll be able to get this curmudgeon here out of the house for George's concert?"

"I'm going with or without him," she replied. "I could always take Tony as my date. He can't seem to get enough of me."

"Takes one to know one, Israel," Harry quipped.

"Touché, Salvatore," Ira laughed.

Ira didn't enjoy getting out much either, though he cherished having visitors. Ira's porch light policy was that if you drove by and the light was on, you were welcome to stop in any time of day or night. He seemed to prefer the company of his friends over one-on-one time with his wife, who was known to be somewhat of a tyrant.

Harry knew this about Lee Gershwin but had always been able to avoid her by sitting with the cigar smokers, whereas it would have been rude for Josephine to decline kibitzing with the other women, especially the host. Lee haughtily held court as though *she* were the real star of the family. She'd been the same way back in New York, but it came across as much more cloying against the backdrop of orange trees and al fresco dining. Still, when it came to hearing George's *Concerto in F,* nothing was going to prevent Josephine from going. She and Harry were among the many Gershwin friends who had not seen the premiere in 1925, when the Symphony Society of New York commissioned George to compose the piece. That was back when he wasn't even sure what the form of a concerto was. Those who missed it the first time assumed they'd probably never have another chance, because George was always working on his next ambitious project. They weren't about to lose another opportunity.

Before the performance, Harry and Josephine joined a group for steaks and martinis at the Pacific Dining Car downtown. Much had changed in the intervening years between George writing the concerto and this concert twelve years later, as the public came to have not only a deeper understanding but an immense appreciation of the meaning of the music of George Gershwin, a pioneer of the hybrid genre of classical and jazz.

"I remember reading in *The New York Times* what Walter Damrosch, the conductor, said about George before that premiere," Josephine said. "He described George as 'the prince who has taken Cinderella—jazz—by the hand and openly proclaimed her a princess to the astonished world, no doubt to the fury of her envious sisters.'"

Everyone raised a glass to this. "Good memory, Jo," someone said.

"Harry didn't marry me just for my hair," she joked.

"Hell, if I'd known how good you were at playing the stock market, I might have married you sooner," Harry said with a laugh.

"Any sooner and I would have been a child bride!" Josephine smiled sassily.

Even for Gershwin's biggest fans, hearing him perform live was a transcendent experience. It made Harry happy to see Josephine captivated by the music, taking in the piece with her eyes closed for much of it. It occurred to him how much he loved her but how bad he could be at showing it. Just as he was beginning to lose himself in his own reverie, alarm bells went off in his mind, forcing him to sit two inches taller. He'd heard something go wrong in the piece. Josephine looked over to find him nearly panic-stricken. For ten to twenty seconds, George froze up, missing several bars of music. Harry scanned the faces of the crowd and was grateful to see that most of the audience didn't notice.

During the applause at the end, Josephine leaned into his ear. "What went wrong?" she asked.

"He lost his place, forgot a few notes. That's never happened with George. Something broke his rhythm."

A look of concern washed away some of Josephine's joy as she stood, clapping. Harry never liked seeing that expression on her face—part of him truly believed in her ability to see deeper than others, and it usually portended things others didn't want to see.

At the Gershwin Plantation one afternoon a few weeks later, George emerged wearing a black-and-white polka-dot housecoat and a handkerchief pulled tightly over his head. He sat down next to Harry by the pool to smoke his pipe.

"Harry, have I ever told you how much I envy all the hits you've written?" he said. "I would give anything to have written just one of them."

Harry laughed. "That's kind of you, though I think it's safe to say there will only ever be one George Gershwin for as long as there's music."

George reached out and touched Harry's shoulder in a gracious gesture. "Ira tells me Sonny wants to study music in college?"

"That's right. Apparently, he wants to go to USC. He seems fairly serious about it."

"This, despite knowing his pop and Uncle George dropped out of high school and have absolutely no formal music education?"

"Well, maybe it's more for the girls than anything else," Harry joked.

"Now, that makes more sense," George laughed before suddenly wincing and raising a hand to his head. He stood up slowly. "Will you excuse me, Harry? I think I need to go lie down a minute."

George kindly waved off Harry's offer to help as he walked through the break in the hedges that led back to his house in the rear of the compound. Ira jumped out of the pool and toweled off next to Harry.

"He's still having terrible headaches," Ira said. "He got checked out after the concert and they didn't find anything wrong, but they also couldn't say *why* he smelled burned rubber after going blank like that. It happened again last week while he was at the barber. And that damn analyst of his keeps telling him he's just neurotic. I said, 'Yes, we're Jewish.' How much does he have to pay this guy to keep overstating the obvious?"

Harry knew Ira was trying to lighten the mood, but his finely tuned ear picked up on Ira's distress.

A few weeks later, Harry's sisters Annie, Carolina, Maria, and Mamie arrived for a long-overdue visit after he'd sent them tickets to ride the *Super Chief* out to the coast, which had begun service in 1936 and boasted even more amenities than the *Chief.* The luxurious train was filled with Hollywood stars shuttling back and forth between New York and Los Angeles. Harry knew the ride alone would thrill his sisters. He picked them up from Union Station downtown in his Mercury Club Coupe convertible. Riding with the top down, they stared up in awe at the rows of palm trees and marveled at the Beverly Hills estates and the elegant people riding horses in English tack on the trail in the median dividing the eastbound and westbound lanes of Sunset Boulevard.

"It's even more glamourous than in the movies!" Carolina exclaimed.

When they walked into the Warren home, a painter was in the kitchen, putting the finishing touches on a mural over the stove. It depicted a chef in a baker's hat, and above it read: "You know what happens with too many chefs."

Maria got the first look at it. "You had this done just in time for our arrival?" she asked.

Harry laughed and said, "It sure looks that way, doesn't it?"

Josephine entered the kitchen to greet them. "We've been planning to do it for a while, but the timing is comical," she said.

Sonny and Cookie ran into the kitchen to welcome their aunts with hugs.

"You're both so big!" Annie said. "Bigger than your Daddy was when he was your age."

"Were you a shrimp, Daddy?" Sonny joked.

Harry playfully grabbed Sonny and tousled his hair. "Funny, Sonny. That's what we should call you."

"And what about me?" Cookie asked.

"Cookie, my bookie?"

"You're the one who like books so much, Daddy."

They all laughed.

"Bookie is a very important job," Harry tried to convince her with mock seriousness. Then he turned toward his four sisters and said, "Speaking of bookies, I have a surprise. Don't unpack."

"You're kicking us out already?" Mamie teased.

"We're going down to the Agua Caliente Casino in Tijuana for the weekend."

The sisters threw their arms around their baby brother. "Really? Is it very fancy, Tuti?" Carolina asked.

"Built and designed to attract Hollywood folks during Prohibition," Harry said. "I'd say it's pretty swanky. Wouldn't you, Jo?"

"Oh, yes. It has steam caves, Turkish baths, and the track," Jo said.

"So we might even strike it rich?" Maria joked.

"I could give you some tips on a few races," Harry said with a smile.

Harry loved horse racing and the ritual of studying up on all the minutiae—which horses preferred to run on mud versus turf, age, breeding, and all the other variables involved in handicapping a race. The following spring, when Harry and Josephine returned to Agua Caliente, they watched Seabiscuit win in dominant fashion. Many agreed the resort and casino at Agua Caliente were the inspiration for Las Vegas, which rose out of the desert some years later. Harry's sisters enjoyed the trip so much, they were not ready to go home when it was time a few weeks later. They reluctantly boarded the *Super Chief* back to New York, promising to come back soon.

"Tuti, I'm so proud of you. I wish Mama could see you now," Carolina said, suddenly emotional.

Harry held her shoulders firmly as he looked into her eyes. "She visits me in my dreams," he said.

As Harry and Josephine were getting ready for another gathering at the Gershwin's, Josephine made an offhanded comment, taking it for granted as common knowledge: "Everyone knows Lee is secretly in love with George but settled for Ira."

"How dare you say that," Harry said angrily. He thought she must just be saying that because most of the wives felt forced into tolerating Lee. "I know she's a despot, but that's low."

"Darling, ask anyone. It's not just my opinion."

Harry felt sick to his stomach. He hated thinking of Ira being stuck with a wife who saw him as second-best.

At the party that night, Harry kept a closer eye on Lee than usual, while he also witnessed strange behavior from George, who kept dropping things. At one point, Harry picked George's lit cigar off the floor for him.

"Never mind him, Harry. He's just acting out to get attention," Lee said as she refilled drinks. A couple guests laughed nervously, afraid to disagree with her borderline spiteful comment. "What?" she asked incredulously. "His psychiatrist says the same thing."

Josephine shot Harry a look as if to say, *Now do you see?* They both agreed with a nod that it was time to go.

Over the next few days, George continued complaining of headaches and dizziness. Late in June, Ira convinced him to go to the hospital for some diagnostic tests, but George declined the most important one of all, a spinal tap, which could have shed light on what was going on internally. He was discharged with the less-than-scientific diagnosis of "most likely hysteria." Ira hoped George just needed extra rest, but when he found him still asleep at 5:00 p.m. the following day, he was alarmed. He woke him and got him into the bathroom, where George collapsed and went into a coma.

Word of this spread fast. When Harry rushed to Cedars of Lebanon Hospital to be with the Gershwins, Ira's voice quaked and he had a pallor Harry had never seen before.

"They called Dr. Cushing, a pioneer of brain surgery," Ira said. "He's retired from operating but recommended the best neurosurgeon, a guy from Johns Hopkins, Dr. Dandy. The Coast Guard located him on a yacht in Chesapeake Bay and is bringing him ashore, where we have a private plane waiting."

"So, George will be all right?" Harry asked nervously. Ira didn't dare answer.

A while later, the team at Cedars told the Gershwins that George was going to need an operation before Dr. Dandy could get there. Dr. Dandy had been working with them over the phone to perform a ventriculogram, a test for which they filled George up with air and performed an X-ray. That's how they found a large tumor on the right side of his brain.

"We're bringing Dr. Naffziger down from San Francisco to do the surgery as soon as possible," the head doctor told Ira. "We don't have a moment to lose."

The next day, the music world experienced one of its greatest tragedies of the twentieth century. George Gershwin had died at thirty-eight years old. The nurse who had been caring for him at home called to inform Harry. Hanging up the phone, his eyes filled with tears. Josephine struggled to say anything that might give him comfort. She put her arms around him.

"This is too young. It's just *too* goddamn soon," Harry whispered. "God, why in the world did you have to take him now?" he asked angrily, looking up.

Harold Arlen called moments later from New York. He too was sobbing as he tried to understand how this could have happened. "I told Ira before I left for New York that George should have been taken to the hospital," he said. "He hadn't been acting like himself for quite a long time."

Harry struggled to picture what things would be like for Ira without George. There was no aspect of his life that was not completely intertwined with George's. They'd written some of the most beautiful and memorable songs in the American canon—"Nice Work If You Can Get It," "Someone to Watch

Over Me," "'S Wonderful," "The Man I Love," "They Can't Take That Away from Me," "Embraceable You"—and one that would hit Harry particularly hard every time he heard it from this point on: "I've Got Rhythm." Seeing Ira so sad and out of balance brought back age-old feelings of Harry losing his mother. He realized that experiencing that loss so young must have meant he put it up high on a shelf somewhere to be dealt with later, and then later never came. It frightened him to think of all the ways it must have affected him.

Late one night when Harry couldn't sleep, Josephine found him staring out the window at the dark sky. "Why bother giving your heart to someone when they might just vanish at any moment, leaving you with nothing but an unbearable memory?" he said.

At times, the relationships between these artists, who had so few people they could relate to, felt like true love without the romance. They were all fellow geniuses to journey with who shared a special language of music that moved so many.

When he saw Ira days later, Harry struggled to be strong for his friend. "I'm so angry about this, Ira. Angry that you're suffering. I would gladly take some of that from you if I could."

"I know you would, Harry. I suppose the only consolation is what the surgeon told us," Ira said. "We should all see this as a blessing. If George had survived the surgery, one side of his body would have been paralyzed and he never would have been able to play piano again."

Just the thought of this was like a dagger in Harry's heart.

George's memorial services were held simultaneously in Los Angeles and New York. Harry and Josephine attended the Los Angeles service at the Temple B'nai B'rith, a stunning Moorish-style domed temple completed in 1929. Funding for part of the dome's interior was provided by MGM's Irving Thalberg; the triple-lancet windows, made of over five thousand pieces of glass representing the twelve tribes of Israel, was paid for Louis B. Mayer. Jack Warner, Carl Laemmle, and many other industry giants were members of the temple. Hundreds lined up outside to mourn the passing of the incomparable George Gershwin.

Days later, when Ira returned from the New York service, Harry went to visit him late one night when his porch light was on. The two sat in front of a fire, Ira nearly paralyzed from shock. The only motion he was capable of was constantly stroking the cat on his lap. Harry thought there might not be any hair left on poor Calliope once Ira was finished grieving his brother, although there was a good chance that day would never come.

The following Saturday night, the weekly open house hosted by the Whitings was a remembrance of George. The Whiting home was described by one friend as a place of "entrances and exits" because there were so many luminaries coming and going. Maggie and Cookie loved to sit on the stairs late into the night, watching the party of the finest songwriters anywhere, although this night was more somber than usual. Richard Whiting had a special connection to George, going back to New York; he'd been the first person to offer fifteen-year-old George a job after hearing him play piano, making George the youngest song plugger on Tin Pan Alley.

Those in the Gershwin circle drew strength from each other to get through the tragic loss. They grappled with the question of why George's brilliant life had been cut so short. Richard often mused about all the music the world would miss out on, having lost such a young, magnificent talent. Then, in a cruel twist of fate, the same untimely end came for him. Just six months after George's death, Richard suffered a massive heart attack—he died at forty-six, at the height of his career. As one of the family's closest friends, Johnny Mercer stepped in to guide Richard's daughter Maggie's career as a singer, while Cookie became a reliable shoulder to cry on for her friend. They were both just thirteen.

The sadness in the Hollywood and New York songwriting circles rippled out into the wider world. This one-two punch was proving difficult to bounce back from. Harry and Josephine started to notice pills around the Gershwin house, first in bottles, then in bowls on the coffee table.

"We just leave them out for anyone who might need one," Lee said.

At the Warren home, the news came that Josephine's mother was in failing health back in New York. Sonny was home sick from school with a terrible cough, but Josephine told Harry she needed to go—she'd never forgive herself if she missed her chance to say goodbye. Harry encouraged her, so she boarded the *Super Chief*, knowing the timing was not great. Now that

Sonny was in his final year of high school, she trusted she was leaving him in good hands with Lucille.

By the time Josephine returned, Sonny had gotten worse. She took him to their family doctor, who diagnosed him with pneumonia.

"How did he ever get that?" she asked the doctor, panic sinking in.

"The good news is that we have a new treatment for it called sulfa," the doctor said. "We'll get him started on it right away."

The doctor sent them home with the new miracle drug, and Josephine sent Sonny to bed right away. His level of fatigue was startling, and after a couple doses of medicine, he seemed only to get worse.

"Why didn't you take him to the hospital when he first got bad?" Josephine asked Harry.

"Dubin gets pneumonia every year and bounces back. Let's take him now!" he pleaded.

"Look at him! He can barely move. He needs to stay in bed until he regains his strength."

No one could have known Sonny was allergic to the miracle medicine. In the middle of the night, they woke to the sound of Lucille weeping. Harry and Josephine found her in Sonny's room next to his bed, where she was praying over him and speaking her native Louisiana Creole. Harry and Josephine stood in the doorway, frozen with fear and shock.

"He's dancing with the angels now," Lucille told them through sobs.

Nothing would ever be the same.

Chapter Nine

The Warren family's world crashed down hard around them, shaking loose emotional debris from every corner of their lives. The trauma of losing a child made the earthquake Harry experienced when he first arrived in Los Angeles feel like a welcome breeze by comparison. After that single terrifying encounter with Mother Nature, he'd always been amazed at how easily he could call up the moment that remained so powerful, the way some actors he knew used sense memory. Just concentrating on it for a few moments made his heart race. He often thought how happy he would be to subject himself to that kind of terror every day for the rest of his life in some grand cosmic bargain to bring Sonny back.

Harry carried tremendous guilt, wishing he had spent more time with his son, the quiet and gentle soul Sonny was. Jo had exhausted herself trying to get him to pay more attention to the children. Whenever she broached the subject, Harry had countered with the need to make money because, he said, "You never know how long the work will be there."

Exasperated, she'd begun firing back with a reference to a play they'd recently see.

"It's like that play, Harry. *You Can't Take It with You*: 'Money ages well; children don't,'" she'd say.

But that was before they lost Sonny. Now, Josephine spent most days in bed, unable to function. Cookie was thirteen going on thirty. She was angry and confused about what happened to her brother, despite her experience being a comforter to Maggie after she'd lost her father. "But where did he actually *go*?" she would ask.

In desperation, Harry and Josephine began blaming each other. "You should have taken him to the hospital sooner," Josephine said, vitriol seeping out between each word.

"I wanted to take him when you got back from New York, and you wouldn't hear of it!" Harry replied. "They could have saved him. This didn't have to happen."

It seemed this conversation was destined to play out between them over and over for eternity.

Early one morning, Cookie overheard them talking in their bedroom. "What's double pneumonia?" she asked, startling them from where she stood in the hallway.

"It's when both lungs are affected, sweetheart," Josephine said, struggling to pull herself out of bed. "C'mon, we need to get you to school. The nuns are going to have my Lutheran head."

"I don't want to go to school! I'm never going back there," Cookie protested. "And why did you say Sonny could have lived if he went in the hospital? Uncle George went to the hospital and he still died."

"We should go back to New York. We're surrounded by death here," Josephine said, storming off into her bathroom and swinging the door shut.

Harry motioned for Cookie to come sit next to him. He smoothed her hair and stroked her cheek with the back of his hand. "I'm sorry for what happened to your brother. Very, very sorry. It's okay to cry," he said.

"You haven't cried, Daddy," she pointed out. And it was true. Harry would remain in the anger stage for a long time.

Once the tragic news reached Al Dubin, he convinced Helen to put their own troubles aside for an afternoon to visit the Warrens. Al's situation seemed to be one in which he was squeezed in a life-sized vise. On one side, he was pressured by his drug and alcohol addiction. On the other, he was crushed by a manipulating mother-daughter team of grifters; the mother was using him to launch her daughter into show business while draining financial resources away from Helen and the girls.

Harry hadn't seen Al since Al left Hollywood behind. It was wonderful to see his old partner again, bringing back all the best memories—a welcome distraction. Lucille prepared lunch and insisted they eat outside. "Everybody out here for the fresh air and sunshine," she said in her lilting tone as she carried a tray to a set table on the back patio. As Harry, Jo, Al, and Helen sat together for the better part of the afternoon, Al grew increasingly emotional. This was a side of him Harry had not seen before.

"I never told you this," Al began. He looked over at Helen

for her blessing to continue and took a deep breath. "We too lost our only son."

Harry and Josephine exchanged a look of surprise and confusion.

"Simon Joseph Dubin. He was four days old," Al said. "I know it's not the same as what you two are going through. I just wanted you to know we've had our hearts broken by a loss of a similar magnitude. We think about Simon every day. That's how we keep him alive in our hearts."

Al began choking on his words and excused himself, tears spilling out of his eyes.

Helen reached across the table to take Josephine's hands in hers. "You know I'm just a few miles down the road. I'm here to help in any way I can, even just to sit and pray with you," she said.

"I don't think I can stay here a moment longer," Josephine said.

"Too many memories," Harry added. "Josephine wants us to go back to New York."

"Maybe I'll go with you," Helen said in a lighter tone. Helen was like Harry in this way—she'd never bought into all the fuss over the Los Angeles lifestyle.

Harry saw Al sit down by the pool and went to join him. They heard voices coming from inside the house and looked up to see Cookie and Maggie. The girls were always dropping in and out before dashing off to some unknown destination. Harry worried about Cookie growing up too fast, especially now that her best friend was on her way to becoming a celebrity as one of the most popular singers of the Big Band era.

Harry and Jo's other friends rallied around them too, doing all they could during this time, but it was their dear old friend Buddy Morris from the Tin Pan Alley days, now head of Warner Brothers Music Publishing, who had the best idea. He and his wife, Carolyn, invited Harry and Josephine to accompany them on an Atlantic crossing to Europe.

"There's no clear-cut answer to how anyone gets through something like this," Buddy said. "One small step at a time is all I can figure. Think of this as a first step on the long road to healing."

"I don't think we'd make for good traveling companions right now," Josephine said.

"That's not what we're asking. We only want to strengthen your spirits—at least, we'd like to try."

Not knowing what else to do, Harry and Josephine agreed to make the six-week trip. As Buddy thought, the change of scenery proved to be beneficial. The time away, however, seemed to make things even more difficult when they returned home to reality. As they resumed their day-to-day lives, Harry faced each new dawn with a rock in the pit of his stomach, sensing Josephine would forever blame him for the loss of Sonny. He told himself this was a sacrifice he was willing to make for the family's sake—allowing himself to be the target of her ire and giving her anger someplace to land. The cost, he knew, would likely be irreparable damage, their marriage transforming from a lovingly handmade quilt to a patchwork of shreds—no longer a functional blanket, let alone a thing of beauty.

Harry felt this was the best he could do to keep some kind of peace, even if it was turning his marriage vow into something of a minced oath, the way some described the song "Jeepers Creepers" Harry wrote with Johnny Mercer that year. The title phrase was a euphemism for "Jesus Christ," a socially acceptable substitution for what one might really want to say—something Harry was becoming skilled at. Harry and Johnny wrote the song for Louis Armstrong to sing and play trumpet on in the film *Going Places.* A colossal hit, the song was nominated for an Academy Award, which only made Harry feel mocked by fate—to lose his son but receive another Academy Award nomination. How was he to feel joy in something so trivial? He was almost relieved when the song didn't win. He didn't feel very deserving.

When Harry and Josephine finally returned to New York, they intended it to be for good. They packed up their home in Beverly Hills to get away from all the memories and moved to an apartment just for Harry to run out the clock on his Warner Brothers contract. But fate had other ideas. Harry received a call from Gus Kahn, who wanted to work with him on the 1939 MGM film *Honolulu,* starring George Burns and Gracie Allen. The studios made the loan-out deal for Harry, who was thrilled to be working anywhere but Warner Brothers. He'd enjoyed collaborating with Gus for many years now. Harry didn't have to put on airs with him, and he could even let his guard down when it came to talking about Sonny and things at home.

"How are you all holding up?" Gus asked in a caring, straightforward way.

"You're German. Why haven't you given me some tips on how to deal with my German wife?" Harry was known to preface his emotional confessions with humor.

"That's tricky, because we're a tough lot. We don't escape into preparing and eating food for days, like Italians," Gus said, winking. "Time—it heals all things, if anything can."

"How is Donald?" Harry asked.

"You'd never know he's German. He's hurting, Harry. I want to be honest with you about that because it's a testament to how good a friend Sonny was to him," Gus said with a sigh. "He told us he doesn't expect he'll ever have such a good friend ever again."

Harry choked up. He'd never heard such a personal account of how much his son meant to someone outside the family. It yanked at his heart in the most awkward and painful way.

Once Harry and Gus finished their work on *Honolulu,* Harry begrudgingly returned to Warner Brothers for a final few days. Even if the studio had offered to renew his contract, Harry would have declined. He was sure they were finished with him just as much as he was with them. He would always believe it was more personal than it was, but the truth of the matter was that they were businesspeople doing what businesspeople do. The only reason the studio had no plans to renew Harry's contract was because it had wrongly assumed the era of the Hollywood musical Harry had revitalized was over.

Ray Heindorf, the beloved orchestrator at Warner Brothers, had been a fellow alleyman of Harry's back when they first met at Shapiro, Bernstein & Company in New York. Ray had worked on most of Harry's films at the studio and made a point of going to see him his last day on the lot. He walked into Harry's office and found him tinkering around with a new melody. "I'm not sure they truly appreciate what they'll be losing with you not being a part of this place anymore," he said.

"I know you'll miss me, Ray," Harry said, laughing. "You're a good skate. I didn't expect any pomp and circumstance for my exit, but no one even cares to say goodbye except you? When they're done with you, they're really through, and that's that."

"No one here could ever get a bead on you," Ray said, explaining the studio brass's bad behavior. "You're a genius, but you don't *act* like one. That's confusing for them."

"I don't run on compliments, you know?" Harry said. "If I did, I would have died a long time ago!"

"You understand what I'm saying, though. With talent like yours, there's an expectation for you to be a real pain in the tuchus," Ray said. "You've kept your head down for eight years while turning out hit after hit and making it look effortless. It's kind of spooky."

"You're very kind, Ray. This almost makes up for not having a cake with a naked lady jumping out of it."

"Wait, who ruined the surprise?" Ray laughed. "Seriously, I

know this may come as a shock to you, but Jack and Hal know damn well this studio wouldn't be where it is right now without you."

Then, with one phone call, Harry and Josephine's best-laid plans to permanently return to New York were upended. Lyricist Mack Gordon wanted Harry to work with him on a 1940 Shirley Temple film for Twentieth Century Fox called *Young People*. For four years, Shirley Temple had reigned as the most popular performer in movies, having celebrated her eighth birthday on the lot with a special non-alcoholic cocktail. But now that she was entering her preteen years, her child-star appeal was fading, and the studio was hoping the right score could help her transition into the next phase of her career.

Harry had long admired Mack Gordon, who apparently had grown tired of a decade working with his partner, Harry Revel. Desperate to keep his mind on work, Harry Warren was excited by the promise of a new collaborator and a new studio. When Gordon mentioned the name Harry Warren to Darryl Zanuck, who was now head of Twentieth Century Fox after squeezing founder William Fox out of his own company, Zanuck was thrilled by the idea. He wasted no time calling Harry's agent, Frank Orsatti, to make the deal. Even though it was just for one picture, Harry privately rejoiced at being in demand by another studio. Despite *Young People* being a flop, it paved Harry's way into Twentieth Century Fox, where he would want to be for the foreseeable future.

∾

One night at the Kahn residence on Arden Drive in Beverly Hills, Harry could tell something was on Gus's mind. The Kahns had invited the Warrens over for dinner frequently since Sonny's passing. Maggie would often be there, working and rehearsing with Grace Kahn, a marvelous pianist and mentor to Maggie, who would also be asked to stay for dinner to spend time with Cookie. Once they'd finished their meal, Gus invited Harry outside for a cigar. As they sat under the stars, Harry told Gus he could tell something was troubling him. "What's weighing on you?" Harry asked.

"You know me well, friend. I hate to even bring it up, considering everything," Gus prefaced. He launched into a story about Ignacio Herb Brown, one of his longtime collaborators, who was best known for writing "Singin' in the Rain." For a decade starting in 1929, Nacio had written dozens of songs with Arthur Freed at MGM and was the toast of the music department. "We've had a project coming up at MGM for months now, something set to star Judy Garland. Suddenly, there's talk about Harold Arlen and Yip Harburg getting the assignment." Harry furrowed his brow. "Do you know anything about it?" Gus asked.

"I don't, but ever since this goddamn gin rummy craze started, it's like they've all lost their minds. Nacio doesn't play, does he? It's Freed and Mervyn LeRoy down there with Zanuck, playing every night," Harry said. "I'm seeing Harold tomorrow and I'll ask him what exactly is going on. It's not like him to do something underhanded."

"It was pretty set in stone. Or so I thought . . ." Gus lamented.

"We're meeting at the pitch and putt at eleven. I'll find out what I can. We've got to stick together in this business. God knows we have enough working against us."

The next day, Harry pulled up along Harold in the parking lot of the pitch and putt. As they grabbed clubs from their trunks, Harold sensed Harry's anxiety. "You all right?" he asked.

"Actually, I'm not," Harry said with a huff. "I detest being put in the middle of things."

"What is it you're in the middle of?" Harold asked, genuinely concerned.

Harry paced a few moments before spitting it out. "Well, what the hell is going on with this Judy Garland picture? Gus tells me he and Nacio had been assigned to it until you and Yip went to some party at Mervyn LeRoy's." LeRoy had started out as an actor before becoming a director, then became head of production for MGM. "I've never known you to be that kind of schmoozer, Harold."

"I had no idea there was another team on it," Harold said, his eyes widening. "Freed started talking to us and it sounded like a great project. I've always loved the L. Frank Baum books and Yip and I said we'd be honored to even be considered."

"Well, it's just politics as usual, then," Harry said cynically. "Nacio's not the big man on the lot anymore. Looks like it's Freed. And if LeRoy hadn't opened the turf club at Hollywood Park, I'd have no use for him either."

"It wasn't my intention to take the job away from another writer, Harry." Harold put his hand on Harry's shoulder, looked him in the eye, and nodded.

Harry took him at his word. He let out a huge sigh, happy to have the confrontation with one of his favorite people behind him. "C'mon, let's go hit some balls," he said.

Despite Harry's attempt to intervene, Harold and Yip were soon announced as the composers for *The Wizard of Oz*. Harry wasn't going to waste his time trying to understand the intricacies of what led to the change in songwriting team. All he could do was relay to Gus that he believed Harold. Gus agreed it wasn't Harold's fault and said he would not harbor any ill will.

Meanwhile, Harold and Yip got down to work, tackling all the movie's big anthems. As they played some songs for Harry, he had to admit it was some of their best work. With Judy Garland's voice behind it, the project was shaping up to be a hit. Harold had been thinking about the big ballad they had to write for an important point in the movie, but he'd been keeping it as the last thing, and he was starting to doubt himself. One day when he called Harry to fret, Harry became annoyed. He overreacted, likely with Gus still in the back of his mind—being caught between his mentor and mentee created nothing but confusion and frustration for Harry.

"Just take your mind off it, Harold!" he griped. "Go do something you don't normally do. Get as far away from it as you can for a while, for chrissakes! Have you not figured out how to do that yet?"

Harold took Harry's advice and asked Anya, now his wife, to a movie at Grauman's Chinese Theatre. While driving there, the song dropped into his head like a gift from heaven. He pulled the car over on Hollywood Boulevard and ran to a payphone.

"Harry, I got it!" Harold gushed. "I took your advice, and it was as if the Lord said, 'Well, here it is, now stop worrying about it'!"

"Oh, so you listen to the Lord but not me?" Harry kidded. "I can't wait to hear it."

Yip added lyrics to the song that would become "Over the Rainbow," then the duo played it for Harry and Ira at the Gershwin Plantation. Ira teared up and Harry was moved, thinking of Sonny. Harry hoped Sonny had been able to forgive him for not taking the necessary steps to save his life.

As Harry was ruminating, Ira rubbed his cheeks and said, "I don't think it ends the right way, though." He came up with a little tag on the spot. "How about, 'If happy little bluebirds fly/ Beyond the rainbow/Why, oh, why can't I?'"

Maybe the right team ended up on the right picture in this case after all, Harry thought, despite any ill-intentioned studio machinations—the circle of songwriters all shared this feeling. Harold and Yip had found the pot of gold at the end of their heartfelt rainbow ballad, and once Judy Garland recorded it, there was no doubt the song would be a bona fide hit.

Not being privy to the daily goings-on with the picture, Harry expected nothing but good things from that point forward. But in a business known for second-guessing, Louis B. Mayer abruptly cut the song after a preview screening of the film, because, he said, "It slowed down the picture." Mayer also didn't think it seemed like something for a little girl to be singing in a barnyard.

When Harold shared this with a couple friends, Harry

became enraged. "It slows down the picture?" he seethed. "Why the hell does he think it's called a showstopper?"

As it turned out, "Over the Rainbow" would have an arc similar to "Lullaby of Broadway"—from studio reject to Academy Award winner.

Across town at Twentieth Century Fox, Harry and Mack Gordon were at work on Harry's second film for the studio, *Down Argentine Way*, starring Carmen Miranda. No one, least of all Harry, would have had the hubris to predict this would be the beginning of another winning streak for him—fourteen films over four years. When the assignment first came up, Harry admitted to Mack that he'd never written a Brazilian tune. Mack shrugged it off, knowing how capable his partner was at writing in any conceivable style. If there was a style Harry had not yet conquered, it was only because he hadn't tried it yet. This was both a blessing and a curse, and likely the reason he never developed a signature style. It had always been his approach to serve the picture, not himself.

On his way home from the studio, Harry stopped at a record store to buy a Brazilian album. When he played it at home, he quickly internalized the rhythm, what he considered the backbone of a song. If he got a handle on the rhythm, he'd have a strong foundation upon which to work. In the case of Brazilian music, the rhythm freed a part of his spirit at a time when everything else in his life felt suffocating. Harry had been familiar with Carmen Miranda before he began work on *Down Argentine Way*—Al Dubin and Jimmy McHugh had written songs for her a few years earlier for the Broadway show *Streets of Paris*. That's when Hollywood first took notice of her and offered her a movie contract.

The first day they were both on the set, Carmen rushed over to greet Harry in her incredibly effusive manner. "I'm sorry to hear you aren't working with Mr. Dubin anymore," she said, "but I love the Brazilian tunes you're writing!"

Harry smiled and confessed, "They're actually just Italian tunes with a Brazilian beat."

"You're so crazy!" Carmen said, lighting up with laugher. Born in Portugal, Carmen had been a recording star and performer from the time she was a teenager in Rio de Janeiro, long before she was cast as the lead in *Streets of Paris*. But it was her film debut in *Down Argentine Way*, featuring Harry's music, that truly galvanized her appeal and earned Harry and Mack their first Oscar nomination as a team.

"I had to figure out that Brazilian music doesn't have roots in Spanish rhythms, like so much of Latin American music; the roots are African," he explained. "I'm mostly concerned with rhythm. I guess that's what drove me to run away with the circus as a drummer when I was a kid."

"Oh, I can just see you doing that!" she teased.

Talking with the magnetic star, Harry had to remind himself he was a married man, though he was fairly certain he would never be intimate with his wife ever again. He went on to develop a fascination for Brazilian music and found himself enjoying the synergy created by his focus on this style brought about by Twentieth Century Fox's concerted effort to develop its presence in Latin America. The studio's profits had begun falling in Europe at the start of the war, forcing them to focus on another segment of the international market. It was Carmen's pure star power and Harry and Mack Gordon's songs that ushered forth a love for Latin dance music in America. Carmen had brought her own band over from Brazil, which Harry delighted in watching perform with gusto. He drew inspiration from these players as he wrote tunes to contribute to their canon, such as "Chica Chica Boom Chic," which he wrote for Carmen for *That Night in Rio*, and "I Had the Craziest Dream," written for Helen Forrest to perform with Harry James and His Orchestra in *Springtime in the Rockies*. Both went to on become bossa nova standards.

Harry and Mack were quickly becoming the songwriting stars of Twentieth Century Fox. What had started as a one-picture deal quickly developed into another American songwriting dream team. When the United States entered World War II, the team was perfectly positioned to provide the soundtrack of peoples' lives with their streak of wartime musicals. In *That Night in Rio,* their second film with Carmen Miranda, Harry watched as Carmen moved from playing herself to playing a character, even though the character was based on her. This was essentially the same part of the larger-than-life, zany lady she would play in subsequent films.

In a departure from Latin American–themed pictures, another inspiration struck Darryl Zanuck while he was vacationing at the Sun Valley Ski Resort in Idaho. After signing Norwegian ice-skating champion Sonja Henie to a contract, he needed a star vehicle for her, and it seemed he'd stumbled upon the perfect setting to showcase her talents. The plot of 1941's *Sun Valley Serenade* lent itself to this with the idea of a touring big band being brought to entertain guests at the snowy resort. Zanuck had the perfect bandleader in mind, Glenn Miller, who would play himself and bring along his own orchestra. Harry and Mack wrote four songs for the picture, and two of them became smash hits: "I Know Why," a romantic and gorgeous tune performed by actress Lynn Bari, and "Chattanooga Choo Choo," a rousing, snappy number starring the tap-dancing phenoms the Nicholas Brothers.

The song that went on to be one of Harry's most enduring hits, "At Last," can be heard twice in the background, even though Lynn Bari's performance of it was cut from the film. *Sun Valley Serenade* was so popular, the studio quickly mobilized to follow it up with another picture built around the winning combination of Glenn Miller performing Harry and Mack Gordon's music. Zanuck made good on his word to always try to find a place for a good song in another picture, which is how "At Last" came to make its debut in *Orchestra Wives*.

The only thing Harry did not care for in his new writing partner was that Mack had to hear the song over and over to the point that Harry never wanted to hear it again. To preserve his sanity, Harry brought in a pianist to work with Mack. This was not nearly as trying as what others had to endure, such as one of the directors on the lot getting fired because, as a German citizen, he had a government-imposed curfew of 8:00 p.m. during the war. It was a strange time, Harry thought one night as he drove over Laurel Canyon from the valley. The vista from the top of the Santa Monica Mountains normally sparkled with millions of lights, but tonight it was completely dark due to the wartime blackout.

Later that year, Harry and Mack also did *Week-End in Havana,* starring Carmen Miranda, which required all the music to be written in four weeks before the star departed for another engagement. Harry worked himself to the bone, becoming ill as a result. When Harry he got so weak that he could barely stand, he sought help from Dr. Sam Hirshfeld, a so-called movie doctor who was known to give everyone injections. When Jo got the bill for all the injections, her eyes went wide. "What are you injecting him with, gold?" she asked.

Harry soon discovered he had a gallbladder problem that required surgery. No longer would he be able to put off his health or get by with mystery injections. While he was recovering in critical condition for some time, he contracted pneumonia and ended up taking off August to October to heal. Harry was more troubled by the pneumonia than anything else because it had caused Sonny's death.

Just as he was finally regaining some strength, he received terrible news. It was October 8, 1941.

Josephine was in a bit of a haze when she received the phone call. Harry heard her speaking in hushed tones, then she came into the bedroom.

"That was Grace. Gus had a heart attack," she managed to say.

Harry pulled himself up to a sitting position, wincing in pain. "Is he going to be all right?"

"No, Harry. He's not." She looked sad and lost, but all the pills she'd been taking had left her numb. Too numb, Harry thought. Lee had given her something to help her relax after Sonny's death, and after trying it, Jo asked her own doctor for a prescription.

"He was only fifty-four," Harry mumbled.

She gave him a strange look, one mixed with sadness and contempt. He knew what it meant—that fifty-four wasn't young compared to nineteen.

"*Another* friend gone?" Harry wailed. "When will it stop?"

It had been a while since Harry had visited Ira, who didn't drive and rarely went out during the day, even in the best of times. On Harry's way home late one evening, he passed Ira's and saw the porch light on. He parked his car and slowly made his way down Ira's front path, still using a cane after the operation. Ira opened the door and smiled warmly.

Moments later, they were sitting in front of the fire, Ira wearing his slippers and stroking the cat.

"How's my favorite carpet slipper man?" Harry asked.

"Oh, you know. Putting one foot in front of the other. Can I make you a sandwich?" When Harry declined, Ira said, "I've missed you, Harry. It's really good to see you."

"Have you been doing any writing?" Harry looked over at Ira's drawing board, where he had lots of words pinned up with thumbtacks so he could move the words around.

Ira shook his head no. "It's been difficult. Things are just so different now."

"Soon there'll be no one worth knowing left," Harry said.

"We're still here," Ira lamented.

"For now," Harry said.

"For now," Ira agreed. He paused. "How about you? Keeping busy with work? You've had quite a year. 'Chattanooga Choo Choo' is a damn runaway train."

"It's all Glenn Miller. He's the one making the songs famous."

"Harry Warren, you listen here. Glenn Miller wouldn't have those songs to make famous if it weren't for you writing them.

"True," Harry said in his typical downplayed fashion.

"Four songs on *Hit Parade* in one week?" Ira said incredulously. "How is it that so much tragedy hasn't affected your ability to write hit songs?"

"Music's the only thing keeping me alive," Harry said. "Don't get me wrong, I have to keep the family together. But Jo hasn't forgiven me, and I don't think she ever will."

"Forgiven you?" Ira asked.

"For Sonny. She thinks it's my fault. At least when she takes her pills, she's not hollering at me all the time," Harry said. "And Cookie—I love that kid, but she's a bit of a hell-raiser, hanging around Maggie Whiting all the time. Who knows what the two of them are up to? Cookie punched a kid in the face at school."

Ira sat silent for a few moments, taking this in. "So, she has a future in boxing, then?" he asked, cracking a smile. They fell into a long-overdue laughing fit.

As Harry got ready to leave for the studio the next day, Josephine said something about their finances that caught his ear.

She knew the studio had stopped paying Harry while he'd been hospitalized and recovering, but she wasn't worried about it, she said. Money was now literally the least of their problems.

Harry stopped cold. "They stopped paying me when I was out?" he asked. He'd had no idea.

"Are you really all that surprised?"

He stormed out of the house and fumed all the way to work. When he got there, he asked if Mack knew about it.

"No, Harry I didn't," Mack said. "You know cheap these executives can be."

"But you were being paid, right?" Harry asked. Mack nodded. "And what were you working on without any music?"

"I banked some lyrics, but nothing for any picture in particular."

Harry stormed over to Zanuck's office, waving his cane around like a madman. "Where is he?" Harry demanded.

The secretary behind the desk was ill-prepared for a song-writer scorned. "I'm sorry, Mr. Warren. He's not in right now," she said, wincing while Harry waved his cane like an extension of his flailing arms. "Can I give him a message for you?"

"Oh, you sure can, sweetheart," Harry growled. "Tell him I never want to see his lying face again!"

At that point, one of Zanuck's underlings appeared from another office, attempting to pacify Harry. "Why don't you come into my office, and we can discuss what's got you so upset?"

"What's got me so upset?" Harry mocked. "Gee, I don't know. Maybe it's that you all like to kick a guy when he's down and under the knife. 'The poor Joe's gotta go into the hospital—let's cut off his paychecks!' And the fact that I have to read about myself in the goddamned daily *Variety*, 'Warren in ill health on the coast'—I wonder where they got that information!" he yelled, releasing years of frustration in just a few seconds.

"It's studio policy not to pay for weeks not worked," the assistant said, "but I'm sure we can come to an agreement about how to make it right with you."

"Too late. I QUIT," he shouted.

Harry's relationship with Zanuck had always been complicated, but he trusted him more than most other studio heads. He knew it was possible Zanuck may not have known about this or was just able to turn a blind eye to the unpleasantries by putting other people in charge of such things. Unfortunately for Harry, despite his dramatic showing in Fox's executive office, the studio refused to let him out of his contract. He begged his lawyer to deal with it, but there was no wiggle room because Fox had every reason to fight to keep Harry. They still had plenty of songs to get out of him—some that would go on to become his biggest hits to this day. But from that point on, Harry would always see Fox, and Zanuck by extension, in a different light. One of the few people he respected from the executive suites had shown himself to be no different than the others. Gone were the days Harry would partake in the gin rummy group with Zanuck, when they'd gamble every night after a plunge and a steam. "They liked to live like Romans," Harry used to say. He was finished with thinking Zanuck was his friend.

Perhaps that's why nothing Zanuck told Harry would ever

make him happy again. Thinking he could get back in Harry's good graces, Zanuck went to Harry and Mack's office after the Glenn Miller Orchestra's "Chattanooga Choo Choo" had been number-one for nine weeks in a row. "I wanted to be the first to tell you," he said cheerfully, "RCA is going to honor Glenn Miller with an actual gold record of 'Chattanooga Choo Choo.' It's sold 1.2 million copies!"

"A gold record? What the hell's he supposed to do with that, wear it around his neck?" Harry said.

As much as Harry scoffed at the silliness of this idea, it didn't stop him from tuning into the live broadcast radio show of Glenn receiving the first-ever gold record. This was long before the Recording Industry Association of America came into being in 1958 and began certifying records as gold or platinum based on the number sold; the first gold-certified single would be Perry Como's "Catch a Falling Star." RCA presenting a gold record to Miller was the label's way of celebrating and publicizing its own success. Harry sat with Josephine in the kitchen and tuned in the radio as the executive from RCA presented it to Glenn.

"Glenn, it's yours, with the best wishes of RCA Victor Bluebird Records," Harry heard the RCA executive say over the radio.

"For the boys in the band and for the whole gang, thanks a million, two hundred thousand," Glenn replied, a clever nod to the number of records sold.

"What about to the guy who wrote the song? And the guy who wrote the lyric, for cryin' out loud . . ." Harry griped. Josephine stared back at Harry.

"Forever the unsung hero," she said empathetically.

Harry didn't hold this against Glenn Miller—it was just more grumble therapy. He admired Miller almost more than any other musical performer he'd ever worked with. He knew Glenn could play anything Harry wrote and arrange it almost magically. With "Serenade in Blue," Harry directly credited Glenn for inspiring him because he knew Glenn had few limitations, which gave Harry free rein in writing a harmonically complex song.

Harry also liked Glenn as a person. He considered him a gentle soul and was quick to correct anyone's mistaken notion that Miller was soft when it came to his musicianship. Harry called him a master. After they finished work on *Orchestra Wives,* Glenn rushed to record all five of Harry's songs from the film, and three became hits: "At Last," "Serenade in Blue," and "I've Got a Gal in Kalamazoo." Then Glenn Miller joined the Army Air Corps. A few weeks later, "Chattanooga Choo Choo" was nominated for an Academy Award.

Despite the song being a runaway success, there was always another train on Harry's mind. "Don't buy anything you can't take back on the *Chief,*" he would tell Josephine and Cookie, threatening to pick up stakes and go back to New York.

Yet neither of these two trains would be the last to figure hugely in Harry's life.

Chapter Ten

THREE ANTHEMS

If it weren't already a widely accepted fact that nothing can stop a runaway train, "Chattanooga Choo Choo" proved the point again when it rolled full steam ahead, right through a radio boycott. As the organization representing the best songwriters and top music publishers, ASCAP had not yet reached a point at which it could collect fair compensation for its artists' licensed works. The folks at ASCAP knew this because when they dispatched representatives to check up on restaurants, clubs, and theaters, they routinely found widespread noncompliance. Between 1931 to 1939, the organization raised royalty rates over a total of 400 percent because there had been such a long way to go toward getting businesses to comply and pay a fair rate.

But when ASCAP moved to double rates again in 1940, it was more than the broadcast radio market would bear. From January through the end of October 1941, not one of the 1,250,000 songs licensed by ASCAP was played on the broadcast stations, including "Chattanooga Choo Choo." Yet the song went on to sell over a million records—becoming a veritable triumph without any help from radio.

Harry was finally recognizing the power his music had. "It's the little engine that could," he told Josephine with a laugh.

In the Oscars race, "Chattanooga Choo Choo" received a nomination, as did Harold Arlen and Johnny Mercer's "Blues in the Night." Harry thought "Blues in the Night" was one of Arlen's best, and he often repeated the story, as Harold had told it, of the first time Harold and Johnny played it for anyone. It was at the Whiting residence several years after Richard died. Maggie had taken over the hosting duties for the songwriters' weekly gathering. She'd already had hits with Harold and Johnny's "That Old Black Magic" and "Come Rain or Come Shine." Johnny had always trusted Maggie's musical instincts and was anxious to get her feeling about the new song. He phoned her to see if they could stop by to play it, and she asked him to wait until about 10:00 because she had guests for dinner. Johnny asked who was there, and when he got his answer, he said, "My God, we're coming right over." They let themselves in through the back door and made their way straight to the piano, where they began performing the song:

My Mama done tol' me,
when I was in knee pants
My Mama done tol' me
Son, a woman'll sweet talk . . .

At that point, the dinner guests—a handful of the biggest

young stars in Hollywood—emerged from the dining room with their mouths agape. Mickey Rooney said it was the greatest thing he'd ever heard. Judy Garland asked them to play it again—and again and again. Harold ended up playing it seven times to satisfy them. Mel Tormé said, "I can't believe it." Maggie and Judy ran to the piano to see who was going to learn it first. Everyone there that night called it pure magic. Johnny and Harold felt that if their song resonated with these youngsters, they must be on to something.

Yet neither Harry nor Harold's song won the Academy Award that year, as popular or arresting as the songs were. Instead, the Oscar went to their good friend Jerome Kern for "The Last Time I Saw Paris," with lyrics by his longtime partner, Oscar Hammerstein II. Harry and Harold were genuinely happy for Kern, whom many called "the dean of popular music," a name reflecting the fact that, as one of ASCAP's first members, Jerry also wrote the music for *Show Boat*. The musical was a first of its kind—more like a serious play with songs, exploring dramatic themes of racism and alcoholism that would have been completely out of place in musical comedy.

Jerry Kern was a man of principle and was distressed over his win, because his song had not been written specifically for the film *Lady Be Good*, for which it had been nominated. He'd written it a couple years earlier and six different recordings of it had already been on the charts. The song evoked a certain poignancy that spoke to the fate of beloved European cities after the Battle of France, in which the Nazis had taken Paris.

After his win for "The Last Time I Saw Paris," Kern petitioned the Academy to change the rule.

Kern also hosted a weekly open house for songwriters to showcase their work throughout the 1940s. Harry, Ira, Harold, Johnny Mercer, and Hoagy Carmichael frequented his Monday-night gatherings. In addition to collectively writing the Great American Songbook, these men had something else in common: they loved pulling pranks on one another.

"Which one of you scoundrels sent an undertaker over here yesterday?" Jerry asked one night.

Harold nearly did a spit-take of some very expensive Scotch.

Ira chuckled, "Not me, but I wish I'd have thought of it!"

Johnny added, "Oh, that's *cold.*"

Hoagy snickered. "It could really only be one person, if you ask me . . ."

Jerry turned around to find the quietest guy in the room. "Harry!"

Harry sheepishly nodded and giggled as the group fell into uproarious laughter. They were always trying to one-up each other, and it seemed this prank of Harry's took things to another level.

As the laughter quieted down, Jerry said, "All right, Harry wins the prize for prank of the century. But Ira has the best story about what happened to him at a big Hollywood party last week."

"Oh, geez. I'd almost forgotten about that. I've been trying to forget," Ira said.

"I thought you hated schmoozing as much as I do," Harry interjected.

"Well, you can be sure it was against my better judgement," Ira replied. "But, brother, it was a regular who's who of Hollywood. When we got the invitation, Lee said, 'We're going, come hell or high water.'"

"Best not to argue with her," Harry chirped. Everyone nodded in agreement.

"There I was, trying to keep a low profile—not get too wrapped up in the whole spectacle. But before you know it, this man starts talking my damn ear off with twenty questions. Finally, I get so annoyed, I lean over to Lee when the guy gets distracted for a second, and I ask, 'Who the hell *is* this guy?' And she whispers back, 'It's Walt Disney, you dope.'" Everyone cracked up. "I told her, 'That's what you get for taking me to a party.' I couldn't wait to get back to my cat and slippers."

Jerry shook his head incredulously. "Oh, the moguls," he said wistfully. "I think their favorite music must be the sound of their own voices. Remember when I was summoned for a meeting with David Selznick at MGM? I was hoping it was a job, but when he finally finished talking, he asked me to play some tunes!"

"He wanted the guy who wrote *Show Boat* and 'The Way You Look Tonight' to play samples?" Harold asked in disbelief.

"Well, let's not be too hard on Selznick, shall we?" Ira said. "Apparently, he's $30,000 deep into Goldwyn from a rummy game last night."

Harry shook his head, laughing at the absurdity of it all.

Widespread gambling in Hollywood was causing reckless behavior in some of their closest friends. "The only person in a bigger hole right now might be Walter Donaldson," he said. "I'll never forget when Gus told me about the first time he went to New York to work with Donaldson and got dragged to the track. It didn't stop Gus from working—he wrote up a lyric right on the racing form. Walter was ecstatic and said, 'I always wanted a partner who could work at the track.' Well, Gus didn't like his attitude. He said, 'Then you'd better find a horse with a pencil.'"

They all fell out laughing.

The laughter all but stopped when Harry got his first royalty checks for "Chattanooga Choo Choo." He was appalled at how paltry they were, given the song's popularity. It was the same for Mack, so they decided to go see the studio lawyer. As they strolled across the lot to the legal department, Harry turned to Mack. "Now, is this the guy who's always in the pinstripe suits with the red carnation and a big cigar in his kisser?"

"Yeah, that's him," Mack affirmed.

They were ushered into the office of a lawyer who looked precisely the way Harry described. The songwriting partners exchanged a knowing look.

"What can I do for you fine gentlemen?" the lawyer asked smugly.

"Well, it seems writing a hit song doesn't make a guy much money these days," Harry said, uncomfortably.

"Our royalty checks for "Chattanooga" are, let's just say, much less than what you'd expect," Mack told the lawyer.

The lawyer reached for a file. "Do you both have a copy of the contract?"

Harry and Mack glanced at each other. "We usually leave that stuff to the agents, so we can, you know, concentrate on writing music," Harry said, barely able to disguise his irritation.

"Well," the lawyer said, spinning the contract around so the songwriters could see it, "have a look."

Harry and Mack stared at it like they were being asked to read a foreign language. The lawyer began pointing out the pertinent information.

"If you see here, it states that 50 percent of the royalties go to the music publisher, 25 percent to Twentieth Century Fox Studios, and 25 percent to the two writers—to split."

"But the publisher *is* the studio," Mack pointed out.

"Technically, yes," the lawyer conceded.

"And that makes it only 12.5 percent for each of us," Harry said.

"Correct," the lawyer said, an enormous smile spreading across his face.

Harry felt the back of his neck getting hot. He leaned back in the leather club chair, crossing his arms. "Why are you smiling like that?" he asked.

"Because I'm looking at both your signatures right here," the lawyer said. "Why did you sign, agreeing to terms you don't agree with?"

Without an easy answer for that, Harry and Mack got up and left the lawyer's office abruptly. Pushing through the double glass doors adorned with a gold-leaf studio logo, Harry growled, "So much for the little engine that could. This train has jumped the track."

"My agent just tells me to sign things, not read them. Isn't that what we pay them for?" Mack asked. "But I think I know why they never put up a fight. All their other clients work here too. They can't afford the risk of the studio taking it out on their whole roster."

"Then what the hell choice do we have?" Harry asked, only getting more agitated. "The skullduggery!"

Harry hated the feeling of being taken for a ride, but given the amount of time his craft demanded of him, there wasn't any left over for worrying about business matters. It only made him wonder more how Irving Berlin was able to put himself in a position to receive higher royalties and make himself a household name by demanding top billing, even over the stars of a film—like with *Irving Berlin's Holiday Inn* and, in ensuing years, *Irving Berlin's This Is the Army* and *Irving Berlin's Blue Skies*.

"How did he ever convince the studios to do that?" Harry asked Harold, who was still one of Irving's closest friends.

"He's very aggressive about these things," Harold explained. "That's not my style and it's not yours, but it's definitely Irving's. Maybe you should hire a publicist if you want more name recognition. Why don't you talk to your namesake, Warren? I hear he's getting into the publicity racket." Harold was referring to Warren Cowan, the son of Rubey Cowan, Harry's first publisher, who had such a fondness for Harry's talent that he named his first child after him. Warren would go on to head up what would become one of the largest public relations firms in the world, Rogers & Cowan.

Harry begrudgingly decided to give it a try and hired a publicist, not sure exactly what he was paying for. A few days later, he went out with some of the guys on a Sunday night to the Café Trocadero, a legendary night club on the Sunset Strip. The next morning, he entered the kitchen and found Josephine drinking coffee and reading *The Hollywood Reporter*. She didn't even lift her head as she said, "This is great. Now I can track your whereabouts just by reading the trades."

She handed over the paper over so Harry could see the picture of himself standing with Al Dubin, Mack Gordon, Leo Robin, Harry Revel, Larry Hart, and Hoagy Carmichael—all in sharp suits, with Harry, Al, and Mack clenching huge stogies between their teeth.

"I look like a schmuck," Harry said, disgusted. "I'm firing that damn publicist!"

Jo couldn't help but laugh.

"What is so goddamned funny?" Harry asked.

"Everybody knows Billy Wilkerson owns both the Troc and *The Hollywood Reporter*. Go to the Troc, you'll see your face in the *Reporter*. You don't need a publicist for that."

"How do you know so much about it?"

"Oh, I don't know much," she said slyly. "Just that Wilkerson published the first issue of *The Hollywood Reporter* in September 1930, and now apparently he's got an interest in who in Hollywood might be members of the Communist Party or even sympathizers."

Realizing a publicist was not the answer to his woes, Harry remained mystified as to why more people didn't know him outside the inner circle of Hollywood songwriters and executives. Sometimes the frustration got the best of him. Once, while having one of his infamous grumble therapy sessions with friends at the Hollywood Park turf club, he said, "They bombed the wrong Berlin." It became a line people couldn't help but repeat, deviously hilarious as it was. It perfectly summed up Harry's dark sense of humor and spoke to the personal injustice he felt of being way ahead of Berlin in terms of hits but remaining largely anonymous. Between 1935 and 1950, Berlin had thirty-three songs on the *Hit Parade*, compared with Harry's forty-two. By this metric, Harry was the most popular composer and Berlin was the *second* most popular.

Whenever Harry complained about this to Jo, he'd ask, "How many people do you think even realize a Russian immigrant wrote 'God Bless America'?"

"Would it have been better if an Italian immigrant had written it?" Jo asked.

"What kind of question is that?"

"It's never enough for you sometimes, Harry. Why can't you just be proud of your success and not worry about everything else?"

"More people know the name of Irving Berlin because of all the patriotic songs he's written. That's all I'm saying."

"Then maybe you should write something patriotic," she suggested.

"I'm not that calculated."

"Well, maybe *that's* why you have more hits than him. Ever think of that?"

Harry knew he had the love and respect of the stars who scored huge hits with his songs. This held with the musical geniuses behind the scenes too, such as with Herbert Spencer at Fox. Much like Ray Heindorf at Warner Brothers, Herbert had a reputation as one of the best orchestrators in the business. Working with him was a highlight for Harry during his time on the Fox lot. Herbert venerated Harry and never ceased to be amazed at Harry's talent and good nature.

"My wife would probably disagree with you about my temperament," Harry joked with Herbert once, while they worked late into the night on an arrangement.

"Harry, your melodies smack of the divine," Herbert said. "Your songs sound like they wrote themselves. How do you do it?"

"I just haven't run out of songs yet, I suppose."

"I know I speak for all the arrangers on this lot when I say it's always pleasure to work with you. I don't know if you know this, but we appreciate when you stick around to work on your songs. Most composers turn in their sketches and leave."

"Are we talking about someone with the initials I. B.?"

Herbert laughed. "We might be, yes!"

∾

Of the films Harry and Mack Gordon worked on for Twentieth Century Fox, one that presented a unique challenge was 1943's *Hello, Frisco, Hello*. It was a period piece set at the turn of the century against the backdrop of the hardscrabble Barbary Coast in San Francisco, the red-light district of the day known for its saloons, brothels, and bar fights. Alice Faye's star scene in the film needed a song that sounded like an old ballad while maintaining a current appeal as a song for lovers separated by war. Their answer to this challenge was "You'll Never Know" with the Glenn Miller Orchestra. The song shot straight to the top of the charts, selling over one million copies and becoming Harry's top seller in sheet music with just as many copies. It seemed Harry had a knack for capturing the prevailing public feeling.

"You'll Never Know" became the anthem of World War II, as well as Alice Faye's signature song, spending twenty-five weeks on the *Hit Parade* in 1943. Never one to rest on his laurels, Harry followed it up with "The Lady in the Tutti Frutti Hat," a song that would forever be associated with Carmen Miranda.

When the Oscar nominations came out, Harry was not surprised "You'll Never Know" made the cut, but he still harbored so much resentment toward Twentieth Century Fox that it tempered his reaction to the news. Nevertheless, it was clear Harry had reached the mountaintop.

That awards season, Harry and Jo were invited to the Gershwin Plantation for a dinner party to honor Harry, although Harry really didn't understand what it was all about. Gathered around the table, Ira took his fork to his crystal glass and stood to make a toast.

"As I look around this table, there is an almost unimaginable amount of musical talent," Ira said. "But tonight, I would like us to raise a glass for our friend Harry, who has done something no other songwriter has done." The guests raised their glasses, but Harry still didn't know what Ira was referring to. "Harry, you've done it. Not once, not twice, but *three* times now!"

"What did I do?" Harry asked. Everyone laughed.

"You, my friend, have written three anthems for three decades in a row, defining the sentiments of an entire generation," Ira explained, rattling off a list of Harry's hits: first in the roaring twenties with "I Love My Baby (My Baby Loves Me)"; "We're in the Money" as the 1930s Depression-era anthem; now "You'll Never Know" as *the* war song for soldiers and their sweethearts. "How on God's green earth do you tap into the zeitgeist like that?"

"I never stopped to think of it that way," Harry confessed.

"I know you haven't! But you're at the top of your game. And I felt I would be remiss in my duties as your friend and fan not to mark this moment."

"Well, if I'm at the top, doesn't that mean there's only way to go?" Harry joked in self-deprecating fashion.

"Just remember, not everyone *makes* it to the top," Ira said. "Here's to you, Harry!"

As the guests toasted Harry, he blushed. Like the great composer André Previn once said of Harry, he's "the kind of man who backs into the limelight and then backs out again."

Chapter Eleven

THE BIRDS SING ALL DAY AT METRO

The Oscars race that year had Harry up against three entries from his mentee, Harold Arlen: "My Shining Hour," "That Old Black Magic," and "Happiness Is Just a Thing Called Joe." As it turned out, the three Arlen songs combined were not enough to stand up to the power of "You'll Never Know," which earned Harry a companion statuette to go with his Oscar for "Lullaby of Broadway."

Still, Harry's emotions remained mixed about Fox—his time there had produced his biggest hits, but the stress of the environment had taken its toll. The headline in *Variety* on May 12, 1943, read: "Warren Leaving 20th." The article stated, "Warren wants to take a long rest due to failing health," something Harry did not recall sharing with anyone as an official quote for publication.

MGM had been making musicals throughout the 1930s, while Harry was toiling away at Warner Brothers, but it wasn't until 1939 with *The Wizard of Oz* that the studio's output began to take on the unique flavor of a Metro Goldwyn Mayer musical.

These musicals were incubated in what was known as the Freed Unit, named after Arthur Freed, which essentially operated as an independent part of the studio. It was MGM's shining success at the time. By the mid-1940s, the Freed Unit was teeming with the most sought-after musical talent in the business—including top vocal arranger and coach Kay Thompson, who later went on to write the children's classic *I Am Eloise* and follow-up Eloise books, said to be inspired by Thompson's goddaughter Liza Minelli, Judy Garland's daughter. The Freed Unit had brilliant orchestrators; coloratura sopranos who could sing anything, no matter how many runs or complex trills; and the Italian classical composer Mario Castelnuovo-Tedesco, who'd written an opera. Harry had been appalled to learn that, as an Italian Jew, Mario's work had been banned on Italian radio and he was no longer allowed to perform publicly.

Arthur Freed was a magnet for top talent and told many people over the years that if he could ever get Harry Warren, he'd put him in an office right next to his. And when he signed Harry to MGM in early 1944, that's precisely what he did. Although Harry started out as Freed's neighbor on the lot, he needed a calmer place to work. "Everybody and their dog would drop in," Harry said of the Thalberg building, where his office was located. So, Freed happily moved Harry to a bungalow, where no one bothered him and where Harry spent the next eight years writing some of his best work.

When anyone asked Harry how things were at work, he'd say, "The birds sing all day at Metro." This was in stark contrast to how Harry felt about Warner Brothers. When asked what made MGM so different, he described Warner Bros. as a place where "the bell rings and you think you're at Leavenworth." He even wrote a song comparing the two studios that he'd sometimes play at parties. It could best be described as two songs in one: a robotic staccato section about Warner Bros. being a cold, dehumanizing place, with lyrics evoking imagery of prison and inmates, alternating with a lilting lullaby section about MGM, meant to conjure a bucolic scene of shepherds tending their flock—in this case, with Louis B. Mayer as the shepherd.

Harry knew he was part of a small minority when it came to adoring the mogul, whom most shrunk in the sight of. The fact was, Harry and Louis B. Mayer belonged to the mutual admiration society; Harry trusted Mayer to put his money where his mouth was when it came to music, and Mayer genuinely loved music and those who created it. When Mayer hired Johnny Green to direct the music department, he insisted on hiring only the best orchestra, composers, and arrangers in the business. Johnny warned him that would cost a lot of money, to which Mayer replied, "We *have* a lot of money." Harry respected Mayer for being decisive and having the good taste to know where to spend it—including on him, because Mayer compensated him more handsomely than any other studio ever had.

Almost as soon as Harry signed with MGM, he was loaned back out to Twentieth Century Fox at Billy Rose's request for the movie *Billy Rose's Diamond Horseshoe*. Few circumstances could have convinced Harry to go back to Fox, but this was a situation he simply could not resist. Forever the schemer, going back to his Tin Pan Alley days, Billy Rose sold his idea for a movie musical based on his nightclub in New York for $76,000 (over a million in today's dollars) and then declared he wouldn't allow its release without his name in the title. Rose got one over on the legal department that had taken advantage of Harry, even if Harry had to admit it was a power grab, a la Irving Berlin—fighting over having their names splashed all over the movie. It was a big-budget musical and the studio wanted as much of a guarantee as it could get. The answer to that was to have songs penned by Warren and Gordon.

On the home front, it was a time for much excitement. On March 28, 1944, Harry and Josephine became grandparents to a darling little girl Cookie named Julia, after Josephine's mother. Cookie was nineteen and had been in a relationship with Richard Wyndham Hoffman, a fellow child of a show business family. Young Richard had his own colorful past, which seemed to endear him to Cookie. Things had happened quickly between them; Harry was playing catch up as he pressed his daughter for details of the young man she'd been seeing before she announced her pregnancy.

"Tell me about this Richard," he said as they sat by the pool one sunny afternoon. "You're running in and out of here so fast all the time, I'm dizzy just watching you."

She laughed. "Sorry, Daddy. What would you like to know?"

"Who the hell is he, for starters."

"He was born in New York, like you," she said with a smile, trying to soften him up. She told him Richard's father was a well-respected neurologist there.

"Son of a doctor? Well, okay. That's a good start," Harry said.

"You'd tip your hat, right?" she teased. Harry chuckled in agreement. "His mother is an actress, mostly stage," Cookie said. "Her name is Janet. Janet Beecher."

"Isn't she the one who's in a cult?"

Cookie laughed, but Harry remained serious. "That stuff's no joke. You'd better watch out, so you don't get sucked right in too." Harry grabbed his rosary beads from on top of the book he was reading: *Napoleon,* a biography written by Emil Ludwig. "Go pray the rosary right now and ask for protection!"

"Don't get hysterical, Daddy. Leave the handwringing to mother."

"Well, what does Richard say about all this?"

Cookie explained that Richard was raised mostly by his father. When his parents divorced, he was very young, and his father got nearly full custody of him. He only spent summers with his mother. Janet had been accused of something called "automatic writing," in which the spirits supposedly take over the pen in your hand. "Don't worry," Cookie soothed. "Richard doesn't do that. He's a perfectly respectable young man."

Respectable or not, Cookie and Richard were not adequately prepared to be parents. Cookie had never wanted for a thing her entire life, and that privilege combined with tragedy created many challenges for her. If her becoming pregnant was not the best timing, it was a blessing for Harry and Josephine, who loved having a baby around the house again. When things got shaky between Cookie and Richard, Cookie spent more time at the Warren home and out with Maggie, by then one of the most popular singers of the Big Band era. It made for a very insular world for Cookie to watch Maggie perform many of Harry's songs.

Before too long, Cookie and the baby were living with Harry and Josephine full time. As much as they loved the extended family, Harry thought it was important for Cookie to develop some independence, so he bought a house for her just down the street—but she never moved into it. As a result, little Julia ended up being raised primarily by Harry and Josephine. She was a delightful child who brought immense joy into a household that had struggled with more than its fair share of sadness.

The Warrens had another semi-permanent fixture in their home around this time as well: Alice Kahal. Alice was the young widow of Harry's friend and fellow songwriter Irving Kahal, who'd died in 1942 at just thirty-nine. Alice had been a fourteen-year-old runaway and one of Josephine's best friends going back to New York, when they spent days commiserating over being left alone all the time. There was an ongoing joke about a suspected affair between Harry and Alice, but Alice laughed the idea off, saying, "Lord, no. Harry's way too cheap!" As a former showgirl, Alice had expensive taste in gifts—that much they could agree on. But she was known to dance around with her skirt lifted like a cancan girl while Harry played piano. Alice had a particular way of taunting Harry, which she did right up to the very end. Her kind of teasing colored their relationship with more of a sibling dynamic than one of illicit lovers, but no one may ever know the truth. Harry, Josephine, and Alice all missed Irving, and that July it was bittersweet when Bing Crosby scored a hit with one of Kahal's songs, "I'll Be Seeing You." The beautiful ballad could easily bring tears to anyone's eyes, being the kind of song that is easy to attach personal meaning to:

I'll be seeing you
in all the old familiar places
that this heart of mine
embraces all day through.
In that small café;
 the park across the way;
the children's carousel;
the chestnut trees;
the wishin' well . . .

The song made Harry long for Sonny more than he already did, especially the part about the park across the way. He often looked out the front picture window at the park across the street from their home on North Beverly Drive, a home Sonny never got to live in.

The song broke Harry's heart in another respect as well. He wished Irving could have lived long enough to see his song—written for a Broadway show that ran for only fifteen performances—find new life six years later through Bing Crosby's star power.

Life was more joyous for Josephine with Julia around, even though Jo continued to struggle and was still taking too many pills. In those days, there was little awareness about addiction to prescription medication, which had reached near-epidemic proportions in Hollywood. The prevailing wisdom seemed to be that if a doctor gave it to you, how bad could it be? Some didn't even seem to be aware of how much doctors were overprescribing for their celebrity patients until it was too late.

But as the holidays approached, Harry felt joyful anticipation knowing he'd be seeing the season through the eyes of his granddaughter's first Christmas. Of their many family traditions, Harry's favorite was making traditional Italian donuts, *zeppoles*, for his birthday on Christmas Eve. Harry's favorite part was taking the zeppoles out of the oil and placing them into the brown paper bag filled with powdered sugar for dusting.

Harry handed Julia a piece of dough to show her how to roll it into a ball in her baby seat. Instead, she put it in her mouth and ate it.

"She can't eat raw dough, Harry!" Josephine chided. "You'd think you hadn't raised children of your own! Babies can't eat raw eggs, not that anyone should."

Kitchen conflict was yet another tradition in the house. Every time they made zeppoles, it seemed the dough ended up flying like bombs.

"It was the tiniest little bit," Harry said in defense. "Trust me, this kid is tougher than you think. You should have seen what she did the other day—"

Jo held out her arm to shush him as she caught something on the radio. She turned up the volume. A BBC broadcaster announced: "Major Glenn Miller, the well-known American bandleader, is reported missing. He left England by air for Paris nine days ago . . ."

The plane had taken off in heavy fog and had gone down in the English Channel, the report said. Harry gasped. Jo stared back at him, a deep sadness in her eyes. Instantly, they forgot what they'd been arguing about.

While Harry reached to turn off the flame under the pot of frying oil, little Julia got hold of the brown paper bag and popped it. As white powdered sugar fell around them like a snowstorm, Harry and Jo didn't know whether to laugh or cry.

Julia grew faster than Harry would have liked. When she began talking, she called him Daddy Warren, becoming an even greater source of light and love. In the afternoons, Harry loved to plop her up on the kitchen counter, get out his day-old bread, salami, and pepperoncini, and make little sandwiches for them to eat together. He enjoyed taking her on outings and no matter how much dysfunction she would witness as the years went on, she would always feel a special closeness with him. Harry came to appreciate her presence in their lives, especially during the difficult times, like when he found out about Al Dubin collapsing on a street corner in New York City from a drug overdose.

Al's wife and his daughter, Patricia, had long been estranged from him when they heard the news on the radio. They called Harry to confirm it. "Harry, is it true?" Patricia asked.

"I'm afraid so. I know you've had your differences, and I'm sorry it had to happen this way," Harry said.

"I thank God every day that he met you and that you two

had the chance to create all the beautiful work you did together," she said. Surprising himself, Harry began to cry. "Harry?"

"I was just thinking," Harry said with a sniffle, "about when Al told me the nicest thing his mother ever did for him. She named him after Alexander the Great, who conquered the world before his thirtieth birthday. I felt sick when he said she used to tie him to the crib so she wouldn't miss even one of her college classes." Harry looked down at Julia pulling on his pant leg. He wiped away his tears and ruffled her blonde locks. "He struggled so much, but he knew I adored him. I'm very sorry for both of you. Come by and see us," Harry said.

With that, he handed the phone to Josephine and disappeared into his studio out in the back of their home. Julia tried to follow him, but Jo scooped her up before beginning yet another sad conversation with a widow of someone dear to their hearts.

Harry was grateful MGM was keeping him busy. Writing for *Ziegfeld Follies* took him back to the old-style revues, as there was no plot, but rather twelve vignettes, each with a different star—Gene Kelly, Lucille Ball, and Fred Astaire, to name a few. In the end, there was enough film and music for two films. *Yolanda and the Thief* came next, which could have reasonably been considered a sequel to the "This Heart of Mine" vignette of *Ziegfeld Follies*, with Astaire reprising his role as a thief trying to rob a wealthy young woman. Arthur Freed, who'd started out as a songwriter, had still been trying to write lyrics in addition to all his other responsibilities of running the unit. Harry feared Freed might be spreading himself too thin; the unit hummed like a well-oiled machine due to the talent doing what they did best, he thought, not by trying to do everything. Harry's favorite of all the MGM talent was perhaps Astaire, whose work ethic was matched only by his creativity and talent. Harry also had a high opinion of the script, which was not always the case. He was happy and interested in working on it, and disappointed that the film was not received more positively.

One day, Jerry Kern paid Harry a surprise visit to his bungalow on the lot. Harry's face lit up at the sight of him. Jerry sat in one of Harry's guest chairs. As was often the case, one of the buttons on his coat was not fastened in the right place.

"Looks like you missed a hole there, friend," Harry said.

Jerry looked down and fixed it. "Why am always doing that?" he laughed.

"Have they started production on your movie?" Harry asked.

"Trust me, I don't think of it as *my* movie. I tried to warn them how boring my life is, so who knows what they're doing to spice it up."

"But it's the story of your life, Jer . . ."

"Well, it's only the first week and the whole process is already making me queasy," Jerry said. "I know they have all the top people here, the best of the best. But I don't mind telling you, Harry. They've made a mess of 'Ol' Man River.'"

"Roger Edens is doing the arranging?" Harry asked. When Jerry nodded, he added, "Have you tried talking with him about it?"

"This may seem odd, but it just doesn't seem like my place to say anything. You don't have to tell me how differently things work out here than on Broadway," Jerry sighed. "I probably should have never come around. I could have stayed blissfully ignorant! But the thing is, they just lopped off the entire opening verse . . . 'There's an ol' man called the Mississippi/That's the ol' man I'd like to be . . .' For people who don't know the musical, where is the context for the song?"

Harry stood. "C'mon. Let's go see if we can't gang up on Edens and talk some sense into him," he laughed.

The two walked across the lot and waited outside the sound-stage for the red light to stop flashing. When it did, they opened the door and strolled onto the set of *Till the Clouds Roll By*. The company was in the middle of shooting the scene portraying the opening night of the Broadway premiere of *Show Boat,* with a set to match the original stage set, a façade of the river showboat. When Harry spotted Roger Edens, he and Jerry went over to him.

"Harry, hi!" Rogers said when he spotted them. "Glad to see you back, Jerry. This must all be very exciting for you."

"Sure it is," Jerry said. "It's an honor."

"The thing is, Roger, and I know you'll agree when they make the movie of *your* life . . ." Harry chuckled, trying and lighten the mood, "Jerry's not sure about the arrangement for 'Ol' Man River.'"

Harry saw Edens attempting to veil his contempt. Edens had gotten to where he was through his association with Judy Garland and worked his way up to producer. Now he had the ego to match.

"Oh, you see, Jerry—and Harry can tell you—" Roger said,

"half the movie-making process happens in the editing room. What you saw and heard earlier is nothing close to the final product. You really have nothing to worry about."

Harry had gotten good at sensing when smoke was being blown his way. "There's some truth to that," he acknowledged. "But the point is, you have the writer right here—the subject of the story. Seems like a good idea to hear him out on what's not working with the arrangement."

"We're on a tight schedule here, boys, but of course I want to hear your thoughts, Jerry. Maybe over the dinner break. Although, I'm going to have to work with a couple of the singers then. We'll figure something out. You're going to be very happy with everything when it's all said and done."

As they walked toward the stage exit, Jerry turned to Harry and said, "He doesn't plan on taking anything I have to say into consideration, does he?"

"No," Harry said sorely, "but we tried. Now might be a good time to unleash that quick temper I've heard about but never seen."

"They tell me that's no good for my health," Jerry laughed.

As production continued on *Till the Clouds Roll By*, Harry poked his head in once in a while to see how Kern's songs were being produced and staged. One morning while he was walking near there, he heard some hubbub. People seemed upset, some stunned. He was about to walk on the soundstage when saw Angela Lansbury step out of her trailer. She had always been friendly with Harry—she was a good skate, as he'd say. "Angie, what's going on?" he asked.

"Jerry was found on the corner of Park Avenue and Fifty-Seventh Street. They think he must have suffered a brain hemorrhage."

"Is—is he—" he stammered.

"He's still alive, but it doesn't sound good. The only ID he had was his ASCAP card, so they took him to the indigent ward at City Hospital first."

"No . . ." Harry muttered. It pained him to think of this happening to Jerry.

"But someone just said he's been transferred to Doctor's Hospital and Oscar is there with him."

Harry was slipping into something of a stupor. "He was so looking forward to overseeing auditions for the revival of *Show Boat* in New York and—and begin work on a new score with Rodgers and Hammerstein about Annie Oakley," he said. Angela's face changed to reflect his pain. "I'm an idiot! Do you know I once sent an undertaker to his house as a prank? What kind of cretin pulls a cockamamie stunt like that?"

"Don't beat yourself up, Harry. I'm sure he found the humor in it at the time," she said.

Harry paused, appreciating her kindness. "You're right, he did. But I just can't bear to think he's had all the laughs he's ever going to have." He turned and slunk back to his bungalow.

Jerry passed away a few days later with his friend and lyricist Oscar Hammerstein II by his side. The show's investors were anxious to move forward, forcing Rodgers and Hammerstein to find another composer fast. Harry heard from Harold that they were going after Irving Berlin.

"You're not going to like the next part," Harold warned him. "Irving wanted them to change the title to *Irving Berlin's Annie Oakley.*"

"Does he think he's the second coming?" Harry snapped.

"The good news is, there was no way they would ever agree to that. But Irving still wanted the job."

"How do you abide that man?"

"He doesn't have many friends," Harold reminded him.

"Maybe because he refuses to pay his dying sister's medical bills? You probably didn't know that did you?"

They sat in uncomfortable silence for a moment before Harold spoke again: "It is hard to imagine two people more different than you and Irving."

Harry knew this to be true, for better or worse. And being the polar opposite of the insecure self-promoting Berlin, Harry never dreamed of standing in the way of Harold's friendship with him.

The following year, in 1946, Arthur Freed was trying to come to grips with the fact that he could no longer work as a lyricist while running the entire unit. He gave Harry his choice of lyricist for the upcoming big-budget movie *The Harvey Girls*, starring Judy Garland in her prime. Harry wanted Johnny Mercer immediately. They wrote ten songs for the film, two of which were cut due to length. The breakout hit was "On the Atchison, Topeka, and the Santa Fe," a set piece that tells the story of the waitresses who worked on the trains and owner Fred Harvey's restaurants all along the route. The song introduces the young women on their way to a new life and adventure as the people in town await the arrival of the train carrying them. Harry and Johnny hadn't intended the song to last nine minutes, but that was the result after the studio added extra lyrics to expand aspects of the story. Harry and Johnny were furious about this, and Johnny was mortified, thinking people would assume he wrote the schmaltzy parts. When the song was nominated for an Academy Award, both boycotted the ceremony to show their displeasure.

To escape all the Oscars hoopla, Harry and Jo went to Palm Springs with a group of friends. It wasn't just the grievance with the studio—Harry also felt melancholy about being nominated alongside Jerry Kern now that he was gone. He missed his friend and felt a huge void, just like with all his other sudden losses—never having the chance to say goodbye to many who were dear to him made him feel like he was living with ghosts.

While driving with Harold to the golf course, Harry turned on the radio to the station broadcasting the awards and heard "On the Atchison, Topeka, and the Santa Fe" had won. Neither of them said a word about it—Harold knew full well all the reasons they were in the desert in the first place. As they exited the car, Harry turned to Harold and in sotto voce said, "Walk two Oscars behind me."

Laughing as Harry walked away, Harold called after him, "You beat Irving again. That must be somewhat satisfying, you rascal!"

By then twenty paces in front of him, Harry waved his hand as if swatting a fly.

~

When Harry returned to Los Angeles after the weekend, he was cornered by a reporter at the famous Hollywood haunt, the Brown Derby, looking for a quote from him for the *Examiner*. "As the first songwriter to win three Oscars, how did it feel walking up there?" the reporter asked.

"I wouldn't know. I was in Palm Springs."

The reporter was crestfallen. "How could you *not go* to the Academy Awards?" she asked.

"You don't have enough ink for that," Harry said. "Sorry, kid, I'm no good at this stuff." He walked away and left her standing in a cloud of confusion.

After lunch, he went to see Johnny at his new office in Hollywood. As one of the founders of Capitol Records, Mercer was in a position to put out his own recording of "On the Atchison, Topeka, and the Santa Fe," and wasted no time doing so. Harry found Johnny's two-room hovel off of Hollywood Boulevard.

"Harry!" Johnny greeted him warmly. "Congratulations, ol' chap. Any regrets over our boycotting the awards? Sounds like we missed a big party."

"Nah. I shot a seventy-nine and had the best osso buco outside of Italy."

Johnny smiled, then got serious. "Listen, I think you should reconsider investing in Capitol. I just signed Maggie. I'm going to make stars out of the singers, not just the bands! And now with the recording strike over—"

"That's good you're looking out for Maggie's career," Harry

interrupted. "I know Richard is up there feeling grateful for it. But you know me, I'm no business guy. I leave that stuff to Jo."

"Then maybe I should talk to her about it," Johnny said.

"Be my guest. She has pretty strong opinions about her stocks, I can tell you that."

The Warrens did not invest in Capitol Records. Instead, a few years later, Jo bought stock with a fledgling company called Xerox that did well for them. Capitol made a tremendous splash with its first three releases, surpassing Johnny's wildest expectations. If Harry had any regrets about not buying Capitol stock, he never said so. Then again, a great deal went unspoken when it came to Harry. In 1947, his business manager sent a letter informing him that the balance of his trust was $110,000 (over $1.2 million today) and suggested end-of-year bonuses to all who worked toward making money for the trust.

Toward the latter part of the decade in the postwar period, people in Hollywood started hearing the name Billy Wilkerson more and more. The journalist, who had started *The Holly- wood Reporter*, kept a running list of suspected communists and sympathizers that was becoming the basis for the Hollywood blacklist.

Harry stopped in on Ira one night to kibitz on his way home from the studio. Harry had heard Ira was in the sights of Jack Tenney, the former songwriter turned lawyer and politician chairing the California Factfinding Committee on Un-American Activities. As they settled into a couple armchairs and Calliope jumped on Ira's lap, Harry asked, "What the hell is this Billy's List?"

"They're stirring up a second red scare," Ira said.

"Who was it who said, 'It's easy to splash red paint on someone and it's pretty hard to wash off'?" Harry wondered.

"I don't know, but very true," Ira replied.

Around this time, a bunch of actors, writers, and directors had started a group called the Committee for the First Amendment. Ira had already been meeting with another group, the Hollywood Independent Citizens Committee of the Arts, Sciences, and Professions, for a while and had learned the group was under suspicion for communist activities. For this, Ira was called before the California Senate. When he returned from that unfortunate experience weeks later, he was shaken.

"What a ridiculous charade. Even the questioners felt foolish. They tried to link the Gershwin name with something un-American," Ira scoffed. "We just can't stand for the harassment, Harry."

Ira told him he was joining some members of the Committee for the First Amendment on a chartered flight to DC to testify before the House. Wanting to put an end to the communist hysteria, they were working on a radio broadcast to let the public know the Committee for the First Amendment was not affiliated with a political party. Calling it *Hollywood Fights Back* with Judy Garland as the host, it would feature short statements from the members sounding the alarm for everyday Americans on facts about the House Committee. Actor and director John Huston was going to talk about the fact that the committee had been around for nine years already, wasting millions of taxpayer dollars investigating what they believed to be subversive activities.

"How they came to believe there's a red under every bed—it's pure hysteria," Ira said.

"I just don't want to see you on the blacklist like Yip," Harry said.

"I know. Harold asked me to work with him on *My Blue Heaven* because the studio will no longer approve Yip."

"It'll be great for you to work with Harold again! What's it been, thirty years?"

"I can't possibly be that old," Ira laughed. "Yip has already gone back to New York, where no one cares about the damn list."

"So, you mean if I get myself on the list, I'd be forced to leave this town for good?" Harry joked.

Chapter Twelve

INVASION OF THE SMALL SCREEN

Throughout the war years, Hollywood dutifully played its part, pumping out product for a hungry audience of moviegoers. But in the period that followed, several events conspired to create a domino effect that would cause the whole system to come crashing down.

In 1948, the Supreme Court ruled in what became widely known as the Paramount Decision that it was a violation of anti-trust law for studios to own theaters. Things had been bound to catch up with the industry eventually; it been building the plane while flying, like so many other industries do in their nascency, and this had not been its first run-in with government regulation. In the decade preceding the Paramount Decision, the studios had been embroiled in litigation over illegal trade practices that forced many industry reforms. As a result of being forced to divest from theaters, the studios recognized they no longer needed to keep their stars on expensive long-term contracts. Additionally, because they would not be solely responsible for keeping theaters stocked with product, they stood to save money and have more control by paying the talent one picture at a time. While this may have convinced some rattled studio heads they'd come out on top, any gains proved to be short-lived once the last domino fell: a change in tax law that allowed actors to form corporations of their own. Once Jimmy Stewart made a deal for $750,000 plus 10 percent of the gross, the moguls were about to be shown the door. The end of the studio system was nigh.

But there was another change in the air in addition to the Paramount decision—one no one in Hollywood wanted to face, some going so far as to call it the "little terror": television. As one MGM advertising executive said, "It's our duty to fight off television if it takes the next twenty years." No one had the slightest inkling of how transformative the little terror would come to be, given its unmistakable immediacy, a highly addictive ingredient not found in film.

Harry was again in the minority when it came to his feelings about television, because he was a gadget man. While he didn't like the idea of something cutting into his earning potential, he wasn't about to let anything stand in his way of being an early adopter of new technology. By the late 1940s, televisions were everywhere and becoming more popular every day. Harry was one of the first of his friends to get one. It was enormous, and Josephine found it unsightly. Not wanting it in any common room of the house, she made Harry set it up in their bedroom. He was determined as ever to tune into whatever was on the air at that time, which then amounted only to a couple hours of programming per day—shows such as a woman painting movie stars' faces on eggs. The problem was that after he'd plugged in the set, he couldn't get decent reception. Someone told him to try an antenna on the roof.

When he came home with the unwieldy contraption, he asked the valet on his staff to accompany him on the roof to install it. Standing on top of the house, Harry saw Cookie and Maggie return from shopping the boutiques of Beverly Hills. They were holding about six bags each.

"Daddy, what are you doing up there?" Cookie shouted.

"Suntanning," he said sarcastically. "What the hell does it look like?" He proudly held up the antenna.

"Trying to make contact with Martians?" she said. He had to wonder where she learned to be such a smart aleck.

Harry loved to tinker with things, despite not having much of a knack for it. He and his valet shifted the antenna in all different directions as Harry shouted down to Josephine, who was keeping an eye on the screen inside. "Is that any better?" he yelled.

Josephine stuck her head out of their bedroom window and shouted back up, "Not ye-eet!"

They moved the antenna in a different direction and Harry shouted to Jo again, only to get the same answer. As this went on, Harry looked down at the girls below, now in stitches over the whole thing. "I'm glad you two are so amused!" he said.

"We'll go inside and see how it looks on the television, Daddy," Cookie offered.

Harry continued struggling with the antenna until he got so frustrated that he threw his arms up in defeat—knocking him off balance and sending him tumbling right off the roof, tangling up in wires on the way down. The wires were still wrapped around him when he entered the house mercifully unscathed. Despite his scrapes and scratches, he could not contain his excitement when he the saw the television screen: "I can almost see Clark Gable's face coming into focus on that egg!" he exclaimed. Josephine, Cookie, and Maggie fell into a fit of laughter.

Harry's love of boxing was one of the greatest motivating factors for him to set up his television. He wanted to watch *Cavalcade of Sports,* which NBC had been broadcasting from St. Nicholas Arena in New York City twice a week since 1946. On Mondays, Harry insisted the family watch with him. Later, Friday nights became *Gillette Cavalcade of Sports*, broadcast from Madison Square Garden. Harry took pride in betting on his fellow Italian Rocky Marciano. Julia would get excited when she saw the show's opening animation, an advert for Gillette. She'd march around the room singing along to the theme song: "Look sharp! Look sharp!"

These days, Harry had been feeling, dare he say, almost *fulfilled* as he began work on what would become his favorite film to be associated with. *Summer Holiday*, starring Mickey Rooney and Gloria DeHaven, was based on the Eugene O'Neill play *Ah, Wilderness!* Perhaps Harry loved it so much for its indulgence in nostalgia, given that Harry was finding himself at the same point in his life—looking back more than forward. He often visited the set at Busch Gardens in Pasadena when the company was on location there, including the day they shot "The Stanley Steamer" number. Even having what he considered one of the best songs he'd ever written, "Spring Isn't Everything," cut from the film was not enough to dampen his affection for this picture. Despite being a critical success, the film didn't find an audience, even though the studio strategically held it for release until 1948. Critic Rex Reed famously listed it as the best movie musical of all time, second only to *Singin' in the Rain*, which ironically ended MGM's long and powerful run of musicals.

The winds of change continued blowing, and when Harry heard about a new Academy rule allowing songs *not* written expressly for a film to be included in the Best Song category, he was furious. Songs such as "Baby, It's Cold Outside" and "White Christmas" garnered nominations as a result, the former winning in 1949.

One night, as Maggie and Cookie were getting ready for a party, Harry voiced his frustration. "I like your recording of that song, Maggie. It's one of the best out there—yours and Ella's," he said. "But Jerry Kern is rolling over in his grave. He fought hard against this."

"Why's that, Uncle Harry?" Maggie asked somewhat naively.

"How hard is it just to plop songs right into movies? An ape could do that. An ape probably *does* do that," he scoffed. "Academy awards are given out for the craft and the skill needed to write a song for a picture's specific needs. Or so I used to think."

"Didn't you write the music for 'Lullaby of Broadway' without any idea how it would be used?" Josephine asked, waltzing into the room. Harry loved and loathed how she was always trying to keep him honest.

"Well, I knew what picture I was writing for. It wasn't my fault there were no book songs! If you remember, there was no script when we started," Harry said. As he thought about it, he grew increasingly flustered, until he announced: "I'm quitting the Academy. This is the last straw."

"Oh, no! Don't do that," Maggie said.

"Then how am I going to see all the movies?" Jo shouted with indignation as Harry marched out.

Harry made good on this threat and sent a letter of resignation to the Academy. He wasn't sure what it would accomplish, but it made him feel better in the short term. It felt good to stick to his principles, especially during a time of so much change and upheaval.

While at the Hollywood Brown Derby one day, he ran into an old colleague from MGM who'd left the studio: Ben Feiner, the brother-in-law of composer Richard Rogers. As they caught up, their conversation turned to CBS Records, where Ben had landed after leaving MGM.

"How do you like it over there?" Harry asked.

"Like it? I love it," Ben said. "Harry, you *have* to come back to the studio with me if you want to hear something extraordinary."

"How could I say no when you put it like that?"

When they left the restaurant, Ben walked Harry right into CBS Records. He sat him down in the sweet spot, equidistant between the two speakers in the control room, and hit the play button. Ben wasn't exaggerating—the fidelity of the sound was astonishing.

"It's recorded on a tape," Ben said. "It's called Ampex."

"This is really going to change things, isn't it?"

"Bing Crosby is already using it a lot now that he's realized he doesn't have to do everything live for his radio show. This way, he can record as much as he wants at his home studio."

"Where can I get one?"

"I thought you might ask that!" Ben said, smiling.

Not only did Harry want a tape machine of his own, but he rushed home to tell Josephine to buy stock in Ampex too. It was one of the few times she gladly took a stock tip from him.

Arthur Freed told Harry to choose a lyricist to work with on 1949's *The Barkleys of Broadway*. Harry wanted to get Ira back to work and he knew this would be a great project for them to team up on. The film reunited Fred Astaire and Ginger Rogers, who hadn't worked together in ten years. Originally, Judy Garland was cast in the part Ginger took over after Judy dropped out due to ongoing health problems, which always seemed to be code for something far worse. Harry and Ira felt this was a shame, as some of the strongest songs they wrote were with Judy's voice in mind. Ginger, gifted dancer that she was, did not have Judy Garland's voice. On the other hand, Harry adored Astaire, whom he called a gentleman's gentleman. He enjoyed working with the polite and soft-spoken Fred, who always discussed his ideas for dances with Harry. For the number "Shoes with Wings On," Harry was in awe of how Fred worked alone on the soundstage from early morning until late at night. Occasionally, when Fred couldn't make something work, he went back to Harry in the most deferential way, asking for an alternate piece of music to try.

One of the comical songs Harry and Ira wrote for the film was "The Weekend in the Country" for Oscar Levant—the multi-talented actor, songwriter, concert pianist, comedian, and conductor. Harry and Ira got a big kick out of Oscar, an eccentric who would likely be considered an obsessive-compulsive individual today. He was always rearranging objects just so, he wore nothing but dark clothes, and he simply could not abide anyone touching him.

One day, Harry and Ira had never laughed harder when Oscar said the strangest thing to Harry. "Have I ever told you, you look like my mother?" Oscar asked.

"Your *mother?*" Harry clarified.

"Daughter of a rabbi? That mother?" Ira chimed in.

"Yes," Oscar said, "my mother. I'll show you a picture sometime. There'll be no denying it. You'll see."

Harry and Ira enjoyed their experience on the production. It almost felt like being back in New York because they were mostly left alone to work. They laughed about Oscar's singing at times, which Harry said sounded like a dying calf. He did his best imitation for Ira: "A-a-a-a-a-a!"

Harry held Ira in higher esteem than anyone, even when challenges arose, like when Arthur Freed attempted to ingratiate himself with Ira, showing up at the Gershwin Plantation with increasing frequency. Before long, Freed began insisting they use a Gershwin tune in the movie. They decided on "You Can't Take That Away from Me," and no matter how much Harry loved the song, it never felt good to have any song interpolated into a score. Yet Harry could never hold anything against Ira, and after he put himself in Ira's shoes (or slippers), it seemed like a way to keep George present in their lives.

For all Harry claimed he didn't socialize in Hollywood, he had many good friends in the business and none outside of it. Aside from Ira, one of his favorite people went back to his Warner Brothers days. The orchestrator Leo Forbstein, who was miraculously still working for the same studio, requested Harry on a loan-out to work on the picture *My Dream Is Yours*. A fixture at Warner Bros., Leo had outlasted all the executives from Harry's time, with the exception of Jack Warner. As Harry arrived on the lot to meet with Leo about this project, one of his earliest and fondest memories of his time in Hollywood flooded back: the first time he'd ever heard his own music played by the magnificent studio orchestra after being arranged by Forbstein. The memory brought tears to his eyes, just like it had all those years before.

My Dream Is Yours was only Doris Day's second film, and Harry was touched that the movie would also be using several old Warren-Dubin tunes. Harry was impressed with Day's rendition of "I'll String Along with You," and he saw how years of singing with bands was valuable experience for her movie career. Like many stars Harry crossed paths with over the years, he found Day charming and aloof in turns, but she delivered where it really mattered for him—scoring two new hits with the title song from *My Dream Is Yours* and with "Someone Like You."

Harry had never expected to work with Forbstein again and

he was grateful for the chance—midway through the project, Leo died after suffering a heart attack. It felt strange, Leo calling him back to the place where it all began. And just as Harry was beginning to feel some kind of positive closure on what had been a difficult time at Warner Bros., he was forced to prematurely say goodbye to yet another dear friend.

"'There but for the grace of God go you and I,'" he said to Jo in a low, defeated voice as he shared the news with her.

Harry returned to MGM after the loan-out and began working on 1950's *Pagan Love Song*, starring Howard Keel and Esther Williams. Harry would have preferred to bring in a lyricist of his choice, but this time Arthur Freed insisted he do it. Harry could hardly believe this—just before *Pagan Love Song*, Freed had wrapped *Annie Get Your Gun* and *On the Town*, and he was in pre-production on *Royal Wedding*, the third *Show Boat* adaptation, and *An American in Paris*. Harry liked *Pagan Love Song*'s title track well enough for Keel's mighty baritone voice, but they fought over Freed's suggestion to instead use a twenty-year-old song Freed had co-written with Nacio Herb Brown for Ramon Novarro to sing in *The Pagan*.

"I think you're doing this because you're too busy to write anything new!" Harry accused Arthur.

"Harry, this is a good song, and it fits this picture. Sometimes we have to compromise," Arthur said.

"You wouldn't have to compromise if you'd have let me bring in a lyricist who's strictly a lyricist and not also trying to produce every picture under the sun!" After a Gershwin tune had found its way into *The Barkleys of Broadway*, Harry was beginning to see a pattern—and it was not one he liked.

Harry got some consolation with his next assignment, *Summer Stock*, produced by Joe Pasternak, not Arthur Freed. Once again, he was free to choose a lyricist and he felt Mack Gordon would be the best match for the film. As they began working, however, it soon became difficult to watch Judy Garland struggling between good days, when she was in excellent voice, and painful days, when every note she sang seemed to have the weight of the world attached to it. On the day she was supposed to record "You Wonderful You," she couldn't sing at all—the entire orchestra was sent home.

Many weeks later, when the production had all but wrapped, Pasternak decided he wanted to record Judy performing Harold and Yip's song "Get Happy." Despite Harry's role in ushering "Get Happy" into the world twenty years earlier, the song's message was largely lost on him in this instance—not to mention the strange feeling it gave him to see Judy singing it at what was the lowest time in her life. Perhaps that's what made it so powerful. It was simply the luck of the draw that Judy recorded it on a good day, delivering what would define a classic performance—a brilliant pairing of song and performer. It proved the staying power of a song that never would have happened without Harry, but it was not enough to take the sting out of the realization that interpolating songs into his scores wasn't just a trick of Freed's, but a new reality altogether.

Like everyone in Judy Garland's orbit, Harry was awed by

her talent. He'd come to know the mercurial nature of movie stars, and with Judy he empathized deeply, given her life experiences. She'd been performing in vaudeville since childhood, she had a terribly harsh stage mother, and the executives were always manipulating her image out of concerns that she was not attractive enough, despite playing the girl next door and standing less than five feet tall. Maggie often expressed her concerns about it to the Warrens.

"I'm sure it hasn't been easy for Judy to come up alongside the other MGM stars, like Elizabeth Taylor, Ava Gardner, and Lana Turner," Harry said.

"It's terrible, Uncle Harry. L.B. loves her, but he also calls her 'his little hunchback,'" Maggie said. Josephine gasped. "Do you know what one of Daddy's friends once called me? 'Wolf child,'" she said. "He asked my father, 'What are you going to do about that wolf child, Margaret?'"

"Who? Who said that?" Harry demanded, his face reddening with anger.

"It's okay," Maggie said calmly. "I've come to terms with it. The person who said that sure can't sing like I can. And the same goes for Judy and all the terrible things people have said about her. She's the biggest moneymaker at MGM."

"Well," Harry said, calming down, "that's mighty mature of you."

Cookie came downstairs, ready to leave for a night on the town. "It was Walter Bullock who said that about Maggie," Cookie said, having heard the last part of the conversation.

Harry laughed. "I don't see that troll winning any beauty competitions!" he said.

"Tell them the story about the teeth!" Cookie said excitedly.

Maggie laughed as she recounted the story: "Judy and I were feeling incredibly grown up one day and decided to have a ladies' lunch at the Brown Derby. She was driving and she asked me to get something out of the glove box. When I opened it, it was just a mess of maps and matchbooks and menus! I told her she really needed to get rid of some of that junk and she said, 'You're right, get rid of all of it!' So I threw it out the car window into some trash cans in the alley. But a moment later, Judy panicked. 'Oh, no,' she said, 'you just threw away four hundred dollars of my teeth!' We had to get out there on our hands and knees and find those teeth so Judy wouldn't get in big trouble with L. B.!"

Harry had heard from someone in MGM's makeup department that they used prosthetic discs to reshape Judy's nose too. It seemed the indignities of Hollywood affected everyone from the biggest stars right on down to the lowly writers of script and song. During the filming of *Summer Stock,* Harry saw Judy's heartbreaking downhill slide occurring in real time.

"I love Judy—but never let her in your house," Harry once darkly joked to a friend who was visiting.

"Why not, Daddy Warren? Don't you like her singing?" Julia asked, overhearing.

"Of course, I love her singing," Harry said, embarrassed. Jo looked on, waiting to see how he was going to get out of this pickle. "But, you see, sometimes Judy takes all the aspirin and then there's none left when someone else needs one."

Jo raised an eyebrow. Luckily, Julia did not have any follow-up questions. "It's okay, she can have my aspirin," Julia said as she skipped away singing "Get Happy."

No one knew *Summer Stock* would be Garland's last film for MGM. Her struggles caused the production schedule to double, stretching into eight long, painful months. If Judy had been at a different studio, she would have been dropped much sooner, but Louis B. Mayer fought for her, trying to keep her on as long as possible. As hard as he was on her, it seemed he did have her best interests at heart.

As the film went on, Harry noted the studio showed disrespect toward Mack Gordon, whose time at Fox had ended abruptly when he failed at trying his hand at producing. Harry didn't know if this was what people were holding against him, but he did not appreciate it. If there'd been any question with the quality of work coming from Mack, Harry would have been the first to notice.

One day while Harry was on the *Summer Stock* set watching Gene Kelly perform "Dig-Dig-Dig for Your Dinner," one of MGM's seventy-five studio policemen approached him menacingly. "Mr. Mayer would like to see you in his office," the officer said.

"Can't you see I'm working here?" Harry replied, not wanting to be ordered around or strong-armed.

"Is that the message you would like me to deliver to Mr. Mayer?"

Harry got up in a huff and reluctantly followed the guard to Mayer's bungalow across the lot. He walked in and found L. B. seated behind the rounded desk in his cavernous art deco suite. As L. B. invited him in, it all felt a bit odd. Or ominous—Harry wasn't sure which. He approached the desk and sat in one of the leather guest chairs.

"I've been hearing rumors," Mayer said.

"About me? Impossible."

Mayer smiled. "That you want to quit."

Harry sighed. If the boss cared enough to call him in and have a chat, he thought, maybe he should just put all his cards on the table. "That might be the first rumor about me that happens to be true," he said.

"Is there anything I can do to change your mind?" Mayer asked.

"I've never had such bad luck as I've had with songs on this lot. It's like no one is pushing them."

"C'mon, Harry, that's an easy one," Mayer said. "All we need to do is set you up with your own publishing company, with offices on Broadway in Manhattan. How does that sound?"

"Sounds like I should have asked for it sooner," Harry said sheepishly.

"Now, is there anything else you need?" Mayer asked, sounding like he'd do anything not to lose Harry.

Harry felt like saying, "Why don't you stop calling Judy Garland your 'little hunchback,'" but he thought better of it. Maybe another time.

With the creation of Harry Warren Music Publishing,

Harry's copyright split was changed to 60 percent to MGM and 40 percent to him, a better deal than he'd had before. But he didn't realize the not-so-minor detail that the company would continue being managed by the same people who ran all the Metro subsidiaries, so pushing the songs harder wasn't likely to happen. Feeling good about the improved terms, Harry had every reason to feel he'd reached a new level of success. And while it was true, he was receiving a greater share percentage-wise, once L. B. left the studio, something else changed. Harry Warren Music was released, and Harry was powerless to stop MGM from ransacking his catalog to get its their first pick of his songs, none of which were split copyrights. He blamed Johnny Green, the head of the music department. There was something between the two that Harry remained reluctant to discuss, even years later.

He slammed the contract on his desk and cursed the day he signed it. "This goddamn megillah," he shouted, Yiddish for something long and complicated. "How can they do this?" he asked Jo.

"I'm sure all the wording is cleverly buried in there some-where," she said.

"Now they want me to go to New York for some meeting. Why should I bother? L. B.'s out. So why should I care? They pillaged my catalog and now I'm the bad guy?"

"We don't want them to have anything else to hold over you," she reasoned.

After Harry flew to New York to meet with the MGM lawyers, he called Jo to give her the report: "They're claiming Harry Warren Publishing lost one hundred fifty thousand dollars. I said, 'Well, I'm not Harry Warren Publishing. I'm just Harry Warren. What do you want me to do about it?'"

"How is that possible? I don't even believe that," Jo said.

"And the head guy, you shoulda seen him. Big heater in his mouth, all puffed up like he's a Supreme Court justice, and he says, 'What are we supposed to tell our stockholders?' I said, 'I don't know. Maybe whatever it is you tell them when you lose a million on one picture.'"

Harry had never been happier to leave New York and get back to Los Angeles.

Instead of Harry choosing a lyricist for his next project, like he had been doing, the studio paired him with Dorothy Fields, one of the few immensely successful female songwriters of the time. The film was 1951's *Texas Carnival*, starring Red Skelton and Esther Williams, doing one of her famous water ballet sequences. Of Dorothy's many hit writing credits, she'd done "On the Sunny Side of the Street" and "Exactly Like You" with Jimmy McHugh, and even more notably, "The Way You Look Tonight" with Jerome Kern, earning them Best Song at the 1936 Academy Awards. Harry was impressed with her track record, but he was unsure how it would be to work with a female partner. The first time she called him at 7:00 a.m., he didn't find the prospects very promising.

"Dorothy, I don't even go to sleep until two or three a.m.," Harry said.

"C'mon, now! Up and at 'em. Get down to the studio and let's get to work!" she chirped.

"Now, wait just a minute. We're partners. I don't take orders from you."

"Well, maybe you should!"

Harry hung up the phone and wished Jerry were still alive so he could ask how he survived working with this insufferable woman. Things did not improve when Dorothy would harass Harry about why he was living in Los Angeles.

"There's nothing for you here," she said. "Why are you wasting your time in Hollywood? You need to get back to New York to write for the theater."

He didn't know if she realized how sensitive this subject was for him, but she returned to it almost every time they were together. He felt he'd just begun making his peace with the whole thing, and she was throwing salt in the wound. They wrote many songs together, but only four ended up being used in *Texas Carnival.*

Harry gave one of their songs to Helmy Kresa, the copyist for the production who also happened to be Irving Berlin's musical secretary. When Harry got it back from Helmy, it had been reharmonized, meaning a significant amount of work had been done to it—work that required several creative choices. With a song's basic melody, there are almost endless possibilities for how to harmonize the accompanying chords and varying levels of complexity. Harry was much more an author of his own music and never actively invited this amount of change. Arranging was one thing, and the arrangements Hollywood orchestrators did on Harry's songs were based on more complete sketches Harry turned in.

Harry was quite uncomfortable with the level of work Helmy had done to "Carnival," and he told him so. "Helmy, that's not how I work," he said. "I know you do this kind of thing for Irving all the time, but not for me. Understand?"

It didn't take long for this comment to get back to Irving, who was furious. He called Harry steaming mad. "How dare you insinuate that I let my secretary reharmonize my songs?" he said.

"Irving, it's all right," Harry said, soothing him. "Everyone knows how you work. You have a modified piano, for chrissakes. You still write damn good songs, so don't worry about it!"

Irving was so incensed, he soon called again to accuse Harry of using part of one of his songs in his own music.

"Which song would that be, Irving?" Harry asked.

"The one I'm working on now!" Irving barked.

"You're lucky Arlen still puts up with you, or you might not have a friend in the world. You hummed an entire symphony to your copyist to have it written out. A symphony!" Harry said before slamming down the phone.

Harry went over to Ira's, still shaken up by Irving's latest accusation. "Nothing we do or say will ever change that man," Harry said.

"I heard a funny thing from Harold about him recently," Ira said. "People started noticing a young man who'd been traveling everywhere with Irving. Like a shadow, you never saw Irving without him. No one knew who he was or what he did for the longest time."

Ira loved dramatic pauses, but Harry couldn't take the suspense. "*And?*" he asked.

"It's his barber! That's how he keeps his hair so black. Who else have you ever known whose hair gets blacker the older they get?"

Harry howled. "Remember when Edgar Leslie said, 'his hair gets blacker while his face gets grayer'?"

As they recovered from their fit of laughter, Ira asked about things at Metro.

Harry dabbed at the tears of laughter in his eyes. "Same old stuff with Freed," he said. "The guy just can't help himself from wanting to do everything. He's spread way too thin again and I think it's beginning to show. The other day I thought, hey, maybe I can take advantage of this mania and tell him an idea I have for a movie."

"Really? Good for you! What's the idea?"

"The life of Jacques Offenbach, the father of cancan music," Harry said. "He was a prodigy, composing complex original work at age eight. The most brilliant composer of light opera of his day. He was the son of a synagogue cantor, just like Harold. He didn't get into writing for burlesque until much later in life. He made cancan respectable and, of course, that is all he's remembered for."

"And for his opera *The Tales of Hoffmann*," Ira added. "Sounds like you relate to this character somehow?"

"Maybe I do," Harry agreed. "The movie would be set in Paris—it could be cinematic and wonderful. Freed wasn't impressed when I told him about it, but they've made movies out of worse subjects!"

Later, Harry became suspicious when many of the ideas in his pitch for the Offenbach story showed up in *An American in Paris*, produced by Arthur Freed. Of course, he couldn't prove anything, but it made him feel unappreciated at best and ripped off at worst. All he could do was move on to his next project, *The Belle of New York*, starring Fred Astaire, who had not made a film in two years. Astaire had turned Freed down once on this film adaptation, seeing it as an old-fashioned holdover stock piece from the last century. But when Freed approached Astaire with the idea again after his two years of not working with the promise of a new score by Harry Warren and Johnny Mercer, Astaire changed his tune and signed on immediately. Despite the material's dated feeling, it called for a big score, and he and Johnny enjoyed being on payroll for twenty-four weeks. The longer it dragged on, the more they hoped for continued production problems, as long as the checks kept coming.

When Harry started on his next picture, *Skirts Ahoy*, he didn't realize it would be his last film for MGM. A military-themed picture about three women who join the Navy to escape problems at home, Harry called on lyricist Ralph Blane, who'd written "Have Yourself a Merry Little Christmas" and "The Trolley Song" for Judy Garland. The film needed several marches, and Harry conveniently loved writing marching band music. But the story didn't quite hold together, so once again producer Joe Pasternak tried to pull a rabbit out of a hat. He added the old vaudeville song "Oh, By Jingo!" as a number for Debbie Reynolds and Bobby Van to sing for the troops. The problem was that he didn't bother consulting Harry, who chafed once again at the interpolation. He vociferously objected—to no avail.

It was time to accept this was now business as usual with Metro, Harry realized as he discussed upcoming projects with them. None came to be, so Harry and the studio agreed to end his contract.

The little terror of television was bringing song and dance shows into people's living rooms on a nightly basis, and another era of the Hollywood movie musical had come and gone. Once again, Harry had contributed some of the best and most enduring songs of the era.

Walking across the lot one day, he bumped into the young composer André Previn, who greeted him warmly and said, "I'm going to make an album of your songs."

Harry thanked the musical savant, but he didn't know if it was all lip service—until the record finally released in 1952 on RCA Victor. Harry was impressed with the arrangements and the brilliant piano playing.

Harry had grown increasingly concerned about the degree of Harold's drinking after he had been found passed out on the lawns of Beverly Hills on more than one occasion. Things came to a head when police showed up at the Arlen residence to report that Harold's car had been left at the Los Angeles airport. Harry's nerves frayed—he recognized Harold was in a downward spiral. Harold's family braced for the worst as his brother Jerry searched for him. Three days went by until finally a call came from

Hawaii. Apparently, Harold had gone from a bar to the airport with the intention of flying to New York, but somehow boarded a flight in the other direction.

Harry knew this was related to Harold's excessive drinking, which had grown worse after Anya's psychiatrist told him she needed to be institutionalized because she'd become a danger to herself and others. While Harold couldn't disagree, having been on the receiving end of her violent rages, he could not bring himself to do it. Instead, his brother Jerry drove Anya to the facility in Malibu. After a few days of imagining his beloved in this environment, Harold went to sign her out. This became a pattern that went on for some time.

At this time in early 1952, Harold had also written about forty songs for five films, with none breaking out. Harry was long overdue for a vacation and knowing what a difficult time Harold had been having, he thought now was a good time to take their wives on a European holiday. He extended the invitation to their mutual lifelong friend Buddy Morris and his wife, Carolyn, as well.

Harry was excited to spend a good part of the trip in the land of his ancestors. Anya ended up having the best time of anyone. Being away from Hollywood, spending time with Jo and Carolyn, atypical Beverly Hills showbiz wives, and listening to Harry speak Italian and crack jokes was what the doctors back home had not been able to provide. The journey took them through London, Paris, Rome, Naples, and Pompeii. The friends reminisced about times from their early days in New York, when Anya was a chorus girl and Breck shampoo model, and when Harry had first brought Harold to the Remick office to work with Ted Koehler, where he first met Buddy.

"You've always had so much in common with Harold," Anya said to Harry.

"Handsome, pretty good songwriter, great golfer . . ." Harry joked.

"Yes," Anya laughed, "but also because you both dropped out of school at an early age and ended up becoming voracious readers. You're always reading several books at once." Harold nodded, beaming at Anya, who seemed back to her old self. "And look at all you've accomplished," Anya said. "You're cultured men of the world—a couple of high school dropouts!"

Josephine raised her glass. "To high school dropouts!" she said.

They clanged their glasses and savored several bottles of champagne.

Restorative as the vacation was, Anya took a dark turn when they returned home. Her psychiatrist suggested in the strongest terms yet to put her back in the Malibu sanatorium, where she stayed for the next six years.

Meanwhile, there was plenty more playing on television these days than just a lady painting celebrity faces on eggs. It was as though the invention of television had been timed with Harry spending more time at home by his post at the pool. He'd become obsessed with everyone learning how to float just in case he or any of them were ever shipwrecked.

One afternoon when Frank Sinatra came on the radio, Julia

made an important announcement: "Daddy Warren, it's one of your songs!"

It was Sinatra's recording of "You're Getting to be a Habit with Me." When Sinatra first started out in Hollywood, he could sometimes be found at the Warren house. Ol' Blue Eyes knew a great songwriter, even back then. But as the singer rose in status, Harry could no longer stomach Sinatra's expansive ego and ever-growing entourage.

Harry shouted, "Well, for cryin' out loud, turn it up, would you?!"

As Julia went to adjust the volume knob, Josephine turned to her. "Promise me you'll never marry an Italian," she said.

Chapter Thirteen

THIS IS YOUR LIFE

The phone rang early one morning, especially for someone who doesn't go to sleep until hours after midnight. As Harry picked up the receiver, the bedside clock read 6:00 a.m.

"Hello?" he said, rubbing his eyes. When he heard the voice on the other end of the line, he felt a twinge of disbelief.

"Harry, are you working?" the voice said.

He felt like saying, "Right now? I'm sleeping!" But it was Bing Crosby. For a split second, Harry thought it might have been a prank, even though most of his fellow pranksters were now gone. "No, I'm not. Is that getting around?" Harry joked.

"How would you like to do a Paramount picture with me?" Bing asked. "It's called *Famous*. I'll be playing a Broadway producer who's been so focused on his career and success that he doesn't realize it's largely been at the expense of his relationship with his children."

Harry felt a lump in his throat. This hit home. He was speechless for a moment and grateful when Bing filled the silence. "Natalie Wood is set to play my daughter and Robert Arthur, the son," Bing continued. "Ethel Barrymore plays a headmistress, and my love interest will be Jane Wyman. Top-notch cast and truly fine script. I can't think of anyone better to write the score."

This was the first time a star had ever reached out to Harry to personally offer him a job. As flattered as he was, he also sensed the shifts in the business happening beneath him; he knew he wasn't going to have a contract with Paramount, but he had to wonder if it really mattered anymore. Those days seemed to be over for nearly everyone except the biggest stars, who held all the power. He agreed to do the film.

Driving under the iconic double arches at the entrance of Paramount Pictures for his first meeting with Bing, Harry drew a deep breath and sighed. He marveled at it all, contemplating the fact that this was the last of the four major studios he hadn't yet conquered, not counting his very first Hollywood assignment for the Gary Cooper film *The Wolf Song,* for which he wrote "Mi Amado." He was gleeful at the chance to finally work on a full Paramount picture and vowed to keep himself nimble in the fast-changing environment, whatever it took.

Harry found his way to the production office, where Bing greeted him like an old friend. Elliot Nugent, the director, would be joining them soon. "Have you given any thought to who you'd like as your lyricist?" Bing asked in the meantime.

"Johnny Mercer would be a great choice for the material," Harry said. "There's really no one better right now, which is probably why he's tied up on so many other things."

"What about Leo Robin?" Bing asked. "He has a long

history here at Paramount and I know you two worked together on *The Gang's All Here* at Twentieth."

Harry agreed they would make a good pair on the film. When Bing told him the score would be big, requiring at least ten songs or more, Harry said, "Then Leo and I better get to work!"

"Fantastic," Bing said. "I'll have Hal get in touch to finalize the deal."

This stopped Harry in his tracks. "Hal?"

"Wallis. You two have a history?" Bing asked, seeing Harry's unenthused face.

"If you call being a thorn in someone's side for seven years 'a history,' then yes," Harry laughed. "We were at Warner Brothers together all that time. He used to think it didn't matter if the actors weren't singing the right lyrics! I never got over that."

"I can assure you that's not how things are done here. Not to worry, you just work your magic. That's what I'm hiring you for." Then Bing leaned in and whispered conspiratorially, "There are dozens of Hal Wallises in the world. There's only one Harry Warren." Harry smiled. "That reminds me of one of my favorite songs of yours—'There Will Never Be Another You," Bing said brightly.

"Ah, that's one of my favorites too. *Iceland* was a tough picture to work on, though. That was a pigpen, that picture," Harry laughed.

Bing got a kick out of Harry's characterization of a challenging project. It wasn't every day Harry was fawned over by a star as beloved as Bing Crosby, and Harry was trying to let himself enjoy it.

It took no time at all for Harry and Leo Robin to establish an easy rhythm working together. Harry found Leo a joy to write with, and as much as he viewed humility—rare in their line of work—he thought Leo was almost too modest at times, especially for the guy who wrote the Oscar-winning "Thanks for the Memory."

"You know what you are, Leo?" Harry asked him one day. "The Mary Pickford of composers."

Leo laughed. "How do you figure?"

"You never take a bow for anything. You're supremely talented without any of the other nonsense."

"Well, that's kind of you to say," Leo said. "I think we've got a great batch of songs here. And by the way, Harry? I could say the same about you. Bing's going to love 'Zing a Little Zong.'"

Leo was referring to an upbeat song that turned all the S-words into Z-words. It was written as a duet for Crosby and his costar Jane Wyman, whom Harry also thought was tops. The song would earn the songwriting team an Oscar nomination.

"Jane is a good skate," Harry said. "I don't understand why she hasn't been given more opportunities to sing. She has a sweet voice."

"She's going to shine in this," Leo agreed.

Harry and Leo played their songs for *Famous* for Bing over a couple days. Harry enjoyed tapping into his love of Latin rhythms once again to write "The Maiden of Guadalupe" for Bing, who had previous success with Latin numbers. Bing signed off on each and every one of their songs—it was the smoothest process Harry had ever experienced on a film. He couldn't help but see the irony of Hal Wallis being down the hall all the while. Harry remembered the days at Warner Bros. when he and Al were forced to hold back songs to make sure they wouldn't be rejected for no good reason.

While Harry and Leo were on set one day, Bing approached them excitedly. He told them the Andrews Sisters were going to record two of the songs for the Decca Records soundtrack album. Bing had a longstanding working relationship with the sisters, going back to the war years. Getting them on the soundtrack was a coup and it wouldn't matter that they weren't in the movie—people who didn't see it would still want to buy the record.

"Now, that's how you push a song," Harry said.

Bing was called over by the director and Harry and Leo smiled at one another. Bing turned back to them. "Oh, and by the way, the name of the picture's been changed. It's now *Just for You.*"

Harry and Leo traded a shrug, not sure whether it was an improvement and knowing it wasn't for them to say.

Title aside, *Just for You* was a smart, funny film that was well-received at the box office. This made for an auspicious beginning at Paramount for Harry. That he did not have his own contract didn't seem to be affecting him negatively, especially considering another big star was waiting in the wings with his eye on Harry's talents. Jerry Lewis was one of the heavy hitters at the time who *did* have a contract with the studio. A true force of nature, he'd been an enormous fan of Harry's for years and requested a meeting with him about his upcoming film, *The Caddy*. Harry was immediately bowled over by the lanky lad's sheer energy.

"Harry Warren in the flesh! Is it really you?" Jerry shouted when they met.

"Is this picture of yours really a musical about golf? How'd I get so lucky?" Harry joked.

"Oh, it's hilarious. You're gonna love it. If you do it! You do want to do it, don't you? Don't go and disappoint me now!"

"Sure, I want to do it!" Harry said.

"Oh, good!" Jerry chirped. "Now that *that's* out of the way—I know you just finished a film with Leo Robin, but I'd like you to try out Jack Brooks for this one. Whattya say? It's not gonna be a deal breaker for you, is it?"

"Jack Brooks?" Harry asked. "I think he was brought in to work on an additional song for *Summer Stock* at Metro after I was already off the picture. That one didn't end too well for me." Harry laughed awkwardly.

"Oh, and I remember hearing about the problems with Judy. Poor thing. L. B. really put her through the ringer," Jerry said.

"I'm not a big fan of having other people's songs interpolated into my scores, even if they happen to be friends of mine and damn good songs," Harry said.

"I don't blame you! I wouldn't appreciate that one iota either. So, here's the deal. Why don't you give Brooks a try, and if you're not happy with him, we'll do the old switcharoo?"

Harry agreed. By the time the meeting was over, he felt like he needed a nap.

Having the option to replace the lyricist put Harry's mind at ease, but as it turned out, there was no need for concern. In Jack Brooks, Harry found his next partner for years to come. Just like with all his previous studio associations, he and Brooks would become the top songwriting team on the lot. They seamlessly wrote six songs for *The Caddy*. Even when a scene featuring a big Italian family dinner called for an traditional Italian song, they were in lockstep about writing a new tune that sounded like it was from the old days. They talked Jerry and Dean Martin, the stars of the film, into letting them have a shot at this. "No one's going to know an old Italian folk song, anyway," Harry reasoned.

Jack's first title for it was "Sorrento," but Harry knew it needed something catchier. "Something with more of an Italian flavor," he told Jack. "How about, 'That's Amore'?"

Jack nodded as he let the ring of it sink in. "Yes! I like that."

The new title quickly became the song's entire hook.

Working on a Jerry Lewis and Dean Martin picture was unlike anything Harry had ever experienced. He saw the ways in which the two were inextricably linked—a marriage of sorts that came with all the requisite ups and downs and partial loss of identity as individuals. Keen to pick up on the feelings of others, Harry sensed the subtle strain between them early on and often watched Dean retreat to his dressing room for long periods of time. Harry imagined it wasn't easy being partners with Jerry, who had a way of draining the oxygen out of a room.

He could also relate to Dean's discomfort with Jerry's more disingenuous side, like when Jerry hosted his traditional luncheon at the beginning of the film, telling everyone on the cast and crew to bring all their best ideas because it was a team effort. Harry saw the skepticism on Dean's face at moments like these because once production was up and running, Jerry was not about to take an idea from anyone. He had an irrepressible need to do everything himself.

Harry told Jack, "It's like he has fifteen arms and forty-eight legs and nine heads. He really has to do everything, doesn't he? He knows everything and runs everything. I'm not even sure who the director is anymore."

Jack laughed. "Lucky for us, he doesn't interfere with the music," he said.

As they watched the filming of one scene in which Jerry literally could not stand still, Harry cocked his head and said, "I think the only thing that could stop him might be an elephant gun."

Just then, a young man holding a script walked up to the two of them. "Harry Warren? I wanted to introduce myself. You knew my mother," the lad said. "Years ago back in New York. Belle Baker?"

Harry was shocked. "The great vaudeville performer?" The young man nodded. "Wait a minute, you're Herbie?"

He laughed. "Herb Baker, yes."

"I think I still have the scars from when you used to ram me with your tricycle when I'd go to your mother's apartment to plug songs." Harry fell out laughing.

"I'm sorry about that!" Herb said bashfully.

"What are you doing on this picture?" Harry asked.

"I wrote it."

"Well, I'll be damned. Good for you, Herbie!" Harry cheered.

As it turned out, there was something that *could* stop Jerry short of an elephant gun: a dangerously high fever, requiring three weeks of hospitalization and bringing production to a standstill. Meanwhile, Dean Martin began grumbling about recording "That's Amore." Born Dino Crocetti, he had worked hard to shed any stereotypical Italian image he thought could be detrimental to his career, and he felt this song could potentially set him back years in those efforts. The fact that he was contractually obligated to record it for the movie soundtrack saved him from himself when it went on to become his first million-copy record ever sold.

"That'll teach you to try to hide your Italian heritage!" Harry told Dean.

"That's Amore" quickly became seen as a shoo-in for the Oscars, until Sammy Fain and Paul Webster started advertising heir Doris Day song "Secret Love," which ended up nosing it out. Harry lost respect for the Academy all over again, just after rejoining it after being away for five years.

"You're supposed to be honored. You're not supposed to go around advertising," he told Josephine.

"I know, I know. But I really like going to the Academy to see all the films," she reminded him, with a cheeky wink.

While dining out with the family at Lawry's in Beverly Hills one Sunday evening, Julia was the first to notice one of Harry's songs being played in the restaurant. "Daddy Warren, it's 'Nagasaki'!" she said.

Harry listened intently. "Good ear. Someone told me Oscar Peterson wanted to record it. Now *that's* a piano player," Harry said.

"You're so hep," she teased. "Why did you ever write a song about Nagasaki anyway?"

"We were all writing songs about faraway places we'd never been to back then. I don't know why!"

Harry was tickled that a song he'd written in 1928 was making a comeback twenty-five years later. Gazing across the room, he spotted a group of studio people from Paramount. Feeling expansive, he thought he should go say hello. He excused himself from the table as Josephine shot a look to the rest of the family.

"For someone who says he doesn't like to socialize, he sure knows how to work a room," she laughed.

"To Daddy Warren," Julia said, raising her glass. No one adored Harry more than his granddaughter.

Harry always liked to say he'd never been to a Hollywood party, but that was not entirely true. Likewise, he often said he wasn't a schmoozer, but the truth was, he just wasn't ready to be a retired person. It had been many months since he'd finished work on *The Caddy* and he wanted to line up another job. When someone had recently referred to him as a sexagenarian, he told his friends it scared the hell out of him.

"Unless they meant it as some kind of compliment," he joked to Harold and Ira.

"You're not sexy—you're sexa!" Ira laughed.

Harry was thrilled to see Ira and Harold working together again on a film: *A Star Is Born*, starring Judy Garland, a remake of the 1937 original. As was the songwriters' custom, they spent afternoons playing works in progress for each other, taking breaks for sandwiches and cigars.

"I got a call out of the blue from Alan Lerner," Harry told them one day. "He asked about us writing together. Sounds like there may be an impending breakup with Loewe." Alan Jay Lerner and Frederick Loewe were the team behind the Broadway shows *My Fair Lady*, *Brigadoon*, *Paint Your Wagon*, *Camelot*, and *The Little Prince*. So far, they had worked on the film adaptations of two of them.

"Would it be for Broadway or film?" Harold asked.

"I'm not sure. Guess we'll have to see. I'm not quite ready to be put out to pasture," he lamented.

It was ironic that Harry used this ranch metaphor when dreaming up his next job. While it may not have been exactly the assignment he was envisioning, he was delighted to be asked to write the theme song for the television show *The Life and Legend of Wyatt Earp*. Harry's song is almost hymn-like, seemingly rooted in church music more than country western, with a strong sing-along quality. By 1955, Harry was beginning to understand how much television was affecting peoples' lives and changing how they consumed their entertainment. He had to admit it was gratifying to hear his theme song ring through his television (now with great reception!) every week.

One day, Harry's brother Charlie, who had worked off and on promoting Harry's songs over the years, called to tell him the extraordinary vocalist Nat King Cole was going to record "There Will Never Be Another You." When Cole scored a big hit with it, it was musical redemption for Harry after what had happened with the song originally on *Iceland*. It gave him a renewed appreciation for how his music endured, as this seemed to be happening with more frequency. It was an unexpected joy to watch many of his songs be introduced to a new generation. The following year, he and Jo moved into a house on Sunset Boulevard—their largest and most elegant yet.

Eighteen months passed before Jerry Lewis called on Harry's services again. His next picture with Dean Martin was going to be *Artists and Models*, starring Shirley MacLaine and Eva Gabor. The film was about an artist and a writer, played by Jerry and Dean respectively, living a hand-to-mouth existence in New York City. It was something Harry related to, especially the bit about eating beans for dinner every night. The characters' luck turns around when Jerry begins sleep-talking, describing fantastical tales that Dean's character steals and sells to a publisher. Despite plagiarizing his best friend's dreams, he shares the spoils with Jerry's character and the two enjoy the good life.

The film's breakout song, "Innamorata," meaning

"sweetheart" in Italian, was another hit for Dean. *Artists and Models* was the sixteenth film of Lewis and Martin, who had been turning them out feverishly. Harry went to all the recording sessions and was encouraged to see real-life jocularity between the pair, but something was amiss. Between Jerry's manic energy and Dean's subdued nature, they could not be more different.

While the duo figured out their next movie, Paramount asked Harry and Jack Brooks to contribute a song for the upcoming film *The Rose Tattoo.* It too had an Italian flavor, featuring a character played by Anna Magnani who was being pursued by Burt Lancaster's character. While Harry and Jack's song did not end up in the film, it was made popular when Perry Como and Percy Faith each recorded it.

Harry, who had long despised interpolation, understood the objections of the film's composer on *The Rose Tattoo,* but now that the shoe was on the other foot, he understood the need to do it sometimes—not to mention that most assignments available to him now were theme songs, because musicals were no longer being made.

Soon, Harry's neighbor Harold Hecht asked him to write a theme song for an upcoming 1955 film. Hecht was producing *Marty,* written by Paddy Chayefsky and based on Chayefsky's original television script. Harry felt theme songs were taking over every movie, but this was another test of his ability to adapt if he wanted to continue to work. There was no doubt in his mind that *Marty* would be a fine film, despite it being low-budget—and he was proven right when Ernest Borgnine went on to win an Oscar for his portrayal of Marty.

All throughout Harry's Hollywood career, he'd been approached to write for Broadway—his first love, which had never waned. The problem was, he hadn't been available until 1953, when he agreed to work on some songs for a show called *Shangri-La*, based on the James Hilton novel *Lost Horizon*. Hilton had come to Harry's home to work with him and the playwright-lyricists on a few occasions, but the author passed away before much was accomplished. The writers and Harry agreed to carry on with the project and made slow progress on it. Then, in 1956, after a preview in Philadelphia at which Harry began to see the problems with the show, it opened in New York.

"As an audition, it's charming," he told his partners. "The intimacy of the room where someone is telling the story is lovely and it pulls you in. But something has been lost with the big sets and larger stage. I'm afraid a lot of the appeal is gone."

Whether or not they agreed with him, the show went on to open in New York on June 13 in the midst of an oppressive heatwave and a subway strike. After the jubilation Harry felt working on a Broadway show again, despite the fits and starts, he was gravely disappointed when the show closed after a three-week run.

Back in Los Angeles, another project was waiting. One of Harry's favorite directors in the business, Leo McCarey, wanted Harry for a film he was doing with Twentieth Century Fox. As Harry discussed it with Leo, he wondered if what Leo was about to embark on had been done before.

"Has anyone ever remade their *own* film?" Harry asked.

McCarey chuckled. "You know, I'm not sure. It could be a first. It's been almost twenty years since the first one. Why should you be the only one to enjoy a resurgence of your works?"

Harry enjoyed McCarey's company and humor. As a fellow Catholic, Leo liked depicting church sequences in his films, as well as children singing onscreen. He'd identified a couple scenes for songs to feature this. Harry considered himself a lapsed Catholic, especially compared to the devout McCarey, but he liked working with someone who shared his faith and lived it. McCarey exuded warmth, class, and a tremendous respect for music and those who created it.

McCarey's original film, *Love Affair*, had to be retitled *An Affair to Remember* as part of the deal between Twentieth Century Fox purchasing the property from Columbia. McCarey didn't learn about the requirement for the title change until after Harry and lyricist Harold Adamson had finished their song. It took quite a bit of doing to rewrite it to fit the new words. Harry felt good about the film's prospects given Cary Grant and Deborah Kerr's star power, and he dug deep for the song, writing twenty-five attempts before landing on *the one*.

"I knew I had to get some sort of melody that would sound good with the old lady playing it on the piano, one that would sound almost classical," he said.

It struck just the right chord—and it would be Harry's last hit.

~

During the production for *An Affair to Remember*, Harry became friends with Vic Damone, who performed the theme song over the opening credits. Despite their twenty-five-year age difference, Harry and Vic were both from Brooklyn and the sons of Italian immigrants. They'd grown up singing in church, and they shared a love of horse racing—both had memberships at the two turf clubs in town, Hollywood Park and Santa Anita. Vic would show up to Harry's house in a black limousine to pick up the family, all dressed up for the track. Julia always joked that she learned to read on the Racing Form, but Harry felt like he'd barely blinked, and she'd become a teenager. It would break her up whenever Vic sang Harry's song "Jeepers Creepers" to make the horse he had bet on run faster—the way it worked in the movie *Going Places*, when Louis Armstrong sang and played it on his trumpet. As fellow Italians, Harry and Vic also shared a respect and healthy fear of organized crime. When they'd kid around about the "Calabrian code of ethics," Julia would ask what that they were talking about and they'd quickly change the subject.

One of the first people to rush to record "An Affair to Remember" was Nat King Cole. Shortly after he put his record out, Cole asked Harry to appear on *The Nat King Cole Show*. A charming but short-lived series in rich black-and-white, filmed before a live studio audience, the episode featuring Harry begins with Cole introducing him and performing "Lullaby of Broadway." Cole tells the audience about many of Harry's other hits before performing "September in the Rain," one of Cole's favorites. Cole's reverence for Harry and his body of work comes through on the broadcast and it's clear Harry has fun being shuffled from set to set for each song, even showing a flair for comedic timing as he and Cole mime taking an elevator up to where a piano and the Randy Van Horn singers are waiting to perform "We're in the Money." Cole invites Harry to accompany them on piano and joins in for "With Plenty of Money and You." Cole then motions toward the three Oscars as he tells the audience the songs Harry won them for, setting up his introduction to "You'll Never Know." To close the show, Cole says, "By the way, our theme was based on 'The Shadow Waltz,' which also happened to be written by Harry Warren."

Another positive aspect of the little beast of television was its incredible reach, bringing Harry's music into millions of homes across the country. It was a pleasure for Harry to do *The Nat King Cole Show* and hear his songs in Cole's liquid velvet voice.

But one morning sometime later, Harry was horrified when he opened the paper. "Why are people such animals?" he shouted.

He startled Jo, who nearly spilled her coffee. "They put a burning cross in Nat's front yard," he explained, still reading the article. "And someone poisoned his dog?" Where do they think we are, Mississippi?" He slammed the paper down.

The racial tension on display in other parts of the country always seemed out of place in Los Angeles, a major melting pot. Harry tried hard to rationalize that the people who did such heinous things were simply acting out of fear and had never known anyone different than them. He remembered when his mother had first told him as a young boy how many people were prejudiced toward Italians and that he should never let anyone change the pride he had in himself.

What Harry had seen coming for a while finally came to pass in 1956, when Jerry Lewis and Dean Martin announced they were going their separate ways—ten years to the day they'd become a team. The next project Jerry came to Harry about was *Rock-A-Bye Baby*. The film marked a more serious turn for Lewis, who wanted to show the public he could deliver a song without the yuks. Despite his respectable singing voice, it would make for a tricky transition from slapstick to a more reserved role, in which he cared for the triplets of a recent widow and the movie star who was his childhood sweetheart. This project marked Harry's first time working with lyricist Sammy Cahn, with whom he was incredibly impressed. Harry marveled at the speed and ease with which Sammy worked, preferring to stay in a room and work with Harry, unlike most other lyricists, who went off on their own. Though none of the songs they wrote had a life beyond the movie, Harry's favorite was "Dormi, Dormi, Dormi," the old Italian-style lullaby duet written for Lewis and the father of the woman he loves, played by former opera star Salvatore Baccaloni.

As Harry hummed this tune while making himself a sandwich one afternoon, he received an eerie phone call. He inspected a few pepperoncini he'd pulled from a jar as he listened for the voice on the other end of the line.

"Hello. Is Sonny there?" someone asked.

Harry felt like he'd had the wind knocked out of him. "Did you say Sonny?"

"Yes, Sonny Warren."

"Who is this?" Harry demanded. It had been thirty years since Sonny's death. "I said, who is this?"

The caller hung up as Jo walked into the kitchen. When she asked who had called, Harry told her it was a wrong number.

The following day on the golf course, he mentioned the strange call to Harold and Ira. "What do you think? Was it a sign from God?" Harry asked.

"Perhaps," Harold said, always seeing the mystical side of things.

"It could have been purely innocent," Ira offered. "Maybe someone Sonny knew as a kid who didn't realize he'd passed."

"Well, it got me thinking, that's for sure," Harry said as he picked out a club. "About the need to atone. I know that's something Jews get to do formally once a year. It's missing in my faith, if you ask me."

"Isn't that what confession is for?" Harold asked.

"No, it's not the same. I go in, I tell one guy my sins, and he sends me off to say a few Hail Marys. I say enough Hail Marys. I need to *do* something." He held up a club to examine it, frowned, then put it back. "I promised Miss Schneider I would always make sure God knew I was grateful for the gift of music, and to humble myself before him. But I haven't done that. I must write a Mass, as a gift to the church. And it must be in Latin."

Harry located the club he was looking for and walked out on the green to hit his ball. Ira turned to Harold. "Who's Miss Schneider?" he asked.

~

As Harry got to work writing his Mass, his old pal Chummy MacGregor called one afternoon. Chummy used to play piano in Glenn Miller's band and was now Bing Crosby's housemate.

"What are you doing next Wednesday?" Chum asked. "Say 'nothing.'"

Harry laughed. "What on earth are you up to this time, Chum?"

"It's a surprise. I'll pick you up at one p.m. on Wednesday," he said. "I'll give you a hint. It has to do with a Harry Warren tribute . . . record."

When Chummy picked Harry up, he was in high spirits but Harry thought he seemed to have more nervous energy than usual. As Harry got in the car, Chummy told him they had a little time before they had to get to where they were going. He suggested they get a drink.

"What the hell is going on, Chum?"

"Are you gonna try to tell me you don't enjoy a midday drink once in a while?"

They went to a Hollywood bar, and Harry grew even more concerned over what this could be about. Looking around at all the barflies, he joked to Chummy, "Did you bring me here to show me my future?"

"No," Chummy said, laughing, "we're here because the studio is right down the street." Harry figured this was true. All the best recording studios were a stone's throw away.

Midway into their second round, Chummy looked at his watch. "Oh! We have to get going. Toss it back, Harry!"

Harry looked at him like he was nuts. Chummy was getting more nervous by the minute. "If I didn't know better, I'd think you were taking me to get whacked," Harry said as he shot a glass of whiskey.

They left the bar and headed east on Sunset, walking past several recording studios. As they were about to cross the street at Hillhurst Avenue, Harry looked up and saw the sign for ABC Television Center. The building used to be the old Vitagraph Studio of Los Angeles, starting in 1913, when the studio had two daylight film stages, production buildings, and a few exterior sets. They walked up to the gate and Chummy whispered something to the guard on duty, who let them on the lot.

"A recording session, huh?" Harry asked.

"Something like that," Chummy told him with a wink.

As they approached one of the soundstages, Harry spotted the logo of a popular television show: *This Is Your Life*. "Are we . . . ? Is this what I think it is?" he asked.

Chummy smiled. "Cat's out of the bag now!"

The stage door opened and someone with a clipboard came out to greet them. Suddenly, Harry wished he hadn't had so much to drink. The first person he saw as he entered backstage was his brother Charlie, who had split his time between New York and Los Angeles promoting Harry's songs. Harry hugged his brother for dear life and said, "Who do I have to blame for this?"

"I don't know, but it's not me!" Charlie said.

Then Harry heard the voice of the host Ralph Edwards announce his name. "Are we ready to meet the man of the hour?" he asked. The studio audience cheered.

Harry walked out onstage and felt a wave of nausea wash over him. As he looked at some of the faces who'd been assembled to celebrate his life, he didn't know whether to laugh or cry.

Ruby Keeler came out and talked about her memories of *42nd Street*, riding the *Chief* out from New York to Los Angeles. "I rode to stardom on your melodies," she told Harry.

Bandleader Guy Lombardo talked about the days when Harry used to go to Chicago to write with Gus Kahn, songs such as "Here We Are" and "Where the Shy Little Violets Grow." Chicago was a big music town and Lombardo reminisced about playing at the Granada Café on the South Side, where Harry and Gus would come to see him.

Mack Gordon, Johnny Mercer, and Alice Faye all followed Lombardo, sharing similar fond memories of Harry. Then came Mack Stark, who'd published Harry's first song, "Rose of the Rio Grande." "Not many get a hit with their first published song," he said, "but I knew Harry was something special as soon as I met him. He was also the most reluctant song plugger I'd ever known. But it's that shyness that has kept him a modest man all his life."

As the whiskey swirled around the nostalgia, Harry struggled to process everything that was going on. At one point, Ralph Edwards told the audience Harry was currently writing *The Mass of St. Anthony* as a gift for the church and that, in fact, they had a gift for him too. Someone carried something out onstage draped under a sheet. As soon as it was unveiled, his heart filled like a balloon ready to burst.

"Mr. Warren, we were able to locate this original autographed musical worksheet with notes written by Puccini's own hand in 1895, while he was composing the opera *La Bohème*. Crest presents it as a gift to you." Harry teared up as he looked at the framed score that would quickly become his most prized possession. "For Mrs. Warren, there's this special gold charm bracelet by Marchal Jewelers—each charm is based on your life."

Harry was grateful Mack Gordon had been a part of the *This is Your Life* episode—Gordon died a few months later at age fifty-five. Harry thought back to when they used to audition songs at Twentieth Century Fox for Darryl Zanuck. When they'd played "I Had the Craziest Dream," Mack didn't just sing as Harry played the tune on piano but went the extra mile to add horn parts with his voice. Zanuck said, "That son of a bitch can sell me anything!"

Harry knew he should be grateful for his health and not worry about petty things like the upcoming 1959 Academy Awards. Still, he couldn't stop thinking about the fact that Jimmy Van Heusen was poised to tie Harry's record of three Oscars for Best Song if he pulled off a win for "High Hopes" in the film *A Hole in the Head*. When Van Heusen was announced as the winner, Harry was surprised to feel mixed emotions. Josephine knew what Harry was thinking without him having to say a word.

"Our envy of others devours us most of all," she reminded him. Harry raised an eyebrow, his way of agreeing.

All throughout the process of working with Jerry Lewis on *Cinderfella,* he was uncomfortable watching Jerry chase a hit on the level of "That's Amore." Harry knew he didn't want to fall into the trap of forcing anything. Like any master painter, he thought, one must know when it's one stroke too many. Jerry's film *The Ladies Man* in 1961 would be Harry's last.

Chapter Fourteen

WHEN THE LEGEND BECOMES FACT

Surrounded by family who loved him, Harry often wondered how and why he'd outlived so many of his friends and fellow songwriters. As he looked around, there was every reason to celebrate his life. He and his fellow writers of the Great American Songbook were beginning to feel the seismic shift brought about by about rock and roll, which was quickly displacing them from the charts. Johnny Mercer, for one, was very distraught about the direction music was going.

One evening in 1960, Maggie and Cookie stopped by to chat with Harry. He asked after Johnny, whom he hadn't seen in a while. He lit up with a smile when Maggie told him Johnny had been working with the composer Henry Mancini lately.

"Oh, he's doing great. Working a lot with Mancini," she said.

"Hank is wonderful," Harry said.

"They called me over to the studio one day because Johnny really wanted to know what I thought of their ballad for that Audrey Hepburn picture that's coming out," Maggie said. "It's a stellar song. Apparently, Mancini wrote it specifically for Audrey's limited range but lovely voice. Except there was this one line in the song they wanted to know what I thought of—something about a 'huckleberry friend.' I had to tell them the truth, that I found it out of place and a little distracting."

"Did they change it?" Harry asked.

"I don't know. They thanked me for my input."

At the 1961 Academy Awards, Johnny Mercer tied Harry's record for three Oscars for Best Song when he won for "Moon River," with the "huckleberry friend" line still in the song. The following year, he was the first to best Harry's record for number of Best Song Oscars for his lyrics to "Days of Wine and Roses," also written with Henry Mancini. As much as Harry's circle of songwriters all fretted about rock and roll dominating music, it seemed there was still a place for beautifully crafted songs in the hearts of American music lovers.

At brunch with Julia one Sunday in the valley, a violinist was playing "Boulevard of Broken Dreams," a song Harry wrote for the 1934 movie *Moulin Rouge,* which later became Tony Bennett's first hit record. The couple seated next to Harry and Julia were racking their brains to come up with the name of the song. Harry restrained himself from butting in as long as he could, until finally he caved in.

"It's called 'Boulevard of Broken Dreams,'" he said.

"Thank you!" the woman said, exasperated. "It was driving me crazy!"

"You're welcome," Harry smiled.

Just when Julia was about to inform the people they were

talking to the actual writer of the song, Harry placed his hand atop hers, softly shaking his head no.

"You get frustrated at feeling so invisible, don't you Daddy Warren?"

He grinned back at her sweet, adoring face. "It's not just me," he said. "Aside from the Gershwins, Cole Porter, and Berlin, no one knows who the songwriters are. On the other hand, when we go out, we don't have to worry about being trampled by rabid fans demanding autographs."

"Oh, can I have your autograph?" she teased, placing a napkin and pen in front of him.

In the mid 1960s, Harry once again celebrated the rebirth of one of his Tin Pan Alley songs when the legendary bebop pianist Thelonious Monk made "Lulu's Back in Town" famous again. Like so many of Harry's works, the song was a dream for a jazz musician, with its endless possibilities for improvisation.

While on the lot at Warner Brother's visiting an old friend in the music department, Harry ran into Alan Lerner, of Lerner and Loewe. Alan spotted Harry first and called his name, taking him by surprise. When Harry made his way over to chat, Alan told him he was on the lot shooting *My Fair Lady*. Alan had written the screenplay adaptation after the studio had paid $5 million for the film rights, an unprecedented sum at the time. "Hopefully, they won't regret it," Lerner whispered.

"So, you left Loewe, but you never called me back," Harry reminded him.

"Oh, Harry, forgive me!" Alan said, embarrassed. "I'd still

like to work together on something. This one just has all the music already written."

Harry was irritated that Lerner had forgotten he'd ever called him. On the other hand, Harry's ASCAP rating was strong, as the seventh-highest earner after Richard Rodgers, Oscar Hammerstein, George and Ira, Cole Porter, and Irving Berlin. He and Josephine had done well financially with their real estate and stocks, and Harry felt secure knowing his family would always be taken care of. Soon, he got a call from the *Los Angeles Times*, wanting to interview him as one of the most prolific composers in motion picture history. After the article's publication, Harry received a letter he never would have expected in all the days of his life. It came on official Warner Bros. Pictures letterhead:

Dear Harry,

I was very happy to read in the Los Angeles Times last Sunday, July 9, about the wonderful things you have done through the years . . . and your association with me here at the studio plus the many, many song hits as well as the people who became stars through the singing of your melodies. I just want to wish you every happiness in the years that lie ahead.

Sincerely,

Jack Warner

Harry set the letter down and laughed. When Josephine asked him what was so funny, he told her about the letter. "That tyrant," he spat. "After all these years—it's funny what time can do to people. The guy who congratulated you once you had a hit picture, then tried to cut your salary. Al and I used to say he had a tin ear. He couldn't appreciate a song unless it was first performed by a star. And the way he'd march around like a colonel with his retinue of lieutenants!"

After the *Los Angeles Times* article, Harry received lots of calls and letters venerating him. He knew one reason he wasn't working anymore was that he'd priced himself out of the market. He told the reporter from the *Times*, "As much as I love it, television has changed everything for what I used to do. That screen is just way too small for the old Hollywood musical. I'm glad I worked when I worked. In retrospect, it was a crazy, wonderful, glamorous era."

Then, just when his working days were over, Leo McCarey—who'd directed *An Affair to Remember*—wanted to do a musical with Harry based on Marco Polo. Harry loved the idea and got to work writing the songs. When Leo died in 1969 at seventy years old, the project fell apart, making it Harry's only unpublished and unperformed score.

After that, Harry could be found most days in his private quarters with crisp white sheets, surrounded by books. Against his better judgement, Los Angeles had become his forever home at some point along the way, as he succumbed to the tonic of orange blossoms and jasmine that blew in each afternoon. He'd burn frankincense and keep rosary beads nearby to pray for all the souls who'd been lost to him, as well as for his own. He hadn't been traveling much anymore, but in the spring of 1971, he and Jo went with Ira and Lee to New York for the Cleffers Hall of Fame First Annual Awards Dinner to honor ten songwriters, including Harry, Ira, Hoagy Carmichael, Sammy Cahn, and others. Ira was a loyal friend and Harry knew how blessed he was to have him in his life and still around.

A few months later, Harry found a hand-delivered letter on his doorstep. It read:

Dear Harry,

I have just read the piece you wrote about me in ASCAP Today, and I'm no longer "president of the Sweet Fella's Club." Like it or not, there's a new president and he's you, elected unanimously by me. Anyone who can say such nice things about anyone else is unquestionably the club's new guiding star. There was a time I thought of resigning in favor of Leo Robin, but I'm glad I didn't resign then. You, Harry Warren, Esq., are the new and true president of the S.F.C., and I bow low to you and, please, you are to consider me always at your service.

Much love to you and Jo.

From Lee and Ex-President Ira

The Warren home had grown quiet. Julia had married Solomon Sturges, an actor and son of film director Preston Sturges. As part of the union, Julia gained a stepdaughter named Shannon, whose mother had passed away when she was two years old. Julia adored Shannon and helped raise her even after Julia's short-lived marriage to Solomon.

Most days, Harry was content to tinker around on the piano and read books. But he developed a new appreciation for the younger generation, who showed an interest in him and his musical legacy. He was surprised to receive an interview request from one of them, a British rock musician named Ian Whitcomb.

"I hope you won't hold it against me that I'm a rock-and-roller," Whitcomb said. "I'm also a musicologist and an enormous fan of yours."

Harry agreed to the interview, set at his home in Los Angeles on Sunset Boulevard. Ian wanted to do some filming in Harry's studio as well. When he and his cameraman arrived at the Warren house, Harry immediately felt at ease, succumbing to Ian's British gentlemanly charm. Ian toted a ukulele in the hopes of playing along with Harry on some of his songs. Harry wasn't sure about this at first, until he learned that Ian was an accomplished musician. The interview consisted of Harry sitting at the piano playing the songs Ian asked about, then telling the stories behind them.

"I really love your stormy Catholic harmonies," Ian told him. "I know you grew up singing in church, so I imagine that's where that influence came from."

Harry laughed. He appreciated the Briton's ear for detail.

"Is there any current music you enjoy listening to?" Ian asked.

"These kids and all their rock and roll," Harry said. "Some of them just put a lot of words together—and most of the time they don't even rhyme—then they add some music and they call it a song. I don't know."

"Can you give me an example?" Ian asked.

Harry pushed up the sleeves of his thick cardigan sweater

and thought about it. "For instance, a guy says, 'I woke up this morning, and I wasn't feeling good. I went into the kitchen and drank some orange juice.' What the hell kind of song is that?"

"Sounds like a fairly terrible one," Ian said through a chuckle.

"They're doing country music to death," Harry added. "They sing either loud or soft and sound like cows. I'm not trying to bring back button shoes, but I just can't get with it. If I see a television show with a bunch of guys with guitars, I turn it off."

"What are you writing these days?" Ian asked.

"I'm just writing for my own amazement and amusement. A lot of piano things—not virtuoso stuff, just pretty things."

After his positive experience with Ian, Harry agreed to sit for a much longer interview—this one an oral history commissioned by the American Film Institute. It meant committing to thirteen sessions from August to November of 1972, but he didn't feel he could say no to the interviewer, who happened to be the daughter of his dear late friend Gus Kahn. He'd known Irene Kahn since the day she was born.

The final product of the interviews became a four-hundred-page tome of Harry's life, going all the way back to Brooklyn, Christmas 1893. In the oral history, he railed against studio executives who made his life difficult, as well as the perennial subject of why he was not better known.

When the conversation turned to preserving film music and history, Irene mentioned a few film buffs who'd been hunting a lost number from *A Star Is Born*. Harry made a face and waved her off.

"I don't understand. What's the big deal?" Harry asked. "I

had a lot of numbers cut out of pictures too. Nobody's looking for them, except for me. And what good is all this going to do anyway?"

"This is your life, Harry," Irene said. "Preserving history, including your history, is important. Even if you don't think so."

Next, Irene asked Harry for his thoughts on the music scene of 1972. "Mancini is good. Probably the best right now—and I'm not just saying that because he's Italian," Harry laughed. "Elmer Bernstein writes great picture music, and Johnny Mandel—he's great. But other than that, I'd rather just listen to my tapes."

It seemed Harry was always humming—until he remembered something that irked him, like his recent appearance on *The Merv Griffin Show*. Irene asked him how it went.

"I couldn't believe the first thing he asked me was my age," he said. "What's behind that kind of question? It must be, 'Look at him, he's still alive. Either that, or it's a damn good embalming job.'"

Harry postponed and rescheduled several of the thirteen sessions with Irene due to travel, film screenings, holidays, the presidential election, and the World Series. But the intrepid interviewer prevailed and did her best to get Harry to talk about sensitive subjects, even if she hadn't been able to get as much out of him as she would have liked. When all was said and done, the interviews amounted to fifteen hours of recordings.

Soon after the interviews with Irene, ASCAP contacted Harry about honoring him at a tribute show it was putting on at Lincoln Center. He'd enjoyed the last time he went to New York, and he wondered how many more times he'd be able to make the trip. Josephine had another commitment in Los Angeles, but she told him he had to go without her. Being that it was a black-tie affair, Harry arrived dressed in his finery and was looking forward to the night ahead—until he was stopped by a security guard at the event entrance.

"Excuse me, sir. This is a private event," the guard said.

"Yes, I'm aware of that," Harry said. He proceeded to try to enter, but the man stepped in front of him.

"That means it's invitation only."

Just as Harry was about to turn around and leave in disgust, a journalist recognized him and stepped in. "This is Mr. Harry Warren, who is being honored tonight. If you don't mind, I'm going to escort him to his seat," the journalist said forcefully.

Harry followed the man's lead as the guard stepped aside. Once they were in the lobby, he let off some steam. "That was a bit humiliating," he said. He told the man it reminded him of how, fifty years ago, in 1922, the Vincent Lopez Orchestra released its recording of "Rose of Rio Grande" and the label was printed without his name on it.

"It must have been a blow not to get credit on the record for your first hit song," the journalist said.

"It didn't feel great," Harry told him, "but it's kind of the story of my life." The man laughed politely, then Harry added under his breath: "And I *really* thought 'Cheek to Cheek' was going to win that one year."

"Are you referring to your first Academy Award?" the journalist asked, intrigued.

"I'm just rambling," Harry chuckled. "But I think I was the first songwriter who ever belonged to the Academy."

"Well, that would make sense because you won the first-ever Oscar for Best Song."

"I don't know. Those statuettes are just broken-down doorstops at my house," Harry said humbly—but in truth, his three Oscars were proudly displayed high on a shelf in his home studio.

Harry's emotions stirred up as he went to take his seat. He wished Josephine were by his side. Suddenly, he was flooded with memories of feeling slighted or underappreciated—it was like the opposite of his experience on *This is Your Life*. His old partner, Al Dubin, flashed in his mind. Harry remembered Al's daughter Patricia saying how much her father had a penchant for changing the details of a story to suit his audience. She had first-hand knowledge of this from when she was a little girl, knowing she could always count on her father for a good yarn.

Was this the moment Harry began to conflate nearly getting turned away at the ASCAP event with his night at the Academy Awards all those years ago, doubting the power of his life's work and legacy? Had the idea of being turned away at one's own party simply become a self-fulfilling prophecy? We may never know for certain, but given all the evidence, it is likely this was the making of a myth that would soon become accepted fact, and one that would be forever and printed in almost every article ever written about Harry Warren—the tale about being turned away at the 1935 Academy Awards. Should we concern ourselves with the minor detail that it simply wasn't true?

Chapter Fifteen

AT LAST

As Harry sat in his favorite armchair next to the piano on Christmas Eve in 1973, he couldn't quite fathom he was celebrating his eightieth Christmas Eve and eightieth birthday. As he lit a cigar someone had brought over as a gift, a private-batch Montecristo, he fixed his gaze on the small flame on the end of the match and caught a memory from his childhood home in Brooklyn—the candles his mother placed in the front windows that faced the street during Christmastime.

Certain childhood images, sounds, and smells had remained vivid to him over time. He hoped this was at least partly due to the effort he put into keeping his mother alive and active in his mind. Despite all the trials of his life and the losses he'd suffered over the years, nothing had managed to break his spirit or rob him of simple joys. He was a survivor.

He felt more energetic than he'd expected to upon making it to eighty—he just wasn't feeling terribly social at the moment. A party was going on throughout the house and he knew that if he wanted company, all he had to do was start playing the piano.

But for now, he was content in his moment of quiet reflection. Then Julia found him in the darkened room, where the only light was the warm glow of the colored lights on the tree.

"There you are!" she said, bouncing into the room. She squeezed herself into his chair and flung an arm around him, resting her head on his shoulder. They stared silently at the Christmas tree.

"I never thought I'd live so long," Harry said after a moment.

"But aren't you glad you have?" she asked with an infectious smile. "What's on your mind, Daddy?"

"I'm happy. That's all." He opened his mouth to say something else but stopped.

"And?" she asked. "Please," she pleaded when he stayed quiet. "You can tell me. I'm your—what did you call it?"

"Confidant?" he offered. She nodded. "Well, at the risk of sounding like a sappy old-timer, I just hope my songs are not forgotten after I'm gone."

She stood and put her hand on her hip. "Daddy Warren, if there's one thing I can promise you with one hundred and ten percent certainty, it's that I will *not* let that happen."

Julia kept that promise. To this day, she runs Harry's publishing company, licensing and placing his songs in popular films and high-profile ad campaigns.

"I know you weren't happy with me when I said I'd pay to send you to typing school. I didn't mean it as an insult," Harry said, regret in his voice.

"Well, it *was* a bit chauvinistic." She winked.

"You're right," he admitted. "You know you'll always be

taken care of, but I want you to have a good life—to get out and meet people. Some who aren't all part of Hollywood. It can be too small of a world, as you know." Harry was referring to Julia's new marriage to Michael Riva, a film art director who became a major production designer. Michael happened to be the grandson of Harry's neighbor, Marlene Dietrich.

"I'm creative too. I just don't know how I want to put it to use yet. Michael is encouraging me to do some set design, so we'll see," Julia said. She stood up and offered him her hand. "Now, c'mon. Let's get you back to your guests."

He took her hand and stood just as Ira walked into the room. "Can I have a turn to watch him?" Ira joked to Julia.

"Sure," she said, just as her little boy, Jean Paul, came in looking for her.

"Happy Birthday, Daddy Warren," the little one said to Harry shyly.

"Thank you, Jean Paul," Harry said. "I hope you're enjoying the party." Jean Paul shook his head up and down very fast.

Harry and Ira sat down, both content to stay out of the larger crowd.

"I've been trying to ask you all night—did you receive a gift from Irving?"

Harry looked surprised. "I wasn't aware I was getting one. We haven't always exchanged gifts in the past," he laughed.

"I don't know for certain, but I did hear he was working on a new painting," Ira confessed.

A look of horror came over Harry. "He didn't paint my portrait, did he? If it's anything like the one he did of George that looks like an alien, I'll need to hang it at your house! We can start a gallery in your garage."

The two of them chuckled and Ira raised his glass. "Happy birthday, Harry," he said. "I am forever grateful for your friendship. You've been like a brother to me. And my brother was a tough act to follow."

"To George," Harry said, lifting his stogie.

Celebration of Harry's eightieth birthday continued into the next year. In March, the American Guild of Authors and Composers held a tribute concert, bringing together some of Hollywood's finest arrangers, conductors, and musicians to perform their favorite Warren tunes. Nelson Riddle—the conductor and arranger who first shot to fame with his work on Nat King Cole's "Mona Lisa" and "Unforgettable," before going on to become Sinatra's top arranger—led an all-star big band throughout the night. Harry watched nearly forty singers take the stage. Before long, the entire place had been put in a trance by the gravity of Harry's immense body of work. To hear so much of it in one sitting was spellbinding. At the end of the evening, the dozens of performers joined together to sing "You Must Have Been a Beautiful Baby" to Harry. To cap off the night, the mayor of Beverly Hills told Harry he planned to designate a Harry Warren Day sometime over the summer. Harry chose another of his favorite Yiddish words to describe how he was feeling: *farklempt*, or choked up.

After the revelry of such a milestone birthday had settled, the years became quieter. One day, the phone rang at the Warren house. Jo answered it before Harry could. When he walked into the kitchen, she put her hand over the mouthpiece and said, "It's Lee." As Jo handed over the phone, Harry felt baffled as to why Lee might be calling him.

"Listen, Harry," she said, "I have someone very eager to meet you—if you're not too busy. I can vouch for him. You know I wouldn't send just anyone."

Lee said his name was Michael. He'd been working with Ira as his archivist for a while now, first getting his LP collection cataloged, then working on Ira's scores and lyrics to get everything in order.

"Shall I send him now?" Lee asked.

"Now? Well, okay. I'll be here," Harry told her.

When the doorbell rang, Harry met his visitor at the front gate, where he found a young man smiling broadly. It looked as though the kid could barely contain his joy.

"Mr. Warren, I've been wanting to meet you for a very long time," he said, extending his hand. "For as long as I can remember, actually! This is one of the great honors of my life. I'm Michael Feinstein."

Harry invited Michael into the house, and he followed Harry into the kitchen.

"You like salami?" Harry asked, starting to assemble a small plate of antipasto. Michael laughed and said yes. "Pepperoncini?"

"Yes, thank you," he said as Harry set the plate before him. Then Michael launched into the details of how he'd been helping

Ira archive his life's work. "I would love to do the same for you," Michael said.

"Gee, I could probably use that kind of help," Harry said. "But would you have to finish with Ira first?"

"I work at Ira's in the afternoons, but I could come here in the mornings." That sounded good to Harry, who no longer slept in as late as he used to since he stopped working.

"Say, how's Ira doing with the Bell's palsy? Such a mysterious thing," Harry said.

"He's growing a mustache to cover the drooping side of his face. I have to keep reminding him it's going to go away, even if it takes a while."

"Ira and I are a lot alike, you know, but not in all ways," Harry said. "I like gadgets. I have to have all the new gear as soon as it comes out. Ira doesn't care so much about that stuff. I tried to get him a better sound system over there."

"Wait, don't tell me," Michael said excitedly. "I think I can guess what he said. 'I don't need a stereo . . .'"

Then, at the same time, they both exclaimed the second part of Ira's refrain: "'I've got two ears!'" They laughed. It was clear they were going to get along just fine.

As promised, Michael began to work at Harry's five days a week in the mornings. Harry enjoyed his company more than he'd expected to. Michael was extremely knowledgeable and passionate about the music created before his time, and Harry felt fortunate that such a talented youngster had found his way to him. He began sharing with him the most intimate details of his life, which surprised young Michael—like when Harry made

Michael promise not to tell Jo that he'd watched an adult film in his studio.

"Video tape has changed everything," Harry told him. "Have you ever watched a film like that?"

Michael laughed. "Well, *if* I have, it probably wasn't quite the same kind." Harry looked confused. "I'm a gay man, Harry."

"Oh, sure! I knew that." At Michael's dubious expression, Harry clarified, "Well, I had my suspicions." Harry had never had an openly gay friend before, and he was suddenly feeling very modern. "We're all God's children," he said, placing a hand on Michael's shoulder. "It's no man's job to judge another. Heaven knows I don't want anyone's judgement."

One morning when Michael showed up, Harry was out of sorts. "My damn equilibrium is acting up again," Harry said.

"I didn't know you were having a problem with that," Michael said, offering to drive him to the doctor.

Harry waved him off. "It just gave me a scare when I was driving home from the golf course over in the valley yesterday. I, uh, veered off the road."

Michael looked concerned. "And this was because of your equilibrium?" he asked. "You mentioned having drinks after a round occasionally. I just don't want you to get in any trouble."

Harry quickly changed the subject and asked how Ira was doing.

"He was extremely happy yesterday, actually," Michael said, giving in. "We discovered something he'd completely forgotten about—the score for a little-known Broadway operetta he did back in 1945 based on the sculptor Benvenuto Cellini. It's called *The Firebrand of Florence*." He offered to arrange for Harry to listen to it.

"Say, do you know the Broadway producer David Merrick?" Harry asked.

"His reputation proceeds him," Michael laughed. As Harry raised an eyebrow, he explained. "He's successful but shady. He's known for outrageous publicity stunts and likes to play mind games. Someone told me he had his office painted dark red to frighten and throw people off when they come in for meetings. And he had his desk and chair custom-built higher than the guest chair so he appears to tower over the person in the other side. Weird stuff! Why do you ask?"

"Apparently, he wants to produce a stage musical of *42nd Street*," Harry said. "He wants to have lunch at the Beverly Hills Hotel Polo Lounge to talk it over."

"Are you going to meet with him?"

"I suppose I should." There was a long pause, then Harry added, "You know what Judy Garland called that place? The polio lounge. She said it's for the truly afflicted."

Michael laughed as Harry steeled himself at the thought of a business meeting—something he hadn't done in a long time.

When Harry arrived for his lunch with Merrick, he was shown to a table. He waited for half an hour, feeling more and more awkward with each passing minute. He would later find out this was one of Merrick's typical tactics. When he finally lost patience and got up to leave, he ran into Merrick, who was just coming in, at the hostess stand.

"Harry Warren?" Merrick said, sailing toward him through a crowd of beautiful Hollywood people.

"You're over a half hour late," Harry said irritably.

"My apologies. Won't you please join me?" Merrick asked.

They went to their table and ordered. While they waited for their food, Merrick launched into his pitch. "I find it amazing that no one has brought *42nd Street* to the Broadway yet," he said.

Harry agreed, sounding quite guarded. "So, what was it you wanted to talk to me about?"

"Well, the music, of course. Getting the rights," Merrick said.

Harry was confused. "You don't know much about Hollywood, do you? I don't own the rights to the songs—the studio does."

Harry watched Merrick's beady eyes dart around, as if someone had just come up behind him and shot him full of adrenaline. "Is that right?"

With that, Harry sensed Merrick had no use for him—and he was right.

Harry was powerless to stop Merrick from moving ahead with his plans. He wasn't sure if he should even *want* to get in his way because, for better or worse, it was Broadway at last. Harry heard through some of his contacts that Merrick's very next stop after their lunch was Warner Brothers Music Publishing. There, Merrick made a deal for the rights to all the songs from the *42nd Street* film, as well as a sampling of other Warren/Dubin tunes from other Warner Brothers musicals—"We're in the Money,"

"Boulevard of Broken Dreams," and "Dames"—that would be thrown into the stage show, making it somewhat of a jukebox musical.

Not long before Merrick approached the studio, Harry had been offended upon learning someone there was balking at the idea of doing a Harry Warren tribute album because they didn't know who he was. Merrick took full advantage of the fact that no one at Warner Bros. realized they were sitting on a gold mine. By the time the studio recognized it had been duped, it was too late. Merrick had made off with all that music for a song. Even so, some observers found Merrick's $3-million gamble to be the move of a madman, because the only other movie musical that had been adapted for the Broadway stage—and quite unsuccessfully—was *Gigi* in 1974.

42nd Street opened in June 1980 in Washington, DC, at the Kennedy Center for Performing Arts, where it received glowing reviews, becoming the show's launchpad to Broadway. On the show's Broadway opening night, August 25, 1980, at New York's Winter Garden Theatre, the cast got eleven curtain calls. Merrick had splashed his name all over the posters and playbills with no mention of Harry at all. A quick glance at the program and one would have thought the music had written itself.

But for anyone in the audience that opening night, the thing they would never forget was how Merrick took to the stage after the curtain calls to announce the director, Gower Champion, had died just that afternoon. Somehow, he'd been able to hold this news from the public and the cast so he could exploit it in true David Merrick fashion, ensuring maximum drama and publicity.

Harold Arlen, who'd moved back to New York some years before, called Harry after he'd seen *42nd Street*. "I really wish you could see the show," Harold said.

"With Merrick's name splashed all over everything? No, thanks," Harry said. He scoffed at the stunt Merrick had pulled announcing Gower's death. "What's he going to do when I expire? Oh, wait a minute—he's never acknowledged me at all. I might as well already be dead."

"You can't worry about any of that. If you could have seen the delight on peoples' faces when the curtain came up and they feasted their eyes on those eighty feet tap-dancing to your music! It filled them up like they were taking in one of the wonders of the world. It moved me to tears," Harold said. "And when I was talking to Irving earlier—"

Harry interrupted. "Ira said you two speak every day now?"

"Yes. Apparently, I'm the only one he speaks to now," Harold said. "Anyway, he told me the two of you went to see the *42nd Street* movie just after it came out. To think of the two of you together all those years ago in that theater, just blocks from this Broadway production, gave me chills. Why didn't you ever tell me about that?"

"I never thought to," Harry said.

Despite the bittersweetness of it all, Harry felt some satisfaction seeing his musical succeed, winning the Tony Award for Best Musical. As of 2019, *42ⁿᵈ Street* remains the fifteenth longest-running show in Broadway history. He'd done it. Maybe not in any way he imagined, but the end result was the same.

Back at home in California, another venue was preparing to premiere a Harry Warren work: his *Mass of St. Anthony.* Named after Harry's favorite saint, the Latin Mass for a mixed choir was going to take place at the Sacred Heart Chapel on the campus of Loyola Marymount University in Los Angeles. Harry and his family attended. When the performance was over, Harry told Jo he needed a moment alone. "I'll meet you all outside in a few minutes," he said.

Jo nodded and ushered their group out. Harry waited for the last few people to exit the chapel, then he pulled out the kneeler. He slid forward onto it, bowed his head, and closed his eyes. What swirled around in his mind was one of his more rambling prayers, when he felt like there was so much he wanted to say to God that he just hoped it didn't come out a jumbled mess on the other end. But when he opened his eyes, a brilliant ray of light from the setting sun burst through the stained glass and cast him in a rainbow, just the way it had back when he and played his first notes on the church organ as a young boy at Our Lady of Loreto in Brooklyn. He took this as a sign that Miss Schneider and his mother had both heard his Mass. It was a promise fulfilled.

Harry soon began spending most of his time thinking about his legacy and whether things could have been different for him had he chosen another name. Should he maybe have just short-ened Salvatore to Sal, or even gone by Tuti Guaragna? *That* name would have been memorable. Ira and Harold tried to convince him his music would endure, and that was what truly mattered.

"Maybe it's just my fate as a Capricorn. They call us 'the hard-way' guys," Harry sighed.

"You should stop worrying about your legacy, Harry. It speaks for itself," Harold assured him.

"You know you're less identifiable because you write so bril-liantly in every conceivable style," Ira said.

"And that's exactly what made you so wildly successful and indispensable in Hollywood," Harold added.

"You're the original *hit man*, Harry," Ira quipped.

Harry laughed, the thought appealing to the darker side of his sense of humor. "And hit men don't need publicists," he chuckled. "Quite the opposite—they need to keep a low profile!"

Harold looked at his mentor soberly. "I have something to show you," he said. He reached down for a book by musicologist Alec Wilder called *American Popular Song: The Great Innovators, 1900–1950.* "Listen to this, would you?" He read from the book:

There is an interesting fact about this man which continues to puzzle me. Why have disc jockeys, ever since there were record programs on radio, almost invariably mentioned his name when-ever they played one of his songs? Harry Warren, Richard Whiting, Walter Donaldson, Jimmy McHugh all wrote great songs. But seldom have their names been announced with a recording as has Hoagy Carmichael's. Theater writers are often mentioned, Ellington occasionally, but other superior pop songwriters, very seldom. I find this anonymity to record program listeners an ill-mannered lapse on the part of the disc jockeys.

"How do you like that?" Harry said with a smile as Harold smacked the book shut. He asked to borrow the book, but Harold let him keep it.

Harry went home to read the passage to Jo and Julia.

"Now, there's a guy who knows what he's talking about," Jo said.

Julia beamed at him. "I agree," she said. "You've written over four hundred songs, for crying out loud."

"And I just heard they want me to write a song over at Fox for a film called *Manhattan Melody.*"

"See? They can't get enough of you," Julia said.

"I've always written music the way I felt it," he told them, starting to wax poetic about his craft. "I write for the public because I feel like the public, the way they would write if they could. You don't have to know anything about music to understand what I write. Mine are simple melodies. In music, there are certain chords that are tender and poignant—it's the universal language."

"Easy for you to say!" Julia laughed.

A short time later, Harry received a phone call from Ian Whitcomb, the British rocker who'd interviewed him a few years earlier. He told Harry the Royal Military Band had just played one of his songs, "You Must Have Been a Beautiful Baby," for the queen's birthday. He'd seen it on the BBC.

"Wonderful," Harry chuckled. "That's what they sang to me

at my eightieth birthday, though I'm not sure it was true!" Harry could now rest easy knowing his music was still appreciated the world over, even by royalty.

"And I also thought you might want to know that I've learned the queen's favorite song of all time," Ian said.

"Is it one I know?" Harry asked.

"It's one you *wrote*," Ian said, his smile audible over the phone. "'You'll Never Know.' But of course, I thought you should know!"

"Yes, indeed. Thank you for telling me, Ian."

"*By their works shall ye know them*," Ian said. "Have a lovely day, Harry."

As the days wore on, Harry's mind continually drifted back in time to his childhood in Brooklyn, when he spent his days playing in the streets. His family brought in a nurse to help him bathe and dress. One day toward the end of his life, he asked the nurse to move him over to the piano, though he'd stopped playing it by then.

When Michael visited him one day, he asked if Harry wanted him to play something. "'My Heart Tells Me,'" he requested of his young archivist. Written in 1943, it was one of Harry's favorite songs he'd written—one of seventy of his that had become standards, recorded by artists such as Frank Sinatra, Tony Bennett, and Nat King Cole. Harry closed his eyes and listened to Michael play. A smile spread across his face.

In the days and months that followed, Harry's health began to fail. His kidneys were shutting down. After one urgent trip to the hospital, his demise accelerated.

Jo fought with the nurse about putting Harry's teeth in. "Would you stop doing that? He looks like Hirohito!" she complained. Harry and Jo were married for sixty-four years, and Harry had been proud of that.

Harry died of kidney failure on September 22, 1981.

As if to prove his music would not be forgotten, the 1982 Academy Awards opened with a rousing, toe-tapping tribute of his songs. Jo had the opening notes of "You'll Never Know" engraved on Harry's headstone, which is notable because there is much about the shy genius of Harry Warren that will forever remain shrouded in mystery. One such instance is looking at his own words and seeing how his accounts of how some of the most important moments in his life changed over time. In *Harry Warren and the Hollywood Musical* by Tony Thomas, published in 1975, Harry described the first time he met Al Dubin:

"I first met Al at the restaurant where so many of the songwriters gathered, Lindy's, and it was an appropriate place to meet him because Al was a large man with an enormous appetite. He loved good food. Eating was an avocation with him, and he spent a lot of time seeking out good restaurants. We hit it off immediately. The chemistry was right."

This description, however, does not comport with the foreword he wrote for Al Dubin's biography, written by Al's daughter, Patricia, that was published eight years later in 1983.

"I first met Al Dubin at the oyster bar in Grand Central Station in New York. I love oysters and so did he. We started to talk, first about food, and then we discovered we were in the same business. We were both songwriters."

In both versions, they met at a restaurant. There was an emphasis on food and how much they both appreciated it. Then the talk turned to music and they ended up as partners. But why did Harry change the story's details in the years between? Was this in fact what happened with the apocryphal story about the 1935 Academy Awards? Was it completely unintentional, or a subconscious way of attracting attention for the being guy who was known for being unknown? Perhaps these questions place too much of the burden on Harry and lets the music-loving public off the hook.

With 450 songs published and performed in ninety films and over a hundred *Looney Tunes* cartoons, Harry may have been the most cantankerous contributor to the Great American Songbook, but he was also the most prolific. Posthumously, Harry has remained one of ASCAP's biggest moneymakers.

He is also the most culturally relevant of these first-generation American songwriters who came to define a uniquely American sound that found its way around the world. Shortly after Harry's death, the Ryan Repertory in Brooklyn changed its name to the Harry Warren Theatre, and the troupe lobbied the city to change the name of the street that runs alongside the venue to Harry Warren Way.

Nowadays, one would be hard-pressed to attend a wedding and not hear the Etta James version of "At Last," a favorite first-dance song the world over. The song ties love, family, and music together—something Harry always aimed to do. When President Barack Obama chose it as the theme song for his inauguration, it was arguably the most apropos choice to celebrate the first black American president. Something Harry would be downright tickled by happened just six years after his passing, in 1987, when "That's Amore" was used in the blockbuster Cher film *Moonstruck*, putting Harry alongside his hero Puccini on the same soundtrack. These are things Harry would be proud of.

There are many ways a person of any age or background encounters a Harry Warren song in everyday life. The popular NPR show *Marketplace* uses a couple different songs to symbolize what kind of day it was on Wall Street. One of those is a Harry Warren song and the other was written by his beloved mentee Harold Arlen. Rough day? Cue up Arlen's "Stormy Weather." A strong showing? You'll hear Harry's "We're in the Money." For these two New Yorkers and veterans of Tin Pan Alley, who better to give us the financial news in musical form? Perhaps it's perfectly fitting that the song by Harry, the "genial curmudgeon," is the one to deliver the more upbeat news. It could be this study in contradictions that, at last, tells us all we need to know about Harry Warren.

ACKNOWLEDGMENTS

To consider there had never been a biography or autobiography written on this giant of American music and cinema remains an astounding fact and one that Robert Barbera sought to remedy by including a book on Harry Warren in The Mentoris Project. I would like to deeply thank the following people, without whom this book simply would not have been possible:

Andrew Justice, Head of the Music Library at the University of Southern California and Scott Spencer, USC Music Library Supervisor, who took me by the hand to lead me to every possible resource, however obscure, allowing me to puzzle together Harry Warren's life and imagination.

Brett Service, Curator of the Warner Bros. Archives at the University of Southern California School of Cinematic Arts, who shared his personal story of a chance encounter with Harry Warren and loaned me his own jacket to use as a hood over a microfiche machine, so I could see well enough to read a transcript of a long-forgotten interview with Harry.

Emily Wittenberg, Archivist, Louis B. Mayer Library at the American Film Institute, who arranged for my many visits to read the oral history of Harry Warren commissioned by the AFI.

Elizabeth Tuico, independent researcher, who dove headlong into the Harry Warren Papers at the National Archives (National Museum of American History) in Washington, D.C. for the love of her cousin and this cause.

And most of all, Julia Riva, Harry Warren's granddaughter, whose memories and storytelling delivered me directly into the Warren home, as it was for her growing up there. Julia's formidable bond with her grandfather has kept Harry's legacy alive and thriving through her management of the Harry Warren archives and his timeless catalogue administered through Four Jays Music Publishing, the company Harry founded in 1955.

ABOUT THE AUTHOR

Stacia Raymond is a freelance writer and editor based in Southern California. With over twenty years of experience in the film and television industry, Stacia's body of work includes fiction, non-fiction, and ghostwriting for clients in the fields of music, film, and technology. Stacia's television writing has been produced by CBS, Paramount, and Lifetime, and she has developed projects with Showtime and ABC Family. In 2013, she was awarded a Fellowship with the Puglia Film Commission as part of a program to bring more production to the Southern Italian region. Stacia holds a B.A. in Communications from The American University and an M.F.A. in Professional Writing from the University of Southern California. She is a member of the Writers Guild of America and the American Society of Composers, Authors, and Publishers. She is currently working on her first book for children, *The Carol of the Ornaments*, and maintains a blog of personal essays focusing on the serendipitous nature of everything. Stacia also wrote *Grace Notes: A Novel Based on the Life of Henry Mancini*.

Building Wealth 101
How to Make Your Money Work for You
by Robert Barbera

Character is What Counts
A Novel Based on the Life of Vince Lombardi
by Jonathan Brown

Christopher Columbus: His Life and Discoveries
by Mario Di Giovanni

Dark Labyrinth
A Novel Based on the Life of Galileo Galilei
by Peter David Myers

Defying Danger
A Novel Based on the Life of Father Matteo Ricci
by Nicole Gregory

Desert Missionary
A Novel Based on the Life of Father Eusebio Kino
by Nicole Gregory

The Divine Proportions of Luca Pacioli
A Novel Based on the Life of Luca Pacioli
by W. A. W. Parker

The Dream of Life
A Novel Based on the Life of Federico Fellini
by Kate Fuglei

Dreams of Discovery
A Novel Based on the Life of the Explorer John Cabot
by Jule Selbo

The Embrace of Hope
A Novel Based on the Life of Frank Capra
by Kate Fuglei

The Faithful
A Novel Based on the Life of Giuseppe Verdi
by Collin Mitchell

Fermi's Gifts
A Novel Based on the Life of Enrico Fermi
by Kate Fuglei

First Among Equals
A Novel Based on the Life of Cosimo de' Medici
by Francesco Massaccesi

The Flesh and the Spirit
A Novel Based on the Life of St. Augustine of Hippo
by Sharon Reiser and Ali A. Smith

God's Messenger
A Novel Based on the Life of Mother Frances X. Cabrini
by Nicole Gregory

Grace Notes
A Novel Based on the Life of Henry Mancini
by Stacia Raymond

Guido's Guiding Hand
A Novel Based on the Life of Guido d'Arezzo
by Kingsley Day

Harvesting the American Dream
A Novel Based on the Life of Ernest Gallo
by Karen Richardson

Humble Servant of Truth
A Novel Based on the Life of Thomas Aquinas
by Margaret O'Reilly

The Judicious Use of Intangibles
A Novel Based on the Life of Pietro Belluschi
by W.A.W. Parker

Leonardo's Secret
A Novel Based on the Life of Leonardo da Vinci
by Peter David Myers

Little by Little We Won
A Novel Based on the Life of Angela Bambace
by Peg A. Lamphier, PhD

The Making of a Prince
A Novel Based on the Life of Niccolò Machiavelli
by Maurizio Marmorstein

A Man of Action Saving Liberty
A Novel Based on the Life of Giuseppe Garibaldi
by Rosanne Welch, PhD

Marconi and His Muses
A Novel Based on the Life of Guglielmo Marconi
by Pamela Winfrey

No Person Above the Law
A Novel Based on the Life of Judge John J. Sirica
by Cynthia Cooper

The Pirate Prince of Genoa
A Novel Based on the Life of Admiral Andrea Doria
by Maurizio Marmorstein

Relentless Visionary: Alessandro Volta
by Michael Berick

Retire and Refire
Simple Financial Strategies to Navigate Your Best Years with Ease
by Robert Barbera

Ride Into the Sun
A Novel Based on the Life of Scipio Africanus
by Patric Verrone

Rita Levi-Montalcini
Pioneer & Ambassador of Science
by Francesca Valente

Saving the Republic
A Novel Based on the Life of Marcus Cicero
by Eric D. Martin

The Seven Senses of Italy
by Nicole Gregory

Sinner, Servant, Saint
A Novel Based on the Life of St. Francis of Assisi
by Margaret O'Reilly

Soldier, Diplomat, Archaeologist
A Novel Based on the Bold Life of Louis Palma di Cesnola
by Peg A. Lamphier, PhD

The Soul of a Child
A Novel Based on the Life of Maria Montessori
by Kate Fuglei

What a Woman Can Do
A Novel Based on the Life of Artemisia Gentileschi
by Peg A. Lamphier, PhD

The Witch of Agnesi
A Novel Based on the Life of Maria Agnesi
by Eric D. Martin

For more information on these titles and
the Mentoris Project, please visit
www.mentorisproject.org